Iain M____ ____ ____ t now lives in the
Englis____ ____ ____ ____ne novels. *Perfectly
Dead* is ____ ____ook in his highly regarded Crowby series. *A
Study In Death, Making A Killing, Killing for England, Cut
Her Dead,* and *Envy The Dead* are also published by Piatkus.

We hope you enjoy this book.

NORFOLK ITEM

30129 080 780 266

*Also by Iain McDowall*

A Study in Death
Making a Killing
Killing for England
Cut Her Dead
Envy the Dead

# Perfectly Dead

## *Iain McDowall*

piatkus

PIATKUS

First published in Great Britain in 2003 by Judy Piatkus (Publishers)
This paperback edition published in 2006 by Piatkus
Reprinted 2012

Copyright © 2003 Iain McDowall

The moral right of the author has been asserted.

*All characters and events in this publication, other than those
clearly in the public domain, are fictitious and any resemblance
to real persons, living or dead, is purely coincidental.*

All rights reserved.
No part of this publication may be reproduced, stored in a
retrieval system, or transmitted, in any form or by any means, without
the prior permission in writing of the publisher, nor be otherwise circulated
in any form of binding or cover other than that in which it is published
and without a similar condition including this condition being
imposed on the subsequent purchaser.

A CIP catalogue record for this book
is available from the British Library.

ISBN 978-0-7499-3671-6

Printed and bound by CPI Group (UK) Ltd, Croydon, CR0 4YY

Papers used by Piatkus are from well-managed forests
and other responsible sources.

MIX
Paper from
responsible sources
FSC® C104740

Piatkus
An imprint of
Little, Brown Book Group
100 Victoria Embankment
London EC4Y 0DY

An Hachette UK Company
www.hachette.co.uk

www.piatkus.co.uk

For Jesse, this time

# Part One

# Chapter One

Sheryl had let the barman from the Poets talk his way into staying the night again. Christ knows why. He had all the chat, she supposed. And he could seem so eager. At the time anyway. You'd never know it to look at him now. Flat on his back, snoring like a porker. In the light of her bedside lamp he looked his age too. His eyes were his best feature. Deep blue, always coaxing a smile. But they were tight shut now and what you noticed instead was the stubble on his doubling chin, the bloated red veins that had started to scar the tip and the sides of his nose, the way his mouth seemed to shudder at the finale of each snore. She turned away from him so that she only had to hear, didn't have to see as well. At least, she thought, he was a bloke. A man. Not some daft lad who'd get possessive, want to move in, start telling you what to do. His wife didn't mind, he said. Maybe, maybe not. Most likely when you looked the way she did you didn't have much choice anyway. The back end of a bus didn't really get it. Unless it was one that had been rammed by a ten-ton truck. He always said he didn't have sex with her any more. Sheryl hoped he wasn't lying. Even the idea of being shagged by the same prick as *that*.

She slid out of bed and got dressed quickly. Jeans and a blue top. A jumper that really needed to go in the wash. She closed the bedroom door behind her quietly but firmly. She'd rather that Anne-Marie didn't know there was anybody on the premises. Not for certain, at any rate. She'd already have noticed the line of empty Super Lager tins in front of

3

the fireplace, the unfamiliar pack of Marlboro next to her mum's Silk Cut. Anne-Marie was ten and brighter than a button: she never missed a thing, could put two and two together all right. A good riser too. Always up and about before you needed to shout her. She was in the kitchen when Sheryl walked through, making sure that the little one, Lucy, didn't put too much sugar on her bowl of Rice Krispies.

'Morning, Mum,' she said. 'I told her it's bad for her teeth.'

'Morning, loves.'

She squeezed round the table, kissing them in turn on the top of the head.

Lucy giggled.

'I dreamed I was a pirate,' she said.

'Did you now?'

She clicked on the kettle, spooned instant coffee into a mug. There was a dismal pile of washing-up next to the sink. But she decided she could deal with it later. When she'd made the coffee she went through to the living room, sank into the sofa, found her fag packet. She always had to have a ciggy to start the day. But no way would she breathe nicotine over their little lungs while they ate their breakfast. She noticed a bra, the one from last night, lying discarded next to her. She picked it up, stuffed it behind a cushion for now. She lit the cigarette, took a few puffs, sipped the coffee. The remote had been under the bra. She put it back on the low, unsteady table, rearranged the pile of magazines into something less un-neat. She couldn't handle breakfast TV, couldn't understand how anybody would want all that bloody noise first thing in the morning, all those bright lights and busyness. She could hear the girls in the bathroom now: Anne-Marie's bossy tones, Lucy still giggling. The big sister was good with the little sister, thank God. Better than good: brilliant, great. Always had her ready on time, always had her turned out properly. In a few minutes they'd present themselves in front of her

4

for inspection and approval. She finished the cigarette and the coffee, checked her hair in the big embossed mirror above the fireplace. It was an ugly fucking thing, she'd always thought. Harley-Davidson in garish lettering along the bottom. The picture of the bike itself always getting in the way. But she'd picked it up cheap. It would have to do for the time being.

'We're ready now, Mum,' Anne-Marie said from the doorway, still fussing with Lucy's scarf. Sheryl pulled on her coat, ushered them out into the unlit, broken lightbulbed hall. She undid the chain on the door and followed them out towards the stairwell. They were never, ever to use the lifts, she'd told them. Never, ever. She never did herself. Not even when shopping was involved. Too filthy, too smelly. Too many horror stories. The stairs led up and down, gave you a fighting, shouting, screaming chance in two directions. The lifts offered you up pre-confined and trapped. A ready meal: a chicken in a broiler.

Outside it was still dark. And pissing down as usual – a wet, ceaseless drizzle. But the girls – or Anne-Marie anyway – skipped towards the bus shelter as if the pavement was the Yellow Brick Road. Just about the only thing you could say in favour of William Blake House was that it was handy for the bus. Some parts of the estate it was a quarter of an hour's walk to the nearest stop.

Sheryl checked her watch once they were settled and under way. The bus was on time for once. Seven thirty on the dot. If it reached the Flowers Street depot on schedule, they'd have a clear five minutes to catch their other bus. The 8.15, not the 8.30. Which meant there would be a chance of getting there on time, of not dashing breathless across the playground at the last frigging minute. They'd told her at the council offices that the journey would be a problem right from the start. That they couldn't be expected to put on a school bus for just two pupils. She hadn't let them put her off. Nor the snooty school secretary neither – when she'd phoned to make an appointment to talk to the head teacher about enrolment. You had the right to send your kids to any school these days. End of. And no way were Sheryl's two little sweethearts going to the local primary on the Woodlands, learning how to roll a joint – how to blag a corner shop – before they even knew how to tie their shoelaces properly. She'd dug her heels in. Simple as that.

The bus took a corner on the sharp side. Lucy elbowed Anne-Marie with more force than the swerve merited.

'Whoo, whee,' she said.

Then again:

'Whoo, whee.'

But Anne-Marie kept her eyes buried inside her book. Sheryl shushed Lucy, stroking the back of her head gently as she did so. Leaning back, she caught her own reflection in the window. Her too-thin mouth looked taut, her eyes nervous and drawn. *I'll take them myself if I have to.* Sheryl had wanted Barton Primary for the girls – and in the end she'd got it. The other side of town. What they called a good area. Doctors and lawyers sent their kids there. Parents with proper jobs in offices. All that. Grant, the young guy from the advice centre, had helped her. He'd sorted out the paperwork, fixed up bus passes for the girls. She'd wondered if he'd been after something in return. But he'd never said. Shy maybe. Or gay, according to one rumour. Too bad if he was – with his nice, quiet smile. Sex with him would be some kind of easy, gentle thing. Not the usual fucking rough house.

The bus pulled out of the estate, heading towards the town centre. Dave the barman would most probably be gone when she got back. He'd see himself out, make sure the door was double-locked, sling the spare key back through the letter box. He was good like that really. Not a bad sort. He'd probably leave her something too. Ten, twenty, maybe even thirty. It wasn't paying for it. It was nothing like that at all. *A young girl like you*, he'd said one time, the notion swimming somewhere under the surface of the conversation: where either of them could look at it when the other one wasn't. *On your own, two little kiddies. Only natural to help out, isn't it?*

She'd laughed throatily before she'd replied, let him undo the buttons of her blouse, nestled her head on his chest. *Don't be soft, Dave. A big handsome man like you always gets it for free.*

Florida Boy and Charlie waited in Charlie's car until the slapper, Sheryl or whatever, and her brats were well and truly on the bus and well and truly off the estate. It would be a clean job, Charlie reminded himself. Straight in, straight out. They were professionals now. Or very nearly: the years of kids' stuff almost finally behind them. Take the car as an instance. Sound until the end of the week. Soundness virtually guaranteed, virtually built in. Yesterday afternoon, he'd fare-dodged Richard Branson all the way over to Birmingham New Street and then out to the NEC. Only kids nicked cars in their own back yard. Professionals brought their transport in from elsewhere. Likewise he'd ignored the amateur opportunities available in the Exhibition Centre car park. Cars that would be missed in hours not days. Charlie had made a plan and he'd stuck to it: taxi ride over to the airport concourse, an inconspicuous latte in the Lavazza franchise, a brisk stroll across to the long-stay car park. He'd instantly rejected anything too new, anything too upmarket, had been looking for something solid and dependable, something that would be virtually invisible.

Florida Boy ran edgy, twitchy fingers along the walnut fascia below the windscreen.

'Just the ticket, Charles, old bean. Just the fucking ticket and all-round bee's knees,' he said.

Charlie nodded agreement. Not that Florida Boy had scope to quarrel anyway. A Rover 216, P reg: a fucking sight faster than it looked and fearsomely boring. No self-respecting dibble would be seen stopping one in a month of Sundays. Besides, if all went well, by the time they needed to get rid, they'd be *in* the bloody firm, feet under the bloody table. That could very well mean taking possession of something sleek and shiny, not to mention legit. Charlie Taylor and Florida Boy Bilston for the use of. Tax disc, insurance, the fucking lot. Permanent membership at babe magnet city. He slid down the window and tipped his ash thoughtfully.

The deal was this. A week's try-out with no questions asked. A few odds and sods that needed taking care of. Jobs the regular crew didn't want bothering with, done to the letter with zero assistance. Fuck up or get caught and they were on their own. Come through clean as a whistle – nothing else was good enough – and they'd be on the payroll, three months' trial.

'The bee's knees and all-round fucking ticket,' Florida Boy repeated.

Evidently Bilston was well pilled up. That could be something he'd have to watch in future, Charlie thought. As it turned out, though, it was probably no bad thing for this morning's first little task. For something of this nature, you needed to go in boisterous, not giving a flying fuck. Especially as it would be mainly down to FB anyway. The way Charlie saw it, he would be there more in the role of a facilitator himself. That was another thing about turning professional: utilising skills to the max, building on the strengths of your associates. The clock on the walnut dash pulsed from 7.39 to 7.40. Taylor stubbed out his cigarette in the ashtray, tapped Bilston lightly on his forearm.

'Right, mate,' he said, as matter-of-factly as he could. 'Time you and me were making a move.'

They got out of the car and Taylor locked it. Casually, but not wasting any time, they walked the thirty or so yards along the pavement and then up to the entranceway.

William Blake House was medium-rise. Ten floors only. There were five other identical blocks standing next to it. A monotonous row punctuated by scrubby patches of grass and potholed tarmac. They stood shuffling outside for a minute, hoods up for the rain as much as anything. FB rattled the main doors but they were locked. The council had forked out for a security upgrade recently. Each block had telecom entry these days. You pressed the number of the mug you'd come to visit and the mug buzzed you in.

The wait for an unofficial entrée took less than another twenty seconds. A young lad in a ripped puffa jacket emerged from the lifts, approached the glass fronted doors. The council had sent every tenant a leaflet. 'Never Let in Strangers'. Florida Boy gave the kid his look as he came through the left-hand door. But the kid was sussed anyway, not even the hint of minor disagreement on his face. He held the door wide open for them.

'Cheers, mate,' Charlie said evenly.

Courtesy cost nothing where it had been duly earned.

They took the stairs up without rushing. A nasty big '4' on the wall told them when they'd reached the right level. Somebody had graffitoed a hyphen and the word 'skin' underneath the number in green paint. Hopeless, unfunny. Charlie pulled open the connecting door that led to the flats themselves. New locks were another feature. Not that bad actually. But Charlie's sister lived three blocks along at Byron House. He'd gone up there last night, put in a worthwhile couple of hours. It had looked like a screwdriver job at first. But practice makes perfect and all that. He could manage it with the credit card now. Simple, quiet: exactly how he liked it. All you had to do was get the angle right, put a bit of weight pressure on. Just so.

'*Voilà*, as they say in France,' he whispered, putting card back in his pocket.

'The dirty foul foreign bastards, old bean,' Florida Boy replied.

Charlie opened the door with infinite slowness, made a sign for quiet, followed FB inside.

Dave the barman was still in bed. Sat up reading the problem page in one of the tart's magazines, it looked like. Plus smoking a half-smoked cigarette.

'Tut, tut. Filthy habit,' Florida Boy said, looming up in the doorway.

He'd crept through the flat like the proverbial fucking dormouse but now he was through with fannying about. Dave cursed them, was throwing back the purple duvet, swinging his legs out. He was a big enough guy but Florida Boy already had the tyre lever out from under his fleece, landed a good one smack across the chops before Dave's big, hairy feet could touch the very, very non-matching carpet.

Charlie had brought a generous length of clothes line, also courtesy of his sister. They trussed the cunt up while he was still stunned from the blow.

'Twatted and all-round stuffed,' Florida Boy said, his eyes pill bright and blinking.

# Chapter Two

There was a pile of unwashed clothes lying in front of the dressing table. Florida Boy picked up a pair of knickers from the top of the pile, stuffed them inside Dave's mouth. Taking a leg each, they dragged him through to the lounge. They'd been told to give him a slapping. Nothing too drastic and with an accent on the face: the deterrence angle, it had been put to them as. Until he healed up, Dave would be a walking advertisement for paying proper respect, for not taking the piss. But also, they'd been told, they had to get the fucker to talk. To explain his misdemeanours in detail, to name names.

They dumped him down in front of the sofa, kicking the rickety table out of the way. Handily the tart had an electric fire. Handily her electricity hadn't been cut off. Charlie liberated the fire from its position in the cheap built-in surround. The cable stretched the distance just about perfectly. Deftly, he unscrewed the protective grille and then switched it on, all three bars. Dave was thrashing around on the floor, his eyes popping like a goldfish on bad acid.

'Now, old bean,' Florida Boy said. 'I remove the kecks from your kisser and you say fuck-all until you're asked. Comprendo?'

Dave stopped struggling, appeared to nod consent, then was coughing – choking – as the air found his throat. Charlie looked at him with contempt as he moved out of the way. Forty if he's a day, he thought, yet taking it upon himself to shag some young, fit slag.

Florida Boy went to work, grabbed the fire by the handle. Like a shield. Holding the bottom bar inch-close to Dave's face, trying out his best maniac grin. Charlie lit himself another cigarette. It was a piece of piss this. Better than the dole. Better than working. Once Dave told them what he knew, FB would give him a swift slapping and then they'd be out of there, vamoosed, mission accomplished.

'Who else is in on it, old bean?' Florida Boy asked, the electric fire twitching in his far from steady grip. Charlie took a confident draw, waited for the answers to pour out.

The firm knew most of it already anyway. It was for confirmation only: that and putting plonker Dave in his place. But Dave said nothing. He'd got his breath back, just lay there: trussed up and staring. Florida Boy put the fire down, punched him hard in the face.

'I asked you a question, old bean.'

Everything would have been all right, Charlie thought later, if only the moron had reacted like a normal person. If he'd just answered, even just made something up. But Dave had evidently seen too many movies, was off on some hopeless macho trip. They way they did sometimes – old guys who dipped it in the fountain of youth, thinking it made them invincible. He'd twisted himself half upright somehow, had caught FB off balance, had managed to knee him. Bilston had fallen onto the fire, the bars burning into his back before the bastard thing finally shorted. Which was when – clambering to stand back up again – FB had utterly fucking lost it.

Charlie tried to pull him off, of course. But he couldn't get near. Florida Boy flailing the tyre lever in every direction: the table, the television, the big ugly mirror taking very nearly as much punishment as the barman's head. Charlie himself most probably, if he'd gone any closer. *You little shits*, Dave had managed once, trying to lever himself up onto the sofa. Not much in the way of last words, Charlie thought. But all too true, mate, all too true.

# Chapter Three

After she'd had her school dinner and checked that Lucy was all right, Anne-Marie preferred to spend the rest of the lunch break in the resources room with her friend, Sarah Adams. It could be a bit noisy at the other end. Where the computers were. Where Sophie Norman and her gang were sending silly emails to some boys at their twinned schools in France and Germany. Here – next to the few racks of library books – it wasn't nearly so bad. Anne-Marie had started reading *The Lord of the Rings*. It was much harder to read than *The Hobbit*. But she'd read that all the way through twice now. And her heart was set on finding out what happened next about the ring. Mum had said they could go and see the films. But Anne-Marie preferred to read. You could only watch a film: you could *live* inside a book.

Sarah, of course, was Harry Potter mad, was reading *The Crock of Gold* for the third time. Most of the kids who read for pleasure at all, as Mrs Harrison called it, were Harry fans. Which wasn't that many. Anne-Marie didn't mind him. But her favourite bit had been at the very beginning of the first book. When he was still living with the Dursleys. Once he'd gone to that dreary old school, it hadn't been nearly as good. Mrs Harrison said it didn't matter what they read as long as they did read. Reading for pleasure was something that would last a lifetime, Mrs Harrison said. It was Mrs Harrison who'd told her about *The Hobbit*. As if letting her into some kind of real magic secret. Then last week, when Anne-Marie had borrowed *The Fellowship of the Ring*, she'd said that *The Lord of the Rings* was more for grown-ups really. Though don't let that put you off, she'd added kindly.

It was certainly a very, very long story. Three whole books. And drawings. Strange and beautiful drawings you could just look at for hours. He must have been really, really clever, Anne-Marie thought. Mr Toll Keen. That was how Mrs Harrison said you said the name. Though it was spelt different. Bilbo had found the magic ring – though he really shouldn't have kept it – and he'd outwitted the Gollum just with a riddle. Also Frodo and him were proper grown-up hobbits. Not specky little schoolboys like Harry.

The two girls sat side by side, absorbed, until the 1.30 bell rang. Quickly, they closed up their books. They would be doing their history project this afternoon. Which was one of their favourite lessons. The Cavaliers and the Roundheads. They both thought the Cavaliers were best because they were on the side of the King.

'I'm going to ask my mum if you can come to tea on Thursday,' Sarah said. 'Do you think your mum will let you?'

'I'll have to see,' Anne-Marie answered.

It was a long way for Mum to come and collect her. Four bus journeys. And Mum hadn't liked it the time Sarah's dad had driven her back. *What's the matter, Mum?* she'd asked her after he'd brought her up to the flat and gone again. Mum had been polishing the mirror above the fireplace. She'd stopped, picked her up, given her such a big hug. *We're just as good as them, sweetheart. Better. Don't ever forget that.*

Most of the rest of the class were already waiting outside the classroom by the time Anne-Marie and Sarah got there. They joined the line at the back behind a very little boy who everybody called Froggy for a reason that nobody really remembered any more. His real name was Tom but only Mrs Harrison called him that. Anne-Marie felt impatient, thinking that maybe Mrs Harrison was late. But then she saw her hurrying around the corner at the end of the corridor. There was another lady with her. In a uniform. A policewoman, she realised, as they came nearer. Anne-Marie drew herself in against the wall, willing herself as small as Froggy, wanting to be invisible like Bilbo. For all the special love that Mum gave her, she still felt like running, still knew that, if they'd come for anyone, it would be her the Filthy Bill would be after.

Two hours later, Marion Adams couldn't park the family's Renault Espace anywhere near the school gates. The whole situation was getting ridiculous. You had to get there practically an hour before they came out if you wanted a space directly outside the school. She drove around the corner and halfway along Barton Avenue itself – parked there and walked back. Which was no joke at this time of year. At least Sarah was on time. That was something, she supposed. For once she hadn't hung around pestering the teacher with extra questions after the final bell had rung.

They hurried back to the car hand in hand, Sarah's pointy little nose turning pink in the sharp, wet wind. Studious. That was how the school reports always described her. Well, studious was all right, Marion Adams thought. But it wasn't everything. The teachers had probably been studious when they were youngsters – and now look at them. Old cars and joke wages. Steve, her husband, had left school at sixteen, didn't have a qualification to his name. And he'd done all right, hadn't he? You'd better believe that he had. More than all right in her opinion. She pointed her key fob in the direction of the Espace as they drew near. She liked the way the tail-lights winked at you as the doors unlocked. As if they were saying an obedient hello. Not many of these in the teachers' car park. Not any actually. Still less than six months old and a strictly limited edition. She felt the wetness of the raindrops on the handle as she opened the door. They seemed to take on the colour of the bodywork as they streamed down the sides. Car sweat: like beady, silver-grey tadpoles.

She'd wanted something warmer looking herself. Something brighter. Cherry red or even a yellow. But Steve had wanted silver, so that had been that. They'd nearly argued too – or as close as they ever came to it – about the personal number plate issue. She'd thought it could be a fun thing, a laugh. But Steve had said that if you bought a new vehicle every year, which they did, then you might as well let everybody know about it. Once Sarah was safely in the front passenger seat and securely buckled in, she turned on the ignition, slid out into the stream of suburban traffic.

The Espace had been a big improvement on the Space Wagon in both their opinions. Not that there was anything really wrong with the Mitsubishi. Just that this was the better model. The next step up. Eight-speaker stereo. Five removable rear seats. Every safety feature imaginable. Going up a gear or six, Steve had joked, driving it away from the showroom. Top-of-the-range air conditioning too: instantly cool in summer, instantly warm on a bitter day like this one.

'Anne-Marie had to leave school early. A policewoman came,' Sarah announced gravely.

Mrs Adams didn't reply, tried to look as if driving was taking up all of her attention. Her method with the Anne-Marie problem was to ignore any mention of her as much as possible. Once Sarah was a bit older, she believed, she'd see for herself that the little bastard – for that's what she was when all was said and done – wasn't an appropriate friend. It was nothing to worry about, Steve had argued. And she'd agreed. It was all just a matter of time.

'Daddy's taking us all bowling tonight, dear,' she said.

A policewoman was just about the size of it, she thought. God knows what the mother imagined she was up to, imposing her kids on normal people. They were always turned out neat and clean, she'd give them that. But who was to say how their clothes were acquired? They shoplifted to order on estates like the Woodlands. She'd read about it in the *Mail on Sunday*. According to Steve, their flat had been disgusting – filthy – the time he'd driven the girl over there. *Thank God she didn't ask me to sit down*: his comment when he'd got back.

'I don't want to go bowling. I want to see Anne-Marie,' Sarah said, her fingers playing with the zip of her bag.

'But you'll see her tomorrow,' Marion Adams replied, resigned at last to acknowledging the topic. But only minimally. Not letting it divert her from the task at hand. 'Tonight's going to be a family night. You. Me. Daddy. The boys. Just us and nobody else.'

They were on the other side of the Bartons now, nearly home. Sarah said nothing for a minute or two. Then:

'Anne-Marie says Toll Keen's better than Harry Potter. But I don't think so. What do you think, Mummy?'

But her mother had never read either.

'I think you can spend too much time with your head in a book, my lamb,' she said, indicating left.

She steered the Espace smoothly round the corner, considered the subject successfully closed.

# Chapter Four

Sheryl and the girls could spend tonight at Candice's. Candice lived on the second floor. Another single mum. But she had a big sofa bed in her front room. They'd be fine there for tonight anyway. Tomorrow, the man from the council had said, Sheryl would need to see the housing officer, work out what arrangements could be made. Candice had only the one kid, an eight-year-old lad called Liam. Liam had a Game Boy and Anne-Marie was keeping Lucy busy, showing her how *Tetris* worked. Liam was ignoring both of them, had plonked himself in front of the television set. Candice and Sheryl sat in Candice's kitchen, smoking cigarettes. Candice opened two bottles of Smirnoff Ice, handed one of them to Sheryl.

Sheryl's eyes were red and she picked nervously at her lips. Neither she nor the girls had anything more than they stood up in, anything more than they'd come home with.

'The firemen said we was all lucky,' Candice said. 'Another ten minutes and it might've spread. Could've been the whole block not just yours.'

Sheryl nodded. But Candice wondered if she was really taking any of it in.

'We didn't have much,' Sheryl said finally. 'But now we've nothing. Nothing at all.'

The flat had already been gutted by the time Sheryl had caught her combination of two buses, had made her way back across Crowby from the Bartons to the Woodlands. The block had been evacuated, the tenants standing around across the way, shivering and complaining in the drizzle. Plus there'd been coppers, fire engines, gawpers. Even a reporter and a photographer from the *Evening Argus*. *That's her now*, she'd heard someone say as she'd run, fearful, all the way from the bus stop. Dave had been a goner before the fire brigade could get to him. Smoking in bed was the theory. Smoking but maybe still napping. *Yes, he was a smoker*, she'd told them. The firemen, the Old Bill, the reporter. The reporter had asked if they could take a photo of her and whether she had one of the girls on her that she could let them borrow. But she'd refused point blank. *No*, she'd said, *mind your own bloody business*.

Candice swigged from her bottle.

'Poor Dave.'

Sheryl just shook her head by way of a reply. Her latest cigarette mouldered in the ashtray, barely touched. Dave was no fool, she was thinking. And he was no kind of morning drinker or druggie either. Both possibilities had been put to her by the coppers: the idea that Dave, out of it, had carelessly set the mattress on fire. She'd lied purely on instinct. *I don't know about drugs. But yes, well, he was a bit of a drinker*. If they were happy enough to think that was all there was to it, then fine. Definitely fine: she had enough on her plate to worry about. But Sheryl knew Dave – and the Woodlands – an awful lot better than to believe anything resembling the lie herself.

Florida Boy had moved off the estate, had a bedsit near Mill Street, paid for by the social. His probation officer had argued that it would help him with his independence, also keep him away from previous associates. FB lay face down on the bed, still moaning about his sodding back. Charlie ignored him. It was nothing like as bad as the plonker was saying. Yeah, he'd been burned. But he'd live, wouldn't he? The human body was a great natural healer and all that. No way they could approach a doctor or the hospital casualty anyway. They might as well take out an ad in the bloody paper. Maybe tomorrow they'd get Lisa to take a look. Lisa was one of Charlie's old slags, had been a nursing assistant for a while: until she'd got caught with her hands in the dispensary. Frankly, FB's burns were the least of their worries. Besides, he deserved to suffer. The stupid fucking pill-head twat.

While Florida Boy moaned and whinged, Charlie paced the length of the room and back again. The tiny mobile in his right hand felt like a dead weight. Oh, fuck it, he thought finally, pressing the keypad then dialling. Get it over with.

'It's Charlie,' he said when the line connected. 'I expect you heard we got a problem—'

*No, mate. You've got a problem. You and your colleague. No one else. The arrangement's cancelled. You're on your own now. Pair of head cases.*

'But—'

*One more thing. You never mention this organisation to any third party. You know what I mean. You don't even hint. You don't know us – we don't know you. You don't phone this number again. Not ever.*

Stephen Adams drove the Espace into the car park of the Crowby Leisure Centre. Steve, Marion and ten-year-old Sarah in the front. Matt, twelve, and Mark, fourteen, in the back. Daytime, he used the white Mondeo, decorated with the company logo and contact details. It was surprising how much trade you got just from somebody noting down the number when they were stuck behind you in a traffic queue. But evenings and weekends – family times – he used the people carrier. What it was for. He parked in a well-lit area, close to one of the CCTV cameras. The Espace didn't have a scratch on it yet. He preferred to keep it that way.

At the kiosk, he paid for two full games plus the hire of four sets of bowling shoes. He'd brought his own pair with him. Plus the bowling ball Marion had bought him for his birthday last year. He paid with his HSBC Platinum card. He didn't see the point in using cash any more except where you couldn't avoid it. You were so much better off with plastic. Just clear the bill in full every month and you were clocking up at least twenty-eight days interest free every time. Let the mugs who borrowed and couldn't pay back pick up the tab. That was his motto all right. Or it had been until recently anyway.

He nodded to half a dozen familiar faces as they shoed up then made their way to lane ten. Almost in the nature of a public appearance. That was the way he suddenly saw it. Making a statement on the eve of the big night itself. Doing things together. Staying positive. What the whole thing was about. What the point was. Bill Elliot and his family were playing on number six. Steve let the others go on ahead, grabbed a word in passing. He'd heard that Billy Boy's building firm was renovating a couple of biggish properties out on the Wynarth Road. Upmarket retirement accommodation. Maybe twenty or thirty flats for some well-pensioned old-age croakers. Complete with wardens, nurses and assorted hand-holders on site. Without a doubt there would be cable or satellite going into both gaffs. And no reason on the planet why Elliot couldn't have a useful word with the developer on his behalf. You scratch my back, et fucking cetera. Cheaper to coordinate the TV and digital side with the general rewiring and fitting. That would be the selling angle.

'They'll save themselves a fortune that way, Bill,' he said.

Elliot looked doubtful but after a bit of coaxing he promised to pass the message on.

Steve patted the smaller man heartily on his shoulder.

'Cheers, mate. I'll owe you one if we get the business.'

Elliot gave him an uncommitted wink, went back to his game.

The Adams family bowling experience followed its usual pattern. The first game was purely for fun. Steve deliberately bowling wide, fluffing shots, treating everyone to a bit of free coaching. Game two, by contrast, was very nearly serious. Himself and the older boy, Mark, going head to head, strike after strike. One of these days the lad would beat him. But that would be all right. Exactly how it should be. Besides bowling was no different to life in general in that respect, he always thought. He'd done better than his dad and the lads would do better than him. Only proper and natural. Maybe even little Sarah too. Now they had equal rights and all that malarkey.

After they'd played, he treated the kids to Cokes and fries. But no burgers. Not when they'd eaten earlier. Marion ordered a milk shake. Strawberry and vanilla. Steve stuck to coffee, grown up and unsweetened. She wanted to watch that from the weight point of view. Even if she *was* down the gym every day and what not. He'd made his position clear on that score often enough, warned her. A fat wife was the one thing he'd never put up with, would definitely draw the line at.

Matt asked if he could play on the flight simulator. No, he told him. They had to get back once they'd finished. Otherwise Sarah would miss her bedtime. The thing with something like Bill Elliot's conversion contract, he thought, was to get in quick. And when he said quick he *meant* quick. Before some smooth-suited salesman from one of the national or franchised outfits started wining and dining the client. Preferably before they even knew there was an opportunity in the offing. Local intelligence: the only way a local firm could keep ahead of the game these days.

Marion sent Sarah straight to brushing her teeth and bed as soon as they got home. Matt and Mark disappeared noisily to their respective rooms. Twice he had to shout up at Mark

22

to turn the bleeding racket down. House music: not in *my* bloody house, thank you very much. Lights-out for Matt was at ten o'clock on a weekday. Eleven for Mark. Mark had complained over dinner that he was still being treated like a kid, that there were lads in his class who could stop out all night if they liked. You'll thank me for that one day, son, he'd told him. When you've grown up without a criminal record or a line of needle marks on your arm. Mark had said nothing in reply, had known better than to argue.

Finally they were alone in the lounge. Just himself and the missus. Marion was over by the drinks cabinet, pouring out a couple of glasses of an Australian Shiraz. She mentioned some slushy film she quite fancied watching. She'd taped it the night before. He considered whether to humour her or whether to insist on the Italian football over on Sky Sports 1. If he opted for the football, she'd probably go upstairs, watch the film on her own on the bedroom set. If he OK'd it, on the other hand, she'd snuggle up beside him, might even fancy a bit afterwards.

'Movie, then, isn't it?' he said, zapping through the channels while the VCR indexed back.

Marion passed him a glass as she sat down.

'Can we just catch the end of the local news first?' she asked.

Give them an inch, he thought, finding the ITV channel for her.

*The headlines again. One man dead and a young family lucky to be alive as fire sweeps through a flat in Crowby's troubled Woodlands estate.*

Now this was news. But it wasn't his family, wasn't his problem.

'Sarah mentioned something was up,' Marion said. 'I think the police must have called at the school for the daughters. Maybe they'll have to stop away for a bit till it's sorted. Give Sarah a chance to make some other friends.'

Steve nodded. It wasn't much of a photograph, he thought. They were recognisable. But only just. It looked like one of those cheap snaps you got in those passport booth things. Angular, badly lit, one dimensional. Blurred and grainy around the edges. The perfect quality of the signal on the equipment he'd installed personally emphasised every single weakness. His entire set-up was state of the art obviously. Thirty-six-inch screen. Nicam surround stereo. Motorised dish system. Et fucking cetera. Had to be really. The ultimate sincere sales pitch: it's what I have myself at home. Still, you could tell it was them all right. The two brats and the mother. Barely more than a girl herself. Twenty-three or twenty-four, as he recalled.

The news ended and he pressed play. They hadn't named the dead man, maybe they still needed to contact the relatives or something. He settled back on the sofa, glass in hand.

'This film,' he said. 'I hope it's not going to be a long one.'

He put his hand casually on the nape of his wife's neck, rubbing it the way she liked.

That short little skirt she'd been wearing the time he'd driven her daughter back over to her. Pretending to dust her mirror or whatever. Showing off her arse more like. And the long, bare legs.

He was working with only one finger now, the fingernail tracing an inch-long line. Up and down. Down and up. He'd be stoking the same old fire as usual later. But he knew who he'd be thinking about.

24

# Chapter Five

A bleak, grey morning. Chief Inspector Jacobson stared out of his office window into the void of the pedestrian precinct, watching the few citizens brave enough to be out and about in the cold, cutting wind. They scurried – maybe even scuttled – rather than walked or ran, their coats flapping, their heads bent. The kind of day when you wondered why out of all the aeons of human possibility, out of all the times past and times to come, your soul had washed up here: Crowby in the middle of February.

For the third time he studied the piece of paper in his hand – the agenda of Greg Salter's ten o'clock meeting. Jacobson had always thought of his old boss, Chivers, as the DCS – Detective Chief Superintendent – or as the Super. But six months after his arrival, Salter was still plain Greg Salter in Jacobson's mental landscape. An interloper, a meddler, a human pinprick.

He turned away from the window, still reading, still pondering whether he could find any kind of reason to absent himself from what would be a wasted hour filled with management-speak, conceivably even two hours. His phone rang: Peter Robinson, Crowby's assistant pathologist. The one who actually did the work – while his senior, Professor Merchant, delivered research papers to attractively located conferences in warmer climes.

'Frank? Glad I caught you.'

Robinson said the name hesitantly. He'd only recently got

over his habit – borne of youth and residual shyness – of addressing Jacobson by his formal rank and title.

'We had a body brought in yesterday. Provisional cause of death listed as fire accident. Only closer inspection says otherwise. Beaten to a pulp would be more like it in layman's terms.'

'I'm on my way, old son,' Jacobson replied.

With his free hand he made a grab for his coat, very nearly falling over himself in the process. His coat rack was ancient and wobbly, almost useless. But so far he'd refused to ditch it for something newer or more efficacious.

The drive took him twenty minutes. On the way he called Harry Fields, recently promoted to DCI and simultaneously appointed as head of the drugs squad. Clean Harry would be another reluctant attendee at Salter's senior officers' meeting. He was hardly a mate. But he was a less overtly devious customer than most of those who'd be attending. At any rate he was as good a choice as any to pass on Jacobson's totally insincere apologies.

The pathology department was on the fourth floor of the new wing of the general hospital. Robinson, growing at last into his de facto role, had taken to using Merchant's office when the great man wasn't there. Which increasingly seemed to be most of the time. He spotted Jacobson making his way along the corridor, stepped out to greet him. Not for the first time, he put Jacobson in mind of an overgrown, affable schoolboy. A likeable variant on the class swot.

'Want to see the actual body or just, er, run through the video of the PM?' he asked.

'The video gets my vote,' Jacobson answered, thinking that even one post-mortem was more than enough to last an entire lifetime. Although he'd more or less lost count of the number he'd sat through over the years, he'd sooner have walked over hot coals every single time.

There was a VCR and a monitor in Merchant's office. Not

to mention the old boy's Cona machine. Without waiting to be asked, Jacobson poured himself a generous cupful before he sat down. Robinson had everything set up, had probably decided in advance that Jacobson would opt for the video record instead of the real, awful thing. He fast-forwarded his way through, pausing the playback every now and then, pointing out what he evidently considered to be the highlights.

Jacobson forced himself to look, forced himself to listen, forced himself not to wince. As far as he could see, the corpse was burnt and charred from head to toe. The first detail that he actually took in properly – actually asked about – was the position of the hands: lifted defensively in front of the body and tightened into fists. Robinson explained that the pose was a typical characteristic of a badly burnt human body.

'Exposure to the heat produces thermal fractures of the distal bones in the forearms. What you're seeing is the end result.'

It seemed to Jacobson that the effect was entirely as if a boxer had been struck by lightning while squaring up to an opponent. A full minute crawled by before he felt able to speak again.

'Yesterday's fire over at the Woodlands, I take it. I suppose we know who this unfortunate bugger *is*?'

Robinson had followed Jacobson's lead, had poured himself a cup of coffee. He took a quick sip before he replied.

'Circumstantially, the assumption is that he's Mr David Carter. Age thirty-nine. Resident on the estate apparently. He's received ninety per cent burns. Ninety-three point three four to be precise. So the formal identification is still pending—'

Robinson lifted the cup to his lips, took a second, deeper mouthful. Then:

'A matter of accessing and checking the dental records mainly. It'll take a few days at least.'

He paused the tape again, freezing the captured image of

his own frame, tall and stooping, bent over the head of the corpse. He wound further on until finally the head itself was in close-up, filling the screen. If you could still call it a head, Jacobson thought. The hair, if there'd been any, had been totally burned off and so had most of the scalp. It was no more than a skull really. With occasional strips of melted flesh clinging to the sides: like the pith on a clumsily peeled orange.

Robinson pointed to the cranial area.

'It's not as easy as you might think to stove in the average bonce,' he said. 'And not usually necessary. A rain of hard enough blows will usually cause internal haemorrhaging in the brain itself before you get to that stage. Result: death or coma – or unconsciousness at the very least.'

Jacobson steeled himself to carry on looking. He'd been lucky this time after all. He was only sitting through the action replay, he'd avoided the live event. But he would still have sworn under oath to a jury that he could *smell* the acrid sweetness of burning flesh.

Robinson tapped the middle of the screen with his long, nail-bitten index finger.

'The parietal bones, Frank. Aka the top of the head. Just look at the amount of fracturing here. Very nearly right through the sutures. You'd need something like a sharp axe or a pick – and you'd need to be built like a brick shithouse – to do very much more damage than this.'

'So you think a blunt instrument was used? Say a baseball bat or a tyre lever?'

'Exactly. Fissuring distributed over a wide area. No clean lines. Whoever did this was either unusually strong or – possibly more likely – completely enraged. In common parlance, it looks like somebody really flipped.'

Jacobson managed to drain his coffee. This far inside the hospital, it wasn't worth even thinking about a cigarette.

'So the fire was an afterthought? A cover-up.'

28

Robinson switched the monitor off, sat on the edge of Merchant's desk, his long legs dangling.

'I'm no fire expert. But there's not a trace of soot in the lungs. That's the most basic test of all. This chap was dead before the smoke hit him. Absolutely no question about that.'

Jacobson did what he could by phone on his way back across town and out towards the Woodlands. From the regular murder squad pool, only DCs Smith and Williams were immediately available. Barber and Mick Hume were in Birmingham for the morning at least, called as prosecution witnesses for a major case at the crown court. DS Kerr was in London yesterday and today, wouldn't be back in Crowby till this evening. Some course or other run by the Met: witness protection techniques, if Jacobson remembered correctly.

Smith and Williams were waiting for him when he pulled up outside William Blake House. A couple of patrol cars had got there too. Two plods per car. All they needed now were the SOCOs and they could make some kind of a start. Jacobson got out of his car and stood on the pavement, his coat collar turned up. He recapped what Robinson had told him for the benefit of his two detectives.

'Beats me why nobody picked up on it yesterday, guv,' Emma Smith said.

'These thing happen, lass,' Jacobson replied, leaving it at that.

The fire brigade's immediate job had been to stop the fire, to keep it from spreading. The paramedics would have taken as scant a look as possible at the torched mess on the bed that had once been a human being. Definitely not alive so definitely beyond the scope of their over-stretched job spec. If anyone was at fault, it had been the police surgeon who'd scribbled the wildly inaccurate provisional death certificate. *Probable cause of death: severe exposure to fire.* But for now Jacobson's priority was to get the job done. Recrimination would have to sit on the back burner till later. He groaned inwardly at the bad taste of the metaphor, turned his gaze to take in the block of flats behind him. The plods called the area the Son of the Bronx, viewed it as a heartland for miscreants, scumbags, toerags, *untermensch*. You'd want to get the tenants out first of course, he thought. Then you could do the decent thing. Flame the whole bloody lot. And start again.

Sheryl sat at the back of the bus, watched out the window as the Flowers Street bus station came into view. Candice had helped her wash the girls' clothes overnight, drying them over radiators and against the boiler in the big cupboard next to the bathroom. The best thing was obviously for them to carry on at school until things got sorted out. Somewhere warm and clean for them to be all day. Somewhere safe. She picked up her shoulder bag and made her way to the exit when the bus pulled into bay five.

There was a little café on the way out of the bus station. She went inside and ordered a cup of coffee. It wasn't much of a place. She doubted if she'd been here more than two or three times before. But that was why she'd chosen it now. Somewhere no one would be likely to recognise her. Or point a finger. She just needed a few minutes on her own, that was all. A bit of time to think, to get her head straight. She still couldn't work out where they'd got that photo from anyway. The local paper. Even the TV. Someone on the estate obviously. Someone she'd given it to and then forgotten, proudly showing off her little sweethearts. She found a quiet table and sat down, took out her packet of Silk Cut.

She wanted a ciggy to go with the coffee. Thank Christ she always took her bag with her everywhere. Without fail. She always kept everything essential inside. Cigarettes were the least of it. Her rent book, her benefits book, any cash she happened to have, the girls' birth certificates. The whole thing was a frigging nightmare. But at least she could still prove who she was, what she was entitled to. It was a habit she'd followed from the first day she'd move into William Blake. Fair enough, it put you at risk from a snatcher. But at least they'd have to take it from you face to face, not get at it behind your back. This way you always had everything that mattered with you. Even if the flat got done over, you weren't going to come home and find that it was all gone. Dave always laughed at her. The way she even kept it in the bedroom overnight. *What's going to happen with me here, lovely?*

She lit the cigarette, spooned a single teaspoon of white sugar into the cup. No more laughing for him now. Not ever. Dave had been OK, had been better to her than most. Whatever he'd done or whoever he'd crossed, he hadn't deserved what had happened to him. But her crying about it, moping, wasn't going to do any good, wasn't going to change anything. You got shat on when you lived at the bottom of the shit heap. End of. There was getting rehoused. There was getting some cash to buy some bits and pieces of furniture, some new clothes for the girls. There was getting back on their feet. Nothing else mattered. Nothing else in the stinking world.

Jacobson had to take his coat off to get into the protective suit. DC Williams offered to hold it for him but Jacobson decided it was an act of deference too far. He slung it on the bonnet of his car then chucked it into the boot once he was suited up. When they'd taken the lift to the fourth floor, there was another delay while they pulled the protective slip-ons over their shoes. Jacobson noticed the scuff marks on the front of his black lace-up brogues, resolved to give them a good old-fashioned polishing once he got home.

The chief SOCO, Webster, showed them into the burnt-out flat, gave them a grudging guided tour. He'd been in touch with the Forensic Science Service headquarters in

Birmingham, he told them. Hopefully there'd be a couple of FSS fire assessment experts arriving some time in the afternoon. Jacobson offered a silent, agnostic prayer of thanks that the force had abandoned its partial, experimental use of commercial laboratories and scientists, had gone back wholesale to the Home Office agency. In the meantime, Webster added, there wasn't that much they could do. The fire had obviously started in the bedroom – you could tell just by the sheer amount of damage – and spread from there. They didn't want to disturb the seat of the blaze before the specialists had given it the once-over. He showed them the lounge last of all, the least wrecked room: where they were going to concentrate their attentions for now. Especially as there could be all sorts left behind in a partially fire-damaged room. Fingerprints on the odd bit of wall or other surfaces, for instance. All sorts.

Jacobson lifted the mask away from his face for a moment. As if he needed to smell the scene as well as see it. A young lass rented the place apparently. Two kiddies. Once the SOCOs had finished – tomorrow maybe, or the day after – they'd let her back in, let her salvage what she could. Not that it would amount to much. Jacobson bent down in the middle of the room, his gloved fingers pulling at the blackened remains of what looked like a pile of magazines. The charred paper crumbled away even as he touched it. Near by he noticed the shell of what might once have been an electric fire, the coils burnt and useless. Strangely, the grille lay a few feet away. On its own, detached. He stood back up, gave Smith and Williams a meaningful nod in the direction of the narrow hallway: leave it to the SOCOs – for the moment, there was nothing useful for a detective to do in the immediate vicinity.

He left the two DCs plus three of the four uniformeds with the unenviable task of door-to-door enquiries in William Blake House. Rearrange the following into a well-known phrase or saying, he thought. A brick wall. Your head.

Banging against. Any neighbours who knew anything, who'd seen anything, would keep it to themselves. At the very least keep it from the coppers. Even if you weren't actively up to mischief yourself, you still needed to be *sound*. Or at least to be seen to be sound. And sound meant being anti-police. Very definitely so. If a tip-off came from the Woodlands, it would only come quietly and in the middle of the night. The caller's voice muffled and hesitant. The caller's number withheld.

His car was sandwiched between the two patrol vehicles and the scene-of-crime van. The fourth plod stood on the pavement, keeping an eye out. A raw recruit. Awkward, inexperienced. A bunch of small boys stood near by on the patchy grass, smirking and giving him the finger. Jacobson ditched the protective gear, retrieved his coat from his car boot, clambered back in behind the steering wheel. According to the uniformeds who'd spoken to her yesterday, the young lass had said that Dave Carter lived on the other side of the estate. With his wife. She didn't know the exact address. But Carter had been on the PNC anyway. Sporadic minor convictions since his teens. Receiving stolen goods, bits and bobs of burglary. But nothing heavy. Nothing that made him an obvious candidate for murder.

It took him ten minutes to find the place. Along past the Poets then take the second left off Wordsworth Avenue: Tennyson Court, number seventy-three. A bleak two-storey house in a seamless row of a dozen others. The front door wasn't locked, wasn't even shut. Jacobson lifted his hand as if to ring the bell then seemed to think better of it, stepped quietly in. A black cat, the double of DS Kerr's, brushed against his legs. Then two more. He found the woman he assumed was Mrs Eileen Carter snoring in the front room, sprawled out on the sofa, oblivious. A big woman. Statuesque or overweight, depending on your point of view. Depending on what you were into. An empty gin bottle told part of the story. That and the blaring, unwatched TV set. Jerry Springer:

33

*My sister slept with my three husbands.* He looked around for the remote control, finally found it next to an overflowing ashtray on the floor. Next to the fag ends he saw a pill bottle, paracetamol 25 mg, cap off and empty. He pointed the remote at the TV, switched it off. The three entirely black cats had followed him in from the hall, meowing incessantly in an eerie kind of unison.

He checked her pulse inexpertly. The reaction to bad news, obviously. I'm afraid your husband's been cooked to a frazzle, madam. Oh, and in a young woman's bed at the time. She might have left the door open on purpose, he thought. Hoping someone would find her before it was too late. The old cry-for-help routine. He put an emergency call through for an ambulance then helped himself to a good prowl round. In the kitchen, he found an unopened tin of Whiskas in the cupboard under the sink. He put it out for the cats in the blue plastic bowl they'd already licked clean. He put some milk and water out too.

Upstairs, there were two bedrooms and a bathroom. The bedroom at the rear was hubby's attempt at a den. Weights, an ancient computer, home brewing paraphernalia, an out-of-date racing calendar. The wallpaper in the other bedroom was pink and peachy. So were the sheets and the quilt. The wife's domain, he thought. At the back of the wardrobe there was a battered-looking suitcase. The kind you snapped shut. It was the only locked thing in the entire gaff. Two hinged combination locks. One on either side, three digits each. He was wondering how difficult it would be to guess the right sequence of numbers when he heard the noise of footsteps downstairs, saw the ambulance's blue flashing light reflected in the window.

The paramedics were non-committal on her chances. One of them said he'd seen a woman one time who'd taken only four and never regained consciousness. Complete liver failure. Dead within sixteen hours. After they'd stretchered her out to the ambulance, Jacobson closed the front door. There was a cupboard under the stairs. Exactly the kind of place where you'd keep any tools you might have at home. Inside a grey plastic toolbox, he found what he was looking for. A sturdy screwdriver and a hammer. Bollocks to wasting time on the combinations. Who could say, he reasoned, who'd been in and out of the premises while the front door was lying wide open, while Mrs Carter was comatose on the sofa? Anyone could have found the locked suitcase – decided it might be worth a look to see what was inside, scarpered in fright when they saw what *was*.

# Chapter Six

Maybe because there was a murder involved, or maybe because it got him out of Greg Salter's still unfinished meeting, Harry Fields himself had responded to Jacobson's call. Along with a couple of his shaven-headed, famously thuggish detective constables. While the drug squad DCs embarked on a thorough trawl of the premises, Clean Harry cast his eye over the busted-open suitcase.

'A regular little Aladdin's cave, Frank,' he said. 'Hash, hash oil, wraps – even a bit of the brown stuff.'

'Heroin?' Jacobson asked.

DCI Fields nodded.

'Only a bit, though. Ditto crack. Dope and pills mainly, the big recreational sellers. Something for the weekend, as the ungodless say.'

There was cash in the suitcase too. Dirty-looking fivers, tens, twenties. Jacobson had already counted it but Fields bent down to do the sums a second time.

'Five grand, right enough. Big money in this part of the world.'

Jacobson had his back to the window. It was barely late morning. But already it felt that the daylight was fading, that the best of the day was already over. He hated drug-related cases. Not least because it meant you had to work with the drug squad.

'Dave Carter was on your books, then, old son?' he asked.

'Not to my immediate knowledge, Frank. But I really only take an overview these days. I've got my records guy looking into it. The Poets is certainly a venue within our remit. Well within. Plus there's a local tradition of the barman dealing. My guess would be that friend Carter was the latest in that long line. Gave offence to somebody on the scene. Not an unusual occurrence by any manner of means.'

Fields was a thin man over fifty in a good suit. Medium height. Grey faced. Neatly cut silvery hair. On first sight a computer salesman or an estate agent as much as the local drugs czar. He was known as Clean because he'd spent ten years in drugs enforcement without once taking a bung or planting evidence. Half a dozen of his colleagues had put in urgent requests for early retirement and/or transfers when his appointment as head of the squad had been confirmed. He should have been Jacobson's natural ally, even his friend. But Fields was an odd bird. His hobby – or maybe just his way of coping with the job – was fire-and-brimstone lay preaching at some kind of evangelical church. Just for the hell of it, Jacobson offered him a B and H before he took one out for himself and lit up. Predictably, Clean Harry declined the offer.

'Gave offence enough for murder?' Jacobson asked.

Fields moved out of the trajectory of Jacobson's cigarette smoke.

'These are edgy times in the illegal drugs business, Frank. Relaxation on the cannabis front. Do-gooding doctors getting the green light to prescribe heroin to registered addicts for the first time in decades. Mixed messages from the Home Office. A lot of firms are getting panicky, looking to their profit margins. Let's say, for instance, that Carter was taking more than his agreed cut or selling for more than one supplier. Either or both would've been a very bad career move in the current circumstances.'

One of Field's detectives stuck his head round the bedroom door.

'Clean as a whistle, guv. No sign of anything being used anywhere. Looks like Mr Burnt Toast's interest was strictly professional.'

Emphasis on *was*, Jacobson thought. Every functioning policeman was callous to an extent. It was how you got through the day. But only the drug squad had made it into an art form.

'I take it you know *which* firm would regard the Poets as *their* outlet then, Harry?'

'These things change by the month, Frank. And like I say, I'm supposed to take an overview only these days. But I'll be speaking to our area operational officer as soon as possible.'

Fields promised to get back to him and to keep in touch. Jacobson promised to reciprocate.

Back outside, the drizzle was still slow, the sky still grey. He got into his car and retraced the last part of his journey. Finally, steering carefully among the shattered windscreen glass and general debris, he pulled into the car park at the side of the Poets. Getting out, his right foot squelched over a couple of used condoms and the putrefying remains of a Chinese takeaway. A top drugs outlet maybe, he thought, but it was never going to get a Family Friendly rating or a CAMRA listing.

It was the only boozer on the Woodlands, and the other breweries weren't queuing up any day soon to open a rival. It wasn't a place for the hard core to score, obviously. That trade would go on via the safe houses and the under-age couriers. But the Poets, as Fields had suggested, would still be a handy source of revenue for whoever controlled the supply. More than handy. Casual pill-heads, occasional users, weekend dopers: anybody who just needed to get off their face for a few hours or for a couple of days. Which – at one time or another – probably meant virtually everybody on the estate who wasn't entirely brain dead, who could still be troubled by dreams of a life that might be something other than shit followed by more shit. Jacobson had no problem with any of that. Just with Clean Harry's subsidiary theory that the trade was important enough to kill for.

Charlie drove Florida Boy over to Lisa's place in the stolen Rover. The Beech Park estate. Aka straight city. Lisa's mum and her old man both had jobs, both worked, were both out all day. They mostly did around here. Factory jobs, a fortnight in Malaga every summer, banged up in front of the telly every night. See the mice in their million hordes. The moron legions. Lisa would do something with FB's back. Stick a dressing on or something. At least stop the cunt's constant fucking whining. Play your cards right, she'll probably throw in a blow job, he'd told him.

Just to be on the safe side – just to stay even slightly professional – he dropped FB off at the door and then drove around the corner, parked in the next street. He snuck across a couple of gardens, arrived by the back door. Lisa let him in. She hadn't dressed for the day yet. Or maybe she'd de-dressed herself especially. Either way all she was wearing was some kind of nightie. Long and high necked. But still capable of showing the tidy bulge of her neat little tits as she double-locked the door after him.

She already had FB prone on the floor of the lounge, the shirt unpeeled from his sorry-looking back. It took her half an hour to do what she could for him. Charlie sat on the couch watching her at work. When she was nearly finished, he rolled a spliff, using the back of the *Radio Times* as a work area.

Once FB was bandaged up, Lisa sat back in what was probably her old man's favourite armchair, her legs wrapped comfily under her chin. Charlie lit the spliff, passed it over to her.

39

'Ain't they hassling you to get another job, then?' he asked her.

'All the time. But they can stuff it. What they going to do, chuck me out?'

'It's been known,' he said.

His own mother had turfed him out when he was fourteen. Not that he hadn't been glad to go, hadn't been eager to get the fuck away. Lisa took a long, deep draw. Then:

'Your friend still hasn't said what happened to him.'

'Stoned, wasn't it?' Charlie answered. 'Fell over and landed on his electric fire. Daft twat.'

Florida Boy nodded. He was facing towards Charlie and Lisa. But still stretched out on his front on the floor. Still trying to ease his back. The fuckwit. There was something weirdly parental in the scene. Himself and Lisa sat up like adults. Florida Boy sprawled at their feet: the moronic, good-for-nothing son.

'Stoned. Fell over, like,' FB managed at last, lifting his head up, shooting Lisa a quick glance then just as quickly looking away.

You couldn't shut the cunt up when he was chemically enhanced. But the rest of the time – like now – he was practically monosyllabic. Particularly around women.

'We do *have* hospitals in this country. It's not blinking Afghanistan,' Lisa commented, taking a second draw.

He watched the fingers of her free hand playing with the ends of her fringe. Her hair looked like it had been recently washed, recently brushed. Plus for some reason she'd painted each of her toenails a different, sparkly colour.

'Brian leads a complicated life, Leez,' he said. 'There's reasons why he can't go through official channels and such.'

Before they'd called round, he'd told FB to stick to his rarely used first name. Even a babe in the woods like Lisa might've read about the famous Florida Boy on some occasion or other, he'd warned him.

There was silence after that for a bit. Apart from a car having difficulty starting up somewhere outside. Apart from the TV in the corner. An old episode of *Quincy*.

'Seeing anyone these days?' Lisa asked him finally, seeming to let the issue drop, handing him back the joint.

'Nobody special. You?'

'Not really.'

So that's what she thought the visit was about. Getting back together. Using FB's accident as a pretext. Charlie weighed up the options. Out of sight was out of mind and all that. They'd be as well off here for a couple of hours as anywhere. Certainly compared to Mill Street or the Woodlands.

'What time's your old mum back, then?' he asked, waving the spliff in front of him.

Without taking his eyes off her, he passed it down to Florida Boy. The consolation prize for you, mate. That and the telly. Both well more than you fucking deserve. You fuckwit moron.

Ten past eleven. The Poets was open for business – just. But there were zero takers this early in the day. Only two glaziers in the public bar. They'd just fixed the broken window in the lounge, were enjoying a couple of lagers on the house. Behind the counter, a thirty-something skinhead had evidently been pouring out glass after glass. He was wearing a Bin Laden T-shirt – Wanted Dead or Dead – and he hadn't bothered to shave. Not today, not yesterday. Must've just put a new keg on, Jacobson thought. The pouring had stopped when he'd walked in. It didn't matter that they'd never clapped eyes on you before. Round here they knew at a glance *what* you were.

'What can I get you, mate?' the skinhead asked, pretending otherwise.

Jacobson flashed his ID then stuck it back in his jacket pocket.

'And you are?'

'Shields. Terry Shields. I'm the manager.'

Jacobson asked him if there was somewhere they could talk in private. Shields put the green drip towel back over the taps.

'This way, mate,' he said.

He told the glaziers not to drink everything in sight, showed Jacobson behind the bar. He led him through a kitchen area dank with the smell of stale chip fat and into the back room. Three straight-backed chairs around a non-functional snooker table. A dusty sofa. A wall-mounted TV set, cheap hotel style. Shields cut the volume but left the picture to flicker on. CEEFAX: the latest prices from the FTSE 100. Vital intelligence in the Son of the Bronx. Not.

'Sure you don't want something bringing through from the bar, mate?'

Jacobson ignored the offer. It was still an hour or so too early for him and he hadn't much liked the latrinal odour he'd detected from the pile of freshly poured glasses. Instead he pulled back one of the chairs, sat down, got straight to.

'Worked here long, Terry?'

If I'm mate, you can't be Mr Shields. Quid pro quo.

Shields slumped into the sofa, sending a flurry of dust into the grey half-light.

'Near enough a year and a half. To be honest with you I didn't make out too well at my last place. It was either here or on your bike as far as the brewery was concerned. Better off jacking it in, most probably.'

'And Dave Carter?'

'Started about the same time. Don't know what the hell I'm going to do without him and that's straight up. Only reliable staff I've got – or had got. More or less kept a lid on the troublemakers, never dipped in the till.'

42

There was a packing case of Chivas Regal on the snooker table. A four-hundred carton of Dunhill. Twenty packs of twenty.

'What exactly have you heard about Dave, Terry?'

Although the fire and the death had made the front page locally, Dave Carter's name hadn't yet been officially released.

'Dead, basically. That's what. That fire over at William Blake. You hear everything first in here, mate. Although I expect the whole estate knows by now.'

'Did the whole estate know about him and the young lass? Did his wife?'

'Young Sheryl? Well, I never knew and I've seen them talking together over the bar more than a few times. Dark horse an' all.'

Shields stroked his non-designer stubble. A thought was struggling to be born in Hobbesian circumstances. Its life would be nasty, brutish and short.

'These questions, mate. It *was* just an accident, wasn't it? Surely to Christ you don't—'

'I asked you about his wife, Terry.'

Shields shot up off the couch and pulled one of the Chivas bottles out of the case. He broke off the cap and took a deep swig. Then another.

'His wife,' Jacobson repeated.

'I-I've never met the woman. Never came near this dump, as far as I know. There's lots don't. Just stop home with the door locked.'

He paused, the bottle limp in his hand. Then:

'But she must have known something was up. If Dave was spending whole nights over there.'

Jacobson stood up too. He badly wanted a fag: association of ideas from the Dunhill carton. Yet he was nearly through. Very nearly. He decided to save it for the car, for the drive back to the Divisional building.

'Did Dave cut you in on the dealing, Terry? Or maybe it was the other way round?'

Shields shook his head as if testing its connection to the rest of his body.

'I don't know what you're on about, mate. I—'

But Jacobson was already on his way out, already finding his lighter and his car keys.

# Chapter Seven

Lunchtime. Stephen Adams parked his Mondeo in the surprisingly ample car park which opened out behind the Top Hat café. The Top Hat was squeezed next to a video rental shop and a tool hire outlet out on Copthorne Road, not far from the old industrial estate where Adams Installations was located. You reached the car park via the narrow gap between the café and the tool hire place. All day long, cars, vans and the occasional fully loaded rig would hold up the traffic while they entered or exited through the concrete slot between the two buildings.

Above the café, there were half a dozen unsavoury bedrooms and a couple of bath-shower rooms it was worth staying dirty just to avoid. Labourers, plasterers, guys like that, stopped there weeknights if they were doing contract work in Crowby from somewhere out of town. The café itself enjoyed a formidable reputation for its dedication to ethnic British cuisine at its finest and most traditional. Fried eggs, fried bread, health-risk sausages, black pudding. Even if they stuck a tomato on the side of your Full English Breakfast, Served All Day, you could rest assured that it had first undergone a rigorous and thorough process to extract and discard any element of flavour or any trace of vitamin and mineral content.

Steve was in the habit of sharing a bite here with some of his crew two or three times a month. He filed it in his mind under the heading of staff relations. It was a less formal meeting place than his office, kept things casual, made it easier for them to talk straight. It reminded them that although he was the boss he'd started out no better than them, that he was still just an ordinary bloke at heart. Only two things made him different from the herd in his own personal view. One: not being afraid of hard work. Two: not being too scared to grab an opportunity when it presented itself.

He ordered a couple of bacon rolls and a mug of tea – large – at the counter, walked over and joined them at their regular table.

He'd barely sat down when Ray Coombs started in on him. The lack of new customers and the lack of overtime: the usual workforce obsessions.

'Some of the lads have done nothing but reinspects this last fortnight, Steve,' Coombs said.

One of Steve's big ideas was his free follow-up policy. Three months, six months, even nine months if you wanted it, one of his engineers would reinspect your system, make any minor adjustments which were needed without any additional charge. Sometimes he went along himself on these revisits. It was a bit of old bollocks really. A way of maintaining contact, of maybe talking the punter into an early and profitable upgrade. It was also a way of keeping his employees busy if real work was slack.

He gaped at Coombs for a deliberate, uneasy minute before he replied. Straight talking was one thing. Fucking cheek was another. Coombs was a new start, only six months in, more or less an unknown quantity up until now.

'There's always a lull at this time of year, Ray. Everybody's spent out after Christmas. I know I am anyway—'

He paused while the young girl called Milly stuck his rolls and the white mug of tea in front of him.

'Ta, love. Things'll pick up again soon. They always do.'

'I saw something on the Business Channel the other night,

Steve. They reckoned the domestic market might be approaching what they call the saturation point,' Coombs persisted.

Steve had his first roll halfway to his mouth. Hot grease trickled onto his forefinger and thumb. He put it back down on the plate before he spoke.

'That's their job, Ray. Nobody watches the telly to hear good news. But they *watch* the telly. That's all we've got to worry about. There's always somebody shopping for something bigger and better.'

Keep this up pal, he thought, and you can have your cards.

'What Steve says makes sense to me,' Colin Paterson interjected.

Paterson was his key worker. Long serving. He'd been with the firm since the early days, acted as a foreman in all but name. Coombs shrugged, giving up, went back to attacking his individual steak pie and chips. Steve took a highly visible look at the three or four others who were gathered around the table, who hadn't spoken, whose no-initiative, needing-to-be-led heads were nodding docilely.

'But then you've *got* sense in the first place, Col,' he said finally, feigning a smile.

And thinking: et fucking cetera.

He stayed another ten minutes, finished his rolls and the mug of tea. He drove back to base with Talksport on the radio. Idiots from all over talking rubbish about soccer. Gave you something to listen to, though, something you could focus on, keep your mind from drifting.

The Copthorne Road industrial estate had developed an elderly, careworn look these days. The units were ancient and difficult to heat. A lot of them stood empty. But the rates were consequently cheap. He parked up at the side of his loading bays. Adams Installations was a workshop, garage space and two cramped offices dwarfed by the Kwik-Fit centre next door. Business at Kwik-Fit was good, which gave a nice busy feel to the immediate vicinity. But Kwik-Fit were on the move, would be bailing out to the Waitrose complex later in the year. Steve was seriously considering following them. Like that African bird he'd seen on the National Geographic channel one time. The one that survived by following the black rhino, living off the bigger animal's parasites or whatever.

He switched off the radio, got out, strolled into his front office, whistling casually. *If you think I'm sexy*. Linda, his clerk stroke typist stroke tele-sales stroke customer services, sat behind her desk doing something or nothing. Emailing a supplier or – just as likely – playing Solitaire. A tall man paced up and down in the middle of the room. Alan bloody Jones, Steve thought. The original time-is-money operator. Checking his bloody watch every five seconds as per usual, wearing out the bloody carpet.

'Alan, good to see you.' He beamed. 'Tea? Coffee? A dram?'

The offer was purely routine. And was always rejected.

'No thanks,' Jones replied, 'I can't stay long.'

Steve didn't press him, ushered him through to the tiny second office. A table, a computer, two filing cabinets and a couple of executive chairs, strictly last year's range.

'It was good of you to come,' he said, possibly meaning it. Jones was his accountant – paid for. His business advice role was purely a matter of unpaid goodwill.

Jones picked the chair furthest from the door, spoke in a near-whisper.

'Frankly, Steve, it's not good,' he said. 'It's not good at all.'

Lisa always liked to go on top, or at least finish up on top. It had amused Charlie at first, irritated him to fuck later. Today, though, he hadn't really minded. With all the bastarding stress since yesterday it had suited him fine just to lie back and let her get on with it. He dozed for a bit afterwards, woke up to find her leaning over him, licking his left nipple.

'Get off, you daft cow.'

He shoved her head away lightly and reached out of the bed, grabbing his pants. Not so much daft as strange, he thought. She'd wanted to do it in her parents' room, obviously. In their bed. That was another one of her preferences, another one of her old tricks. There was no reckoning her really. But he did love those little tits, firm and pointed. The way they'd barely jiggled as she'd bounced up and down. 'Course, she thought they were *too* small. Too big, too small: there was no slag anywhere happy with the size.

'Gotta go, Leez,' he said. 'Stuff to do.'

But letting her kiss him full on the mouth as he slid his feet on to the floor.

Downstairs, Florida Boy was gawping at *Rugrats*. Just about exactly the twat's mental level. Lisa had put her nightie back on, followed them out to the hall. He let her kiss him again, told her he'd call her or text her, send her something well filthy. They'd meet up. Do something. Soon. No question.

Out of doors, the drizzle continued to drizzle. Charlie and FB walked to the end of Lisa's street and then turned left. Twenty yards farther on they'd turn left again: into the street where Charlie had parked the Rover. He realised he must have slept for longer than he'd supposed. It was gone half four now, the overcast sky already blacking up for the long February night. They were right on the corner, very nearly *around* it, when his brain interpreted the signal his eyes had already processed. Blue light not yellow. And flashing not street lamp. He shot out his right arm, managed somehow to stop FB from blundering on. They retraced their steps a few feet then crossed the road, walked passed the junction on the opposite side. Further away from the patrol car and the bystander commotion. *Casual, mate, casual. Just keep walking.*

When they got to a bus shelter they stepped quickly inside. FB saying precisely nothing, waiting as always for Charlie to do the fucking thinking, to come up with the master plan.

'You and your fuckwit back.'

Then:

'Leez and fuckwit Beech Park.'

Charlie found that he was whispering. Even though there was no one else in the shelter, no one else within earshot. The problem with straight city was the straights basically. Nobody on the Woodlands gave the slightest fuck when they noticed the tell-tale signs of a repeatedly hot-wired car: the damaged plastic casing around the ignition key, the exposed metal of the ignition barrel, the four dangling wires. Evidently it was a different story around here. Too many curtain twitchers and dog walkers. Too many *Crimewatch* fans. Too many nosy gits who couldn't mind their own business. *Police! Police! A stolen car! Stop, bastarding thief.*

The only thing to do, he decided, was to revisit Lisa. Staying where they were was too risky. So was legging it over to the shops in the middle of the estate. The dibble wouldn't bust a gut over a stolen vehicle. But once they'd slapped a Police Aware sticker on the windscreen, they'd at least do a quick tour of the area: on the lookout for known, obvious toerags such as himself and FB. Her mother wouldn't be back till half five anyway, she'd said. And her old man was on overtime. Seven till six. They could say the twat's bandages had got too loose or too tight. Something like that. Anything to get them off the street for the next half-hour. After that, they'd be OK.

Yeah, OK, Charlie thought, turning his hood back up. OK apart from being transport-less. OK, apart from being totally out of the firm before they were even in it. OK, apart from having a useless, needless, fuckwit killing on their hands.

Sheryl had only just caught the bus out to the Bartons on time.

She'd been three hours at the housing office. Which meant she hadn't been able to visit the social until the afternoon. She'd had to leave before her ticket came up. Which meant she'd have to go back tomorrow morning, join the queue all over again. And still the frigging bus managed to be late. Caught up in the roadworks at the Flowers Street junction before it had even got out of town. Now, to cap it all, here was Lucy and Anne-Marie standing outside the school gates with Anne-Marie's friend, Sarah, and Sarah's snooty, stuck-up cow of a mother.

'I didn't want to leave them here on their own,' Marion Adams said. 'I was sure you'd be along as soon as you could.'

'That was decent of you. Thanks.'

Lucy reached up and grabbed her mum's fingers tightly.

'The bus is an old slowcoach,' she said.

Sheryl smiled despite herself.

'You can say that again, my love.'

'Old slowcoach,' Lucy repeated.

Her fingers felt sticky in Sheryl's grip: sweets at lunchtime most probably.

Marion Adams saw her chance to be patronising and took it.

'Public transport these days,' she said, shaking her head. 'We could give you a lift, if you liked. As far as town anyway. I need to pick up our evening wear from the cleaners for tonight. Then I need to get over to Sainsbury's if I've time. I don't know – the big shop never seems to last the week these days.'

Which must be such a blinking inconvenience, Sheryl thought. No flaming thanks. I'd rather frigging walk the whole frigging way.

'No, you're all right,' she said flatly. 'It's usually quicker on the way back anyway.'

Anne-Marie and Sarah had been deep in a whispered

51

conference. Sarah nudged Anne-Marie forward. She stepped over to where Sheryl was standing, took hold of her mum's other hand.

'Mu-um.'

Then:

'Sarah says I can go over for tea tomorrow night. I could even stay over.'

Sheryl scanned Marion Adams' face for a reaction. The cow was knocking thirty-five, had to be. But you couldn't deny she didn't look it. Even after three kids. Maybe a little plumper than was ideal. But not by much. And perfectly styled, shining hair. Clear, untroubled blue eyes. What money couldn't do wasn't worth doing.

'Please, Mum,' Anne-Marie said.

'Please, Mum. Ple-eez. Ple-eez,' Sarah said, taking her own mother's hand.

Marion Adams looked as surprised about the news as Sheryl. About as unhappy too. But the truth was that Anne-Marie deserved a break. More than. She'd been even better than usual since the fire. Keeping an eye on Lucy, telling her everything was going to be OK. It would be good for her. A night in a nice, big, warm house instead of hunkered down like a refugee in Candice's front room. There *was* a flat coming up, they'd told her at the housing. But it would be Thursday at the earliest, the day after tomorrow, before they could possibly move in. Sheryl put on a smile before she spoke. A big, phoney ear-to-ear smile.

'Well, if Sarah's mum says it's OK.'

The cow and bitch was cornered, *knew* she was cornered.

'We'd-we'd be happy to have you, my lamb,' Marion Adams said. 'That's agreed.'

*Especially under the circumstances*, she might have added. Might have been thinking of adding. *Especially now that*.

But Sheryl never took her eyes off her: warning her, daring

her. Don't say it, you cow. Don't say anything like it. Not one frigging word.

'Cool,' said Sarah.

'Cool,' said Anne-Marie.

Sheryl let go of their hands, hugged their shoulders. Her little sweethearts.

'It's really kind of you,' she said. 'Really decent.'

Then:

'Come on, loves. We don't want to miss that old bus again.'

When Alan Jones had gone, Steve made himself a pot of tea and stuck one of Linda's weird tea bags into a mug for her. Egyptian Spice, it called itself. A genuine ayurvedic blend, according to the box. Whatever the hell that was.

He always had to leave early on a Tuesday. But it was in a good cause. And it was the only day – bar the occasional Friday – that he did so. He'd got into the habit of grabbing an extra cuppa first – to keep warm out on the pitch, to keep himself going. For five years now, he'd coached the Barton Juniors; coaxed, humoured and chivvied them, transformed them into one of the best teams in the After School League. Contenders for the shield this year. In his view, the Tuesday training sessions were paramount, central, for the purpose. A team that was unprepared to win was a team that was prepared to lose.

He checked up on the new-prospects file while he drank his tea. There'd been only six enquiries since yesterday, Linda told him. And one of those had been an OAP in Wynarth who'd sounded like she'd gone half daft from too much of her own company. Who'd probably just wanted to talk to somebody, to hear another human voice for five minutes.

'Six is better than nothing, Linda. Six times better to be precise.'

He suggested she call them all back again tomorrow.

Especially the old dear. They could send Colin Paterson over with a couple of brochures and a line of friendly chat to do the estimate. Col was always good for a bit of tea and sympathy.

He went out of his premises via the workshop, treated the lads to a bit of motivational bullshit re the remote possibility of landing the retirement flats contract. There was a big job in the offing, he told them. It was more or less a done deal already. Smiling. Patting a couple of backs. Whistling: *Things can only get better.* Sod Alan *frankly* Jones.

He switched over from Talksport to Classic Gold this time, took the back exit from the estate. That way you avoided the worst of the teatime build up on Copthorne Road itself. Jonesy had a point, of course. A couple of dozen points, to be honest. Steve's turnover for the last quarter, was down on the previous quarter which was down on the quarter before that: et fucking cetera. *You can't go on sustaining losses like these, Steve. I'm the one who's got to make the figures add up. And – frankly – you can't go on paying yourself a director's salary that your volume of trade doesn't remotely justify.* But when all was said and done, Jonesy was an accountant, not a risk-taker. Plus he hadn't had to build himself up from nothing, carve out a niche from effing scratch. Not the way that he had anyway. No real education to fall back on. No poncy degree. Besides, with all the good publicity that would come after tonight, who was to say that the phones wouldn't soon be buzzing like buggery again? The lovely Linda might even have to start skipping on her lunchtime yoga classes.

# Chapter Eight

Jacobson and Harry Fields plus DCs Smith and Williams squatted illegally in an empty meeting room on the third floor of the Divisional building. Smith and Williams took possibly all of thirty seconds to revisit what they'd found out door to door. As predicted, nobody in the block had seen or heard anything. But no one. But nothing. Candice Thompson, in whose flat the burnt-out family had spent last night, was virtually the only neighbour who'd admit to knowing about the mother's relationship with Dave Carter. It wasn't even clear, Williams added, who exactly had phoned the fire brigade. The caller's number had been withheld. And only a curt message delivered in a monotone on the 999 tapes. *Fire, William Blake House.* End of. All he could really say was that the voice was male. Probably.

Jacobson's own afternoon had hardly been more fruitful. He'd spoken to the fire damage experts after they'd made their inspection, cross-checked back again with Robinson out at the mortuary. He knew more now than he did before about domestic fire damage. But the upshot hadn't changed: the flat had been torched *after* someone had beaten Dave Carter to death. The only tiny little problem was *who*. He was sitting well down the table from the others, turning his head away from them every now and again to exhale his fag smoke in the opposite direction. Rumour had it that a new generation of smoke detectors were already under requisition. They were alleged to be sensitive enough to detect the smoke from just one cigarette. It was a bridge Jacobson would cross only when he had to.

Clean Harry spoke next – between mouthfuls of a pork pie. Seemingly he wasn't entirely without sin himself.

'According to our area officer, the Poets outlet is linked to a chain operating out of Birmingham. Which puts any activity on the premises into Regional Crime Squad territory. Which means my guy's restricted purely to monitoring and observation.'

Jacobson shook his head eloquently. The usual drug squad quagmire: taking out a few dealers now and again to keep the papers and the hack councillors quiet. But hitting the low-level cohorts only. Strictly the common foot-soldiers. Most of their time seemed to be spent on surveillance and intelligence-gathering: preparing for the next big regional crackdown. The one that would be putting the major players away. The one that hardly ever got actioned. Or got bungled in the execution when it did. Or fucked up by the CPS retards if any cases ever actually got so far as a courtroom.

'I suppose I'm at least allowed to know what your lad's found out?' he asked.

Clean Harry finished his pie, wiped the crumbs from the corners of his mouth.

'Friend Carter has – or had – the local franchise, just as I suggested, Frank. A two-man operation by the looks of it. Carter plus the bar manager. Name of Terry Shields.'

'I've already had the pleasure,' Jacobson said. 'What about your theory that Carter was doing the dirty on his regular supplier?'

'Now that was news to my guy. But he agrees that it's a likely explanation. More than likely in fact, he says. He seemed surprised they'd stretch as far as murder, though. Punishment beatings are more this lot's usual style, apparently.'

'Happens in Brum, guv. So why not here?' Emma Smith

asked. But didn't get an answer beyond the worried expression on Fields' grey face.

Jacobson got up and found a waste-paper basket. Then bent down and stubbed out his B and H.

'Your lad have any further intelligence for us, Harry?'

'He's not keen on the idea that it was just a simple case of pocketing more than they were entitled to. He reckons the firm's accountancy is too tight for that to be possible. Keener on the alternative supplier thesis.'

Jacobson stayed on his feet and walked to the top end of the table, where the blue bulk of an overhead projector had been stationed. Ready for the kind of meetings that were legitimately supposed to happen on the third floor. Serious stuff: the ACCs' standing committee on paper clips. That kind of thing.

'Any ideas as to *who* the new supplier might be?' he asked.

'Come on, Frank. As it happens, we don't – not a clue. But you know the score as well as I do. I couldn't tell you just like that even if we did have an inkling. All of this stuff is *sub* the Regional Crime Squad. I'm sticking my neck out as it is without the proper *imprimatur*.'

Jacobson played with the mirror on the OHP, adjusting the angle to one that he fervently hoped would be useless and out of focus. He liked the 'imprimatur' anyway. The force needed as many Latin scholars as it could get. Badly.

'And the Birmingham fuckers?'

The question was for show only. Merely for the purity of form. Greg Salter had already paged him to call into his office. As soon as. By now Salter would have taken instruction from the RCS and/or the Chief Constable, would be ready to pass on the agreed party line. From what Fields had just intimated, you could bet the price of a decent Balti that the hierarchy were about to insist on the regional boys taking control of the investigation, squeezing out the Crowby side. From the

RCS point of view, Dave Carter would be just one less toerag wasting space and oxygen. They wouldn't allow his demise to fuck up any of their grandiose, big-scale strategies. If necessary, they'd be prepared to conveniently not find the ex-barman's killer or killers. If he behaved himself, Jacobson could just possibly aspire towards making them the odd cup of tea while they did so. A role that Salter would refer to as crucial liaison. Probably with a straight face.

Clean Harry Fields shrugged.

'My lips are sealed until upstairs says otherwise, Frank. Sorry.'

End of meeting evidently. Jacobson took the lift to the top floor: level eight, senior management country. At least Smith and Williams had agreed to put in an extra shift later, repeat their tour of the kingdom of the blind, deaf and dumb. There was always the chance, he'd reminded them, that a useful contradiction could emerge between the first telling of a pack of lies and the second. Something that might even resemble a pertinent fact.

Detective Chief Superintendent Greg Salter. Jacobson couldn't get his head around this precise combination of five straightforward words, still couldn't shake his sense of their sheer incongruity. The DCS: the highest-ranking detective on the force. CID's ear in the corridors of power. The acolyte with the direct line to the Chief Constable. But here Salter was anyway. Arrived from nowhere. Yet sitting behind the DCS desk, arse parked comfily on the DCS Parker-Knoll.

'Frank, good of you to take the time.'

The usual insincere greeting. The weird pretence that Jacobson had just dropped in for a sociable chat, wasn't remotely under anything as old-fashioned as an order to do so.

'I see you're settled in then, *sir*,' Jacobson said, sinking into a low chair and casting his eye around the room.

Like DCS Chivers before him, Salter had made it known

that he preferred to be on first-name terms with his senior officers. It was an informal rule that Jacobson took a modest pleasure in ignoring.

'Getting there, Frank, getting there.'

Chivers' cabinet of golfing trophies had disappeared. So had his wall display of the force's history in photographs. The Chief Constable of the day meeting King George. A corpulent sergeant behind the wheel of a tram during the General Strike, the buttons of his uniform gleaming in ancient sunlight. Straining plods, some with their hats lost, holding back the lines of screaming girls outside the Palace of Varieties the evening the Beatles had played there. In their place: bar charts, pie charts, graphs, spreadsheets. A diagram showing the force's chain of command in six colours. The force's mission statement, itemised bullet point by bullet point. Plus the big framed poster of a smiling dolphin which had been chosen by the Salter focus group – aka Mrs Salter – to foster an unconvincing illusion: that Greg might have an imagination buried somewhere deep underneath his Hugo Boss suit.

The speech was pre-prepared, glibber than glib.

*No local incident room. No local officers seconded. An RCS operation from start to finish. I've spoken to the Chief Constable, Frank. And to the RCS Commander—*

Or more precisely they've talked to you, Jacobson thought.

*A full murder investigation certainly. But linked to the major War on Drugs initiative, subject to the operational priorities thereof—*

He noticed that Salter had some kind of executive toy on the top of his desk. Small chrome cubes hanging on thin strands of wire.

*There's three forces involved, Frank. Eighteen months' work for the officers on the ground. I'm sure you'll appreciate the sensitivities—*

Appreciate. Verb transitive. To estimate justly. Yes, I can do that all right.

*A liaison role for yourself and Harry Fields, naturally. You'll need to make yourself available to provide local intelligence as and when required, Frank. But only as and when. It's possible that the RCS team might need access to the localised crime database also. Steve Horton will be the contact point for any such enquiries—*

Salter fingered the lapels of his jacket, brushing off imaginary dust.

*There are very large operational issues at stake here, Frank. We let the regional boys get on with it. We stay out of the way. We don't interfere—*

'And when does Supercop take over?'

*Nine am tomorrow morning, Frank. At which point the case is officially out of our hands.*

Jacobson grabbed a plate of double egg and chips in the police canteen. Plus a glass of orange juice, his usual compromise with nutrition. He buttoned his coat up against the wind and the rain before he quit the Divisional building via the revolving doors at the main entrance. Halfway across the pedestrian precinct, a couple of twenty-something ladettes – already the worse for wear from some after-work Happy Hour or other – were harassing a *Big Issue* seller: a teenage girl who looked half frozen. Jacobson flashed his ID, sent the women away with a flea in their cleanly scrubbed ears. He gave the lass a couple of quid but didn't take a magazine.

In the Brewer's Rest, he ordered a half-pint of beer and a single malt. For once he hadn't bothered to argue, had given a nod that could easily have been taken for agreement. But only by a blind horse.

Soho. Somewhere near Greek Street. Somewhere so up itself that it didn't bother with a name plate outside. Detective Sergeant Ian Kerr was in no hurry to get back to Euston. No hurry at all. But he had no great desire to stay where he was either. He waited for Rachel to finish her concoction of vodka and mango juice, idly counting the lava lamps in the immediate vicinity, giving up at six. He'd asked for a Becks himself. Usually a safe enough bet anywhere upmarket. But not here apparently. 'We have *Budvar*, sir,' the girl behind the bar had said, as if making the rarest of concessions. 'Fine,' Kerr had retaliated. And don't have one for yourself.

At last Rachel drained her glass. She leaned close and kissed him, their heads sinking together on to the back of the pink couch. They'd discovered that it was too low and uncomfortable to sit on for any length of time. Although Kerr guessed that wasn't the point.

'We need to go, Rayche,' he said, a moment or so after she'd stopped.

She was fussing with her bag and jacket and the posters she'd bought herself at the National Gallery. Almost as if she hadn't heard. Then:

''Course we do. Back to Deadtown. Back to the wife and kids.'

She said it brightly, smiling. A joke. I'm only joking. But both of them knew that she wasn't.

They gave up on the black cab idea at the third attempt. They wandered through the crowds to Leicester Square and took a crammed, jerking tube the rest of the way. The escalator brought them up into the main station from the bowels of the Underground, Kerr behind Rachel, not letting her remotely out of his sight. In front of the Carphone Warehouse outlet, two paramedics were failing to resuscitate a collapsed down-and-out. Army and Navy Surplus coat. Matted grey hair. One of his feet shoeless. An old-school wino more than a modern beggar. Kerr and Rachel let themselves be swept on by the mass of the Great Travelling Public. Only a couple of Japanese students bothered to slow down and witness the last heavings of the dosser's clapped-out heart.

They stopped not quite in the centre of the concourse, her face pressed into his neck. According to the departures board, her train was ready, would be leaving on time. He said to call him as soon as the train pulled out. So he'd know she'd caught it OK. He said he'd call her too, later, make sure she'd got back all right. He knew the fuss irritated her – like she couldn't look after herself – but for once she didn't argue. Just nuzzled closer. Ludicrously, he found himself wondering how long the transport police held on to their CCTV footage. Half a dozen times now, maybe more, they'd replayed this brief, miniature scene. Their Euston rush-hour goodbye: too risky, they always decided, to share the same train back to Crowby. Thirty seconds maybe. Maybe not even that. A kiss on the lips and then she was gone, heading towards the platforms.

He had half an hour to kill before the next scheduled train, the one he'd take himself. Empty time. And just the start of it. There would be whole empty weeks before they might get away like this again. Together. Even then it would only be for the nights really. If your pretext was a Metropolitan Police training course, you had to turn up for it. At least put in the minimum required hours.

He bought an *Evening Standard*, drifted into the human chaos of the food court, made a choice purely on the basis of the length of the queues. The tables all seemed to be taken but he found a vacant stool along one of the side bars. He cleared away the remains of somebody's hamburger and fries, put his tray down. Tea and a bacon and Brie baguette: harmless looking enough he supposed. He stowed his overnight bag where he could see it, clocked every face in the vicinity for signs of criminal intent or madness. Or both. Less than a year ago, he recalled, a woman – somebody's wife, somebody's mother – had pursued a bag snatcher across the concourse and out into the street. She'd jumped on the bonnet of the robbers' car, trying to halt the getaway. The junked-out driver had dislodged her: then ran over her head just to make sure she was dead. It had been taken – desperately – by some as an instance of surviving British decency that the case had hit the national newspaper and TV headlines for a day or so.

He'd pulled the plastic rim off the polystyrene cup – was just pouring in the contents of the tiny milk carton, when his mobile rang.

'Rayche? That was quick—'

But of course it was Chief Inspector Jacobson calling.

# Chapter Nine

Stephen Adams got back from football coaching at precisely 6.30. He went straight upstairs, slung his clothes off and stepped into a long, hot shower. Thereafter, he dried himself with a clean, warm towel, shaved, brushed his teeth – having first fitted a brand-new head to his electric toothbrush – and got dressed at a leisurely pace. For company as he did so, he stuck on Sky Sports 2: motocross coverage. Marion had left his clothes out for him, even polished his shoes it looked like. White shirt, dinner jacket, black tie. She'd given a lot of thought to what they should both be wearing. Obviously. The way they did. DJ for him, she'd decided in the end. And a little black number for herself. One with a Nicole Farhi label, she'd said, emphasising the point. From which he'd assumed it had cost an arm and a leg, as per usual. Which of course it should do – her being *his* wife – this being the Big Night.

Whistling '*Do You Think I'm Sexy*', he adjusted his shirt collar and tie in the mirror, gave himself the once-over. You'll do, mate, he thought. The news from Alan Jones had been bad, even grim. But he'd promised himself one thing: he wasn't going to let it spoil his evening. Not tonight of all nights. He stopped whistling for maybe ten seconds, practising his smile for the cameras. As a final afterthought, he dabbed on some aftershave. Cerutti Image. His fingers seemed to relish the smoothness of the freshly-shaven skin on his neck and chin. He resumed his attack on Rod Stewart. You'll do. No worries. The rest was just bollocks. Nonsense. Just rubbish in your head.

Jacobson filled some of the waiting time by driving back out to the hospital. Mrs Eileen Carter was in the intensive care unit, her bulk wired up to a life support system. In the corridor outside, Dr Chaudhury, the liver specialist, was gloomily polite.

'The blood plates look bad, I'm afraid.'

He waved the thick file he'd been carrying in his left hand.

'Long-term alcohol abuse. The last thing this patient's liver needed was paracetamol. Even the normal prescribed dose could have been life threatening. We're doing everything that can be done.'

Jacobson had a vague memory of reading something in the science pages about advances in liver transplantation. Or maybe he'd seen it on TV. He mentioned it anyway.

Chaudhury shook his head. His smile was very nearly non-patronising.

'The newspapers, Inspector. Fantasy Island for the most part. Definitely so in a case like this.'

'So there's no chance?'

'We cling to hope. Always. But a woman of this size. A smoker, of course. Heart and lungs less than tip-top.'

Of course. Jacobson thanked him for his time, checked with the duty nurse that there would definitely be a call placed to the Divi in the apparently unlikely event that Mrs Carter regained consciousness. Aka a miracle and a sign from God. For as long as it took him to walk out of the building, he entertained the sure and certain knowledge that he'd be packing it in any day now. Soon. At least this year.

Candice's kitchen. The woman copper sitting opposite, her notebook open on the table. A smug-looking bitch. Not even ugly. The other one, the man, standing with his back to the sink. This afternoon another pair had taken her fingerprints. For elimination purposes. They'd be destroyed later, they'd told her. *I bet.* That had been a man and a woman too. Maybe it was the frigging breeding season. Scene of crime officers, they'd called themselves. SOCOs. The bloke had wanted to do the girls as well. *I'd like to see you try.* But the woman had said no, you're all right, it's not necessary.

Sheryl had only one fag left in her Silk Cut packet. She took it out and lit it anyway.

'I've been through all this all ready. Yesterday. All I'd like now is some peace, yeah?'

'Soon as we can, Sheryl. But maybe there's details you remember now that got forgotten before?'

The cow was smiling at her, some kind of trust-me smile they probably took exams in at copper school.

'Look. Dave was just a bloke. He stayed the night a few times. He was fast asleep when I took the girls to school. Dead before I got back, according to you lot. Apart from where he worked, I didn't know that much about him.'

She tipped ash into the Kronenbourg 1664 ashtray. Something else that had come from the Poets. The smoke felt weak on her lungs. All this frigging hassle: she'd be back on a high-nicotine brand at this rate.

'In your statement you say that Dave liked a drink. Had he been drinking much the night before?' DC Emma Smith asked.

They'd had two cans of Super Lager each. Plus she thought there'd been a couple of empty wine bottles in the waste bin, ready for the refuse. She put the cigarette on the groove in the side of the ashtray, rested her hands steadily on the table. Keeping them motionless, still. Something had just been thrown onto the floor in the lounge where Candice was keeping the kids amused. Or trying to.

'He was already six sheets to the wind when he came round

to mine. Had some wine with him, some beer. But we just –
you know – we just went straight to bed. "I'll finish this little
lot off in the morning." That's what he said.'

She kept her eyes on the woman, except when she looked at
the man. She'd seen a programme on Channel 4. Psychology
and all that. How to lie and get away with it.

Jacobson collected Kerr from the railway station, brought him
up to speed as he drove out of the town centre in the direction
of the Woodlands estate. They rendezvoused with Barber and
Mick Hume – barely back an hour from Birmingham – in the
car park of the Poets, held a hurried case conference in the
pissing rain. They were joined by a couple of patrol cars,
two plods in each, sent out by Sergeant Ince, who was owed
favours on his shift as usual. Going in mob handed wasn't a
typical Jacobson gambit. But he'd realised a long time ago
never to exclude any approach *a priori*. You didn't fit up, you
didn't beat up. But otherwise you did what was necessary.

There were less than half a dozen sleepy-looking, elderly
drunks in the public bar. But the main lounge was jam packed,
gearing up for a karaoke night. Big Cash Prize: according to
the orange poster above the fag machine. The jukebox blared.
'Murder on the Dancefloor' following So Solid Crew. Not
that Jacobson recognised either. There were two women in
their twenties serving behind the counter. A blonde and a
brunette. Plus Terry Shields, poised over the cash register
like a ferret sniffing a drainpipe. Mick Hume was ready to
carve a burly path to the bar but a way opened up for them
anyway. Automatically. Almost by telepathy.

'Thought you'd have done a runner by now, Terry,'
Jacobson said.

Shields closed the till. He'd pulled on a clean sweatshirt and
a pair of almost smart black jeans, but he still hadn't shaved.

'I told you this morning, mate. I don't know what's
supposed to have been going on. But I swear I—'

Jacobson told him to save it, that swearing wasn't nice. Mick Hume caught the blonde's eye.

'Turn the racket off, love.'

The barmaid looked to Shields for guidance.

'Now hold on, mate—'

But Hume went behind the bar anyway, elbowing a couple of drinkers in the process, started clicking off any switches he could find. The room plunged briefly into darkness before Shields himself killed the jukebox and restored the lights.

Mutterings. Oaths. Finally silence. Jacobson grabbed a cloth from the bar, used it to wipe clear the blackboard on the wall where someone had earlier misspelled the list of daily specials. All two of them. Baterd Cod and Chip's. Chilli Con Carney.

'Chalk,' he said.

From somewhere behind the bar the blonde found a grubby stalk of white chalk. Mick Hume took it from her. Then walked over and handed it to Jacobson.

Jacobson wrote a telephone number up on the board.

'Dave Carter and Terry Shields did more than serve pints here, as you all know. I couldn't care less about that. But it pissed somebody off so much that they beat Carter to death and then burned his body. That's something I *do* care about. Something that pisses *me* off.'

He tapped the board with the piece of chalk as he spoke.

'Anybody knows anything – anything at all – they phone this number and they leave a message. Any time. Twenty-four hours. Nobody will be tracing the call. Nobody will give a toss who's calling. The only interest will be in what's said.'

Kerr and DC Barber stood by the bar. Kerr scanned the faces around the room. But they were harder to read than Sanskrit. A podgy, under-aged-looking kid near the silenced jukebox looked as if he might be tempted to leg it. But two of the uniformeds had positioned themselves by the door. Plus Mick Hume, displaying body language that very clearly read just stay right where the fuck you are.

'Look at it this way,' Jacobson said. 'Unless someone gets put away for this, the next over-greedy bastard gets it could be you.'

He drew a thick line under the number. The chalk made the kind of screeching sound that had always drawn Kerr's teeth when he'd been at school.

Message over.

Jacobson put the chalk down on the counter on their way out, told Terry Shields he wanted the number left there until closing time: then he wanted it rubbed off.

'As for yourself, Terry, it could be a good idea to memorise it. You never know when it might come in handy.'

He'd thought that Shields might protest his innocence again. But in the event he said nothing. Then switched the music back on.

It took Jacobson ten minutes to find the gaff they were after in the dark and the rain. They'd left Barber and Hume parked up near the pub. The podgy kid might be nervous about some unrelated offence – might just be nervous. Even so, Jacobson had said, they could follow him later, find out where he lived, maybe have a word. He cut the lights and the engine, used his mobile to check on the non-progress of Emma Smith and DC Williams back at William Blake House. He told them to keep at it for as long as they could stomach. Tonight was their only crack at the case. Tonight was *it*. He turned towards Kerr.

'Ready, old son?'

'Jesus, Frank,' Kerr said.

Give fifty or so hard core toerags your personal mobile number, he'd been thinking. Invite them to communicate directly with you. Stow the official channels. Reveal sensitive lines of enquiry on the eve of a visit from the Regional Crime Squad.

'Jesus,' he repeated.

Compared to which a spot of illegal, unwarranted breaking and entering virtually amounted to a standard textbook procedure.

# Chapter Ten

Sarah complained about having to change out of her usual jeans and sweatshirt into a pink dress. But not as much as the lads moaned about being forced into suits. Mark left his shirt collar unbuttoned behind his school tie – also whinged about – as a faint protest. Steve let it go. As long as everybody was sorted on time. That was the main thing. Finally they were all together in the lounge. All ready. Marion poured herself a G and T and a Scotch for him. Single malt, not blended rubbish. Steve thought she looked great. She'd had her hair done, obviously. And the dress. You'd still fancy it if you were meeting it for the first time. That was always the test.

The door bell rang just as he was taking his last sip.

'They're here,' Marion said.

Meaning the photographer and the reporter from the *Argus*. The chauffeur would stop with the vehicle most probably.

Steve told Mark to get the door.

'Look sharpish, lad.'

The photographer was a man of about Steve's own age but the reporter looked like he'd have problems getting served in a decent pub. Still, he was smartly turned out. Plus he was plonking champagne in an ice bucket on the coffee table. Marion found some fluted glasses and Steve himself popped the cork. Smile for the camera, et fucking cetera. Yes, the lads could have some too, he announced. No harm on a special evening, was there? Sarah tried some from her mum's glass but made a face at the taste.

Matt and Mark brightened up even more when they got into the stretch limo, courtesy of the *Argus*, spent most of the journey perfecting pop star waves to imaginary legions of fans. There was a second bottle of champagne inside. Steve and Marion clinked their glasses, the photographer grabbed a few more happy, smiling snaps. Only Sarah seemed unmoved by the occasion, just sat quietly watching the darkened streets of Crowby rolling past.

In some recess of fantasy, Steve had maybe imagined there might be a crowd outside waiting to greet them. But although it seemed busy enough, everybody around seemed to be either other guests arriving or hotel staff. Whatever: there was still a red carpet at the entrance, the chauffeur was still helping Marion out of the limo cap in hand. The photographer and the reporter were already standing on the pavement. Steve glanced up at the banner above the entrance, rippling in the wind. EVENING ARGUS ANNUAL CIVIC AWARDS. Then the camera flashed again and they were being ushered inside. Even though it was owned by one of the big chains these days, the Crowby Riverside Hotel still retained a degree of local cachet on the basis of its snobbier past. The automatic doors closed smoothly behind them. Steve recalled that the original, unrefurbished building had a set of revolving doors. It had been a game they'd played as kids, try and sneak past the uniformed doorman, ride the doors round then back out.

The dinner would be in the Flowers banqueting suite. But the private pre-dinner reception – awardees and dignitaries only – was in a separate lounge with a wide view over the nearest bridge and the river. Though at this time of the evening – this time of year – all you could really see through the windows were the strings of yellow light bulbs in the trees along Riverside Walk. The trees themselves were black shapes only, the River Crow's fast-moving current all but invisible under the clouded sky. Another *Argus* reporter – a woman, someone more senior – attached herself to the party, made sure they did the necessary rounds, that they weren't unduly neglected. The mayor, an ashen-faced old codger with bad breath, buttonholed Steve. Plus a vicar in evening God kit – discreet dog collar only – whose name Steve didn't properly catch.

'The family. That's the keynote,' the mayor said.

'Family life. Family values,' commented the vicar. 'Absolutely.'

'What it's all about, isn't it?' Steve agreed.

He finished off one glass of wine, grabbed another from the tray of a passing waiter. A spumante or some such only in here. Not the real McCoy. But drinkable at least.

'I mean – if you don't take care of your home pitch, you can forget about the rest.'

'Very nicely put, Mr Adams' – the vicar beamed – 'very nicely put indeed.'

Steve gave them another five minutes, sank another glass, then escaped to the Gents.

He found an empty cubicle, snibbed the door after him. Amitriptyline 50mg. The full-whack dose. It was very nearly a sensuous thing. Sliding the strip of tablets out of the neat white box. Pushing two out, breaking the tiny round seals, holding them, weightless, between your fingers. He collected some saliva together in the front of his mouth, then popped the pills in, swallowed them down.

The doc had tried him on Prozac for a while. But he hadn't really got on with it. Brought him out in night sweats. Give me the old ammies any day. He wasn't supposed to mix them with alcohol, of course. And he was only supposed to have one a night, not two. He lifted the seat, unzipped his fly and took a leak, seeing as he was here. But he didn't take them every night anyway. You did that, you were like a zombie for half the next working day. Which was all he bloody needed. More in the way of recreational use was what it had become. Weekends mostly plus maybe a couple of times midweek. A

73

night like this you wanted to enjoy yourself was all. You wanted to float, forget your worries. A couple of ammies, he'd found, and everything else went down so much better of an evening: booze, food, conversation. You'd look back in the morning and every memory would seem charmed, golden, the purest bloody magic.

He flushed the toilet then exited the cubicle. After he'd washed his hands, drying them under the hot-air dryers, commandeering one per hand, he walked back in on the reception. Marion was talking to a younger woman in something yellow and low cut, green streaks in her hair. The wife of Crowby FC's striker, it transpired. Steve didn't really follow the local team any more. They were forever just on the verge of promotion to the premier league – yeah, right – and Steve had found he preferred to follow the big team action on the box. Arsenal, Man U, Real Madrid. It was still nice, though, that the player joined them, shook Steve by the hand, wished them success. Thanks. Cheers, mate. He tried not to look too obviously down the wife's cleavage. The lads came up to be introduced, obviously well impressed. Sarah stood over by the nearest window, drinking Coca-Cola and gazing out into the night. A good kid, Steve thought. But a dreamer.

The dinner had been set up properly, he'd give them that. Silver service, roses for the finer sex, the top table on a long, raised plinth. Morricone's Jazz Express were playing their jazz twaddle while everyone found their seats. But they packed it in, thank God, before the first course put in an appearance. Marion sat on Steve's right, then little Sarah, then the boys. On his other side was a fireman and his wife. Something to do with the rail crash the previous summer. A hero in person, no less. Not that much further along the table was Chief Constable Bentham. Steve could most probably have asked him to pass the butter or what have you if he'd really wanted to. Beyond Bentham, Marion whispered in his ear, was Dr Croucher, the top dog at the university. The fireman's wife turned out to be Bill Elliot's cousin on his mother's side.

'Small world,' Steve said brightly, taking in the news.

They were nearly finished with the final course when Sarah said she was feeling sick. Marion took her off to the ladies' room. The fireman's wife smiled indulgently.

'Too much cola, isn't it,' Steve explained.

He'd argued at one point for leaving the kids at home, especially the little one. But the paper had obviously wanted the whole family group. And Marion had said it wouldn't do any harm, surely. Not for just the one night. Steve supposed she was right. But he'd still insisted that arrangements were made to get them home after the meal and the presentations, to leave himself and the missus free to let their hair down. Steve was on brandy now. And cigars. He offered one to the fireman. A decent enough type once you got to know him. More than, as a matter of fact. Everybody here was, Steve reckoned. Real people, proper folk. Though it wasn't a job Steve could envy. Sticking your neck out every day. And for peanuts most probably. Steve lit the fireman's cigar, asked him if he'd been at the Woodlands yesterday, meaning the fire at the tart's flat – Sarah's little pal's mother. But apparently he'd been on a later shift. He'd heard they'd been lobbing stones at the fire engines again, he told Steve: they were worse than animals, some of them. Steve puffed his cigar, watched Marion and Sarah hurrying their way back through the tables, became aware of a hush descending. On the other side of Bentham and Croucher, the managing editor of the *Evening Argus* had got to his feet, was starting into the speeches.

Family of the Year was a new category, the reporter had told him. As such it had been decided to make it the last award in the running order. Virtually the stars of the show, Steve thought now, ordering another brandy *sotto voce*, making it a double, feeling that everything everywhere was just right, would stay just right, would carry on staying just right. Especially – it was almost a prayer – everything in the vicinity of Stephen Adams.

Terry Shields lived right on the end of a row of two-storey houses which stood at the very edge of the Woodlands estate. There was an abandoned play area off to the left. Two sets of wrecked swings and a sandpit of dog turds and broken glass. In front: the main road prefaced by a strip of access road and a sloping patch of unhealthy-looking municipal grass. Jacobson had pulled up right outside the gaff, a spot that was also well away from the nearest functioning lamp-post. Not that anyone would be very likely to give a fuck just because they noticed an unfamiliar car in the street. He got out, followed Kerr along the front path.

The place was in darkness. Kerr rang the bell just in case but it didn't seem to be working. He tested out the door.

'More than a credit card job, Frank. Strengthened, it looks like.'

They walked back up the path and then around the back. On the way, Jacobson had second thoughts and locked his car. Kerr tried the handle of the back door a couple of times, even shouldered it.

'No go. We really *will* have to break in.'

'Do it, old son. I'll be lookout,' Jacobson said.

Kerr would have preferred even a vaguely professional approach. Stick some masking tape on the kitchen window, say. At least muffle the sound of breaking glass. But, apart from his winter gloves, he hadn't come kitted out for burglary, and it was clear that Jacobson wanted instant results. He looked up warily at the back of the neighbouring house. There was a light on in a bedroom behind drawn curtains. Also the thud of dance music. Basement Jaxx possibly. Something he'd heard before anyway, maybe at Rachel's. He poked around in the gloom, finally found what he was looking for. A pile of garden debris: rocks, planks, stones, a nice fat brick. There

76

was always one around somewhere, he thought. He motioned Jacobson out of the way then lobbed it cleanly through the window. They waited a couple of minutes, ready to do a runner. But there was totally zero response from next door.

'Deaf, doped out of it or don't give a fuck,' Jacobson said.

'Or all three,' Kerr replied.

He'd smashed in the main pane, making it possible to reach his hand through and open the side window as wide as it would go. Thirty seconds later he was inside, switching the lights on. Two minutes later he'd found a set of keys inside a biscuit tin. A minute after that Chief Inspector Jacobson strolled casually through the opened back door, his hands deep in his coat pockets.

Downstairs and upstairs, the layout was identical to Dave Carter's place on the other side of the estate. At least there were no cats in need of a feed this time, Jacobson thought. No wife or girlfriend either, by the look of things. Or long departed if there'd been one in the past. They worked their way through the house systematically. Shields had an unpleasant collection of video porn in his front room, a stack of out-of-date BNP literature in his loft. *Death Camp Lesbos* versus *The Myth of the Holocaust*. But there were no signs anywhere of drugs, drugs use or drugs cash. Just as bad from Jacobson's point of view was the absence of any address book or even of a contact scribbled on the back of an envelope. There were no messages on the answerphone; the only correspondence lying around was a final demand for an unpaid gas bill.

Kerr seemed to read Jacobson's mind.

'He's had all day to slip back here, Frank. Do some spring cleaning,' he said.

Jacobson nodded. Probably accounted for Shields' change of clothes, at any rate. In an ideal world, Jacobson would have put a tail on him since this morning. But then in an ideal world Shields wouldn't exist. They were back in the kitchen now, Jacobson leaning against an ancient washing machine while Kerr completed a few standard checks: rifling through cornflake packets, emptying out jars of instant coffee, taking apart a torch he'd found in the cupboard under the sink.

'Come on, old son, we're wasting our time here,' Jacobson said.

He helped Kerr tidy up. When they were ready, Jacobson left by the kitchen door. Kerr locked up after him, returned the set of keys to the biscuit tin, checked all the lights were back off and exited by the side window, shutting it as best he could from the outside. Apart from the smashed pane, which nothing could be done about, Kerr wanted to leave as few traces behind as possible. The back door had been bolted from the inside and none of the spare keys fitted the deadlock on the front door. It was a bit of a performance, he thought, but potentially worthwhile: Shields might even be thick enough to convince himself he'd just been the victim of some unconnected vandalism.

Jacobson drove them over to William Blake House, smoking a B and H en route. Kerr rolled down his window, vastly preferring cold air to secondary nicotine. He could have done without the lot of it, to be perfectly honest. Left to his own devices, he'd have taken a taxi straight home from the station. Home in time to see the twins bathed and put to bed. Home in time to seem keen to be there. Back – as Rachel had said – to the wife and kids. He'd phoned from the train, obviously. But Cathy hadn't answered. He'd left a message but she hadn't called back. She'd have been busy at the time, most likely – and sulking at his prolonged absence afterwards. He wondered idly what his life would feel like if its arithmetic were suddenly reversed. So that he had to spend most of his time with Rachel, sneak off only when he could to see Cathy and his son and daughter.

*

The podgy kid emerged from the Poets forty minutes after Chief Inspector Jacobson's visit. He jumped clumsily over the low wall of the car park and set off across the adjoining waste ground. Seen from the air, the Poets sat on the rim of an empty circle of muck at the centre of the Woodlands. The original planners had dreamt of a complete community and leisure complex at the heart of the estate. But only the pub and a shed-like youth centre, draughty and under-used, had ever got built. Add on a grim row of steel-shuttered shops farther down the main drag and you had a virtually complete inventory of local amenities, Son of the Bronx style. Barber and Mick Hume watched the kid long enough to be reasonably sure of the direction he was taking. Then Hume started up the car and they drove slowly, drawing up again behind a white van that had been conveniently parked close to the point where they thought he would re-emerge. Five minutes later there he was: crossing the road into Coleridge Crescent, his eyes darting left, right, left.

It would be trickier to follow him now. Hume was in favour of just pulling him off the street, finding out who he was, what he knew. But Barber argued caution. If the kid did know something, it would be better if they came by it in a way that wouldn't look bad in court. Hume shrugged, eased the car round the corner, killed the lights and the engine. The kid was approaching the corner with John Clare Avenue when he broke into an ungainly, shuffling run. Hume had his fingers on the ignition key but Barber was shouting in his ear.

'No, Mick, don't. Trust me on this one.'

Along the avenue and then turn left again, he was thinking. Three minutes running. Less if the kid helped himself to a route through a couple of back gardens. Barber played his hunch, used his mobile. He phoned Emma Smith, who phoned Jacobson. Jacobson answered on the fourth ring tone: just as he was cutting his own engine – a handy twenty yards or so down the street from William Blake House.

# Chapter Eleven

Ryan Walsh and his mother lived in a chaotic flat on the fifth floor. Jacobson and Kerr did the interview while the rest of the team sat around outside in the cars. Writing up their notes, chatting idly or – in Mick Hume's case – arguing with his wife on the phone about a plumber's estimate for a new shower room. Walsh had looked likely to scarper when he'd pressed for the lift and the doors had opened to reveal DCs Smith and Williams. But he'd given up when he'd glanced behind him, clocked Jacobson and Kerr peering through the glass-fronted entrance doors. Copper, pig and filth written all over the four of them.

The mother wasn't there – *bingo in town, isn't it?* – but although Ryan looked about fourteen and three-quarters it turned out that he was actually nineteen: old enough to be spoken to on his own. The front room was awash with CDs, computer peripherals, a Sony hi-fi set still in its box. There were at least two brand new PlayStations that Jacobson could see. Walsh perched his flabby body on the edge of the sofa. He was still out of breath from running. His face, white and pasty, looked like unset dough. Jacobson found a piece of carpet where he could stand without cracking any CD cases.

'There'll be receipts for this lot, Ryan, no doubt.'

'I suppose so. I expect me mam—'

'There's a couple of warrants out, Frank,' Kerr interrupted, standing by the window and putting his mobile back in his jacket pocket. 'Didn't show last month for a shoplifting charge in Coventry. Hasn't been keeping his probation appointments. Behind on his fines.'

'That's all sorted,' Walsh protested. 'I'm back in court Thursday. I was down the probation yesterday morning—'

Jacobson changed tack.

'Would that have been before or after the fire, Ryan?'

Walsh stared at the laces on his trainers.

'It's a simple enough question, old son.'

'Half seven. No. No – seven more like. That's when I left. You can ask me—'

'A bit on the early side for the probation service,' Kerr commented.

Walsh lifted his head slightly.

'I had to frigging walk all the way into frigging Crowby, didn't I? Me mam was hacked off with me. Wouldn't give me the bus fare, would she?'

Jacobson yawned. The call to the fire brigade had been placed at ten past nine. But it takes a while to start a fire. And first there had been the time needed for murder.

'Did you notice anything – anybody – unusual on your way out? Hanging around the entrance maybe.'

'No. It was dark.'

'Seven or half-seven? Which was it?' Jacobson persisted.

Walsh had small eyes and a big face. He tried to look like he was concentrating.

'Seven. Yep. Definitely seven.'

'OK. Get your coat, Ryan.'

'Wha— ?'

'You're nicked, Ryan,' Jacobson explained. 'Suspicion of handling stolen goods.'

Walsh flung himself deep into the sofa.

'You can't do that! This ain't even my place. It's me mam's.'

Jacobson placed himself between the lad stroke youth and the door.

'I might nick her as well when I see her,' he said. 'Now get your coat.'

They stuck him in the back seat of Jacobson's car. Kerr got into the front, keeping watch. Jacobson had a word with the rest of his officers under the light of a street lamp. They stood in a huddle, speaking quietly. Ryan Walsh apart, they'd got exactly nowhere. No one had seen a thing. No one had heard a thing. No one had even reported the fire. Not personally anyway. No one knew who had. Jacobson yawned a second time. They might as well call it a night then, he told them. He appreciated their efforts. They'd put themselves out for him. But a brick wall was a brick wall. If the RCS got any further, it would only be because they had intelligence sources and information denied to lesser mortals.

Even on a wet Tuesday evening in February, processing Walsh took well over an hour. The custody suite at the Divisional building was being refurbished and the cells were operating at only half the normal capacity. Plus there'd been arrests and trouble at a student night in Club Zoo. The upshot was that they had to squeeze Walsh in with a drunk and disorderly over at Crowby Central. It was 10.30 by the time the paperwork was done and dusted – and they'd persuaded Central's fastidious custody sergeant that Ryan Evans Walsh was old enough to be kept out past his bedtime. Kerr tried Cathy on his mobile again as they were driving, illegally for an unmarked car, along the pedestrianised street that was a short cut through the town centre. No answer. Probably in bed by now, he thought.

'Bugger it, Ian,' Jacobson said. 'I'm going to hit the BR for the last hour. I'll drive you home first, if you like.'

Kerr thought for a moment. Then:

'No need. I'll join you. I'm in the shit by now anyway on the domestic front.'

The Brewer's Rest wasn't a coppers' pub as such, though plenty used it. Mainly because it was close – but not too close

– to the Divisional building. A couple of Harry Fields' DCs were standing over a fruit machine when they walked in. Fields himself was a teetotaller, of course, was never seen on licensed premises outside the line of duty. The main bar was an L shape, darker and quieter at the top end. Jacobson found an out-of-the-way table where they could talk shop if they wanted to. Kerr brought the first round over. Jacobson generally favoured lager over the so-called traditional ales, associated the latter negatively with beards, social workers, the doers of crossword puzzles. But on a cold night like this one, he was prepared to sink as low as a tepid pint of Bass. There had been a country pub he used to drive to with Janice in the old days, when they'd not been long married, where the landlady had kept a poker in the fire on winter evenings to warm the beer through. Thinking about it now, he realised that his memory of the taste had completely gone. He could still picture the scene but for some reason his mind could no longer access the strange, smoky flavour.

'So what, then, Frank,' Kerr said after a moment. 'Going for early retirement on grounds of mental illness, is it?'

Jacobson said nothing, took a deep mouthful of beer.

Kerr pressed him.

'First the phone number stunt. Then a bit of breaking and entering because you couldn't ask for a warrant. Finally, you bang up the kid. Er – why?'

Jacobson took a second mouthful. A third. Then:

'I'm just trying to keep some channels open, old son. Once the RCS take over they'll tell us precisely fuck all. I don't know about you, but if there's a killer walking around Crowby, I'd like to be fully apprised of the situation.'

Kerr had ordered a pint of Stella Artois. He sipped half an inch or so off the top. He supposed he could concede some risky sense in Jacobson's strategy with regard to the phone number. The Woodlands, despite poverty, was exactly like every other layer of English society in one typical respect:

it was a cesspit of jealousies, petty resentments and score settling. If the killer or killers had a local connection, it was entirely possible they'd have local enemies too – somebody who'd hate them enough to grass them up. Likewise, if Jacobson had been luckier, the illegal fishing trip to Shields' gaff might have usefully revealed a link either to the Birmingham dealership or to the alternative supplier Carter and Shields had been using.

The beer was over-chilled but he drank another mouthful anyway.

'Mainly what I don't get,' he said, thinking aloud, 'is why the hell we lifted Ryan Walsh.'

Jacobson lit a cigarette with the faded silver lighter that he never seemed to be without.

'One: he lives right above the crime scene. Two: he's a streetwise little toerag who knows the score, meaning that he's highly unlikely to have had an attack of the jitters just because he's got a stack of shoplifted goodies sitting back home.'

He put the lighter back in his pocket.

'I think he saw something, Ian. Or somebody he recognised.'

'Maybe so. But I don't see how locking him up helps.'

Jacobson held his cigarette in his left hand, away from Kerr.

'Happen it won't. But short of rubber-truncheon tactics it's all we've got. If the lad does have information, he'll want to keep *stumm*. He'll be a fucking sight more scared of being caught grassing than he will be of us. Except that once word gets out that he's lifted, someone might assume he'll grass anyway. Which might – I only say *might* – give him a reason to be cooperative.'

For a *Guardian* reader, Kerr thought, Jacobson could be harder than nails.

'But something like this – if it came to court, the lad could be under a real threat. His mother as well, most likely.'

'Only if he's called as a witness, old son. Besides, there's nothing to stop them moving away, is there? Get him out of the Woodlands, maybe out of Crowby altogether. Jesus Christ, Ian, it would be like winning the lottery for a kid like Walsh.'

Kerr didn't reply. If it was so easy to get out, he was thinking, why would anybody live there at all?

Jacobson put his fag down, finished the rest of his pint in one long mouthful.

'You'll have another?' he asked, standing up. Then heading for the bar without waiting for an answer.

# Chapter Twelve

They'd stopped in the Brewer's Rest until well after last orders. Even Kerr had gone on to shorts: singles at first, then doubles. Neither of them said anything more about the case. Jacobson had no option but to leave his car where he'd parked it. The rank in the pedestrian precinct had a long chucking-out-time queue so they walked round to the taxi office in Flowers Street, took a cab from there instead: out to Wellington Drive for Jacobson and then over to the Wynarth Road and the Bovis estate for Kerr.

Back in his flat, Jacobson eased off his shoes, tossed his coat and jacket onto the sofa. With a tremendous effort of will, he walked through to the kitchen, ran the cold tap, poured himself a glass of water. It was the best preventative he knew for a hangover, kept the system from dehydrating while you slept. The major pitfall with the method was, of course, the fact that the more pissed you were – the more you needed it – the less you entertained any notion of drinking anything as tedious as plain $H_2O$.

While he forced the water down, he stared at News 24. He switched the set off after a couple of minutes, decided that he didn't need wars, disasters and sport intruding into the fleeting sense of well-being and rightness that came after a few drinks. He finished the glass, walked through to his bedroom, resisting the temptation not to bother undressing, to crawl straight under the duvet just as he was. Come to that, there was an entire list of stuff he didn't need. Greg

Salter. The Regional Crime Squad goose-stepping around Crowby. Ryan Walsh, his life fucked up before it had even started. His sole aspiration nicking. And not even good at it. And a hundred thousand like him. His ex-wife, Janice, sunning herself in the Caribbean with the oleaginous property speculator, Mackeson. The retard, Shields, with his Bin Laden T-shirt and his back copies of Wogs Out Weekly. Dave Carter's clenched fists, burnt and skeletal.

He dumped his clothes over the chair, switched out the lights, enjoyed the satisfying creak his weight made on the bed as he fell into it, more or less already asleep.

Steve shot bolt upright, wide awake and sweating. In the dream, the firing squad had refused him a final cigarette because he was being executed for bankruptcy. That's not allowed in a civil case, the commandant had said. Yet he'd nearly got away, so very nearly got away. He'd heard the footsteps running in the corridor, the commandant barking his orders. But one of them had stopped right outside, had flung the door wide open. It had been good to get out into the daylight anyway. He hadn't liked the rats and the spiders that were sometimes snakes. The walls hadn't quite been walls either, had felt like mucus or fungus, something wet and filthy you didn't want to touch. Or maybe it had been as if they were living, breathing. Like the belly of some great beast.

He wiped the sweat from his forehead, waited for his eyes to adjust to the darkness. He deciphered the warm orange digits on the front of the clock radio: 3.19 am. There was something comforting about the pulse of an LCD display if you woke up in the middle of the night. Electricity was still out there, it told you, gridding the land. Life was carrying on. Marion had moved right over to the other side of the extra-king-sized bed. He could hear her snoring softly, fast asleep, face down on the pillow. He couldn't sleep like that himself, or on his back; reckoned he changed from one side to the other and back again all night long. He got up as quietly as he could, found his dressing gown, padded towards the door. He couldn't use the en suite or the main bathroom, didn't want to wake the whole house. So he used the downstairs loo but didn't flush it. Boris, a cocker spaniel, pure bred, stirred dozily in his wicker basket when Steve turned on the kitchen light. Then slavered, reclosing his rheumy, sleepy eyes. The poor dog was getting on in years. One day soon he'd take a trip to the vet's and not come back. Although Marion had said it might be better to opt for a house call, let him pass away in his familiar surroundings. He opened the fridge, sorted himself a glass of milk. She might have a point, at that.

He turned the dimmer switch back down until the kitchen was bathed only in moonlight, falling through the windows and through the glass doors that led out to the patio. He pulled a chair out from the kitchen table, sat down with the milk. His mouth felt like a parrot's cage and his brain felt like soup. But so what? You couldn't fault the occasion anyway; that was definitely one thing. Croucher, the old boy from the university, had done the honours, as it turned out. And not too bad a job: there'd been several plugs for the business among the rest of the rigmarole. Stephen Adams had left school with no qualifications – there must be a message to the teaching profession in that, old Crouchy had said, not missing a trick. He'd built up a successful business by dint of his own hard work and personal effort. And helped by the solid partnership with his wife, Marion. Here was a family, as well, who were putting something *back* into the community. Both lads were in the youth football team which their dad coached. A little bird had told him that Sarah Adams was in the running to be the new editor of the school newspaper. They'd lapped that one up all right. Applause all round.

He felt better after the milk, considered having another one. Maybe with a dollop of whisky this time. Maybe more than a dollop. Well, why the fuck not? He needed to get back to sleep, didn't want to wake up in an hour again, strapped into the electric chair or some other nonsense. Like that one last week: where someone or something had forced his head under deep, black water and he hadn't even struggled – hadn't even *wanted* to struggle. He poured out another glass, walked along the hall to the front lounge. Still not using the lights, still undecided about the whisky. He drew back the thick curtains on the windows an inch or so. Just enough that the room wasn't in complete darkness. A shaft of moonlight illuminated the coffee table, the empty bottle of champagne still in its bucket. Dimly, next to the bucket, he could see the four empty champagne glasses. It was probably just the booze combined with the pills, he thought. Like eating cheese late at night when you were a kid. He was bound to be worried – wasn't he? – with business dipping off to zero. That was a normal thing too, wasn't it? Business worries. And trying to find other ways out of the hole. It was what you did. What everybody did. Worried. Coped. Sorted it. It was all normal. The rest was just daftness. Only in his head. Not important.

He made the drinks cabinet rattle, scrabbling around inside. There was a word. Tangible. That was it. It was only what was tangible that mattered. What you could see, feel, touch. Nothing else. It would be easier to see with a light on. But I want it kept dark. Don't ask me why. I just do. He found the Johnnie Walker's. No point pouring good malt into a glass of milk. The dark you knew could keep out other dark, maybe. Listen to yourself, mate. You'll be talking back to the radiators next. He swallowed down the milk and whisky, then drew the curtains tight shut again. It had been a good night all right. Laughing, dancing. A smoochy little look from the fireman's wife when they'd been leaving. Even Bentham, the Chief Constable, had grabbed a few words with him. If only some of the young tearaways had been given the chance of a decent family background, a proper start. Et fucking cetera.

He took the milk glass through to the kitchen. This time

the dog gave a half-hearted half-bark before settling back down. From a mid-point at the foot of the stairs, Steve could see the moonbeams streaming through the kitchen windows, the porch light refracted through the oval of stained glass in the new front door he'd fitted himself. He was sure that the moonlight really was that bright. Really, tangibly. It was always that bright if you were tired and it was the middle of the night, wasn't it? I've got my feet on the ground all right, mate. Tiny strands of something like smoke in between the shafts. Coiling and uncoiling for ever. The beams and shafts of light. Millions of them. Millions without number. And a noise like the sea roaring.

He went upstairs, not running, not looking back. Just quiet, in-the-middle-of-the-night normal. Sweat but no worries. They had five bedrooms. A guest room. A room each for the three kids. They were doing all right. You reached the master bedroom last. The door was to the left of the little window at the end of the landing. Marion had curtained it like all the rest in the house though it wasn't one where they ever bothered to draw them across. But there was no moon shining now anyway. Only a grey blanket of clouds rolling slowly across the sky.

# Chapter Thirteen

Charlie carried his mug of tea to the one free table and sat down. An earlier customer had left their copy of the *Sun* behind. He glanced disinterestedly at the sports pages while he waited for the tea to cool and for his plate of sausage, bacon and eggs to put in an appearance. He was sitting in a café in Midland Road, maybe five minutes' walk away from Mill Street. He'd just spent an uncomfortable night on a musty sofa over in Longtown. Courtesy of a couple of tame students he used to sell the odd wedge of blow to back in the days when he'd done bits and pieces of minor dealing. Strictly speaking, he was currently of no fixed abode. He'd been crashing on the floors and armchairs of acquaintances for two months now. He'd stopped at his sister's a few times. But her cunt of a boyfriend had made it clear he wasn't welcome to stay more than once or twice a week. Occasionally, he'd slept rough. Less occasionally – meaning less times – he'd slipped between the sheets with some slag or other. It was one of the problems the apprenticeship with the firm had been supposed to solve. The first month's wages would have set him up with the deposit for something half decent – someplace where they didn't take scumbags who were on the social. No chance of that now. Zero. Fucking sod all.

He cut the sausages up neatly when his plate arrived, dipping each piece in egg yolk before forking them into his mouth. He did much the same with the bacon, using the slices of fried bread – finally – to mop up the remains of the egg. They had Crowby FM on behind the counter. With a bit of effort, he managed to catch most of the 9 am news bulletin above the general din. But the only local items were about job losses out at Planet Avionics and a load of bollocks about the Civic Awards night. *Crowby's Oscars*, the daft twat of a reporter had said. Not a word about the fire or about Dave Carter, deceased. He drank up his tea and left.

He'd expected Florida Boy to be still asleep. But FB surprised him by opening the door on the first knock.

'Charles, old bean. Charmed. Come in, come in,' FB said.

The bedsit, which had been a mangy tip of unwashed clothes and unfinished takeaways the day before, had been remade and remodelled. The sudden descent into tidiness had only one possible explanation: Bilston was pilled up again, twitchy with chemical energy. Charlie entered the room, closing the door behind him. Without asking, he switched off FB's television set which had been blaring out *Teletubbies*.

'I've been thinking,' he said. 'What we need to do is get out of this town. Right out – at least for a while anyways.'

Florida Boy went back to what he'd been doing: stacking newly washed and dried cutlery in a drawer in the tiny corner of the room which functioned as his kitchen.

'Foreign parts, old bean, why not? Take in the sights and highlights.'

Charlie plonked himself onto another lumpy, busted couch.

'Cut the crap, Brian. This is fucking serious,' he said, exasperated.

FB had a bread knife in his hand, made a few stabs in the air, sub-Kung Fu style.

'Never take your eyes off your opponent, grasshopper.'

Charlie rolled a spliff. Maybe it was hopeless. Maybe he should just leg it by himself. Leave the moronic twat to take his chances. But the problem was that Bilston hadn't the brains to keep it shut if they lifted him, hadn't the nous not to get caught on his own. When he'd built the joint and lit it, he took a couple of draws, tried again.

'Listen, mate. I phoned my sister at Byron House. What she's heard is CID were at the Poets last night, asking questions. They know it was Dave Carter. They know it wasn't no fire accident.'

FB finally put the knife down.

'But yesterday, old bean. The papers – they was only saying about the fire. Didn't even identify Carter.'

'Could be they're holding back on the media and all that,' Charlie commented, relieved to be getting somewhere at last. 'Fly bastards, isn't it?'

Jacobson closed his office door, glad for a few moments on his own. He sat down in his creaking chair, slung his feet up on his desk at a comfortable angle. His first meeting with the RCS, just completed, had been confoundingly low key. In the first place, they'd only sent three officers. One detective inspector plus two detective sergeants. In the second place, all three of them had been full of conciliation and light. They understood it wasn't an ideal situation. Nobody liked outsiders on their patch. Of course they didn't. But there it was. The decision had been taken on high and all the mugs on the ground could do was get on with it, grin and bear it. They'd asked for copies of the reports Jacobson's team had filed so far, ditto Harry Fields, and for anything forensic likewise. It might even be, the DI had speculated, that the killing would turn out to be purely local in character, some grudge or other that was unconnected to the Birmingham firm. In which case – as soon as that could be established – they'd be more than happy to leave Jacobson to it. They'd be out of his hair, gone.

He played with his B and H packet but didn't take one out. He'd had a wake-up cigarette, obviously. But that had been two hours ago and nothing since. He'd be like this for a few days, he supposed. Maybe even a week or two: until the hospital memory of Mrs Carter stated to fade from his overcrowded brain. He stared idly at his photocube of Janice and his daughter, Sally. Maybe it was finally time to give the photo of Janice the heave-ho. The phone rang, interrupting his reverie: Emma Smith out at the Woodlands. Smith and Williams had clocked on early, had just completed a Section 18(1) search – no warrant required – *chez* Walsh.

'Nothing that shows up on the recent stolen list, guv. But we've noted a few serial numbers, we can do a more thorough check when we get back to base. He's got what looks like an eighth in his bedroom, though. Also some, er, women's underwear in need of a wash.'

'Pervy little sod. Don't bother with the blow, though, lass,' Jacobson said, swinging his legs back off the desk and standing up. 'We're not *totally* desperate. How's Mrs W?'

'At her wits' end, I reckon,' Emma Smith said. 'Wants him kept locked up, she says – or chucking in the army.'

The line was crackling. Jacobson pressed the phone closer to his head. Ryan Walsh, the human sandbag, he thought – an ideal piece of equipment for trench warfare.

'OK, then. Better beat a retreat before the RCS trio turn up. Thanks anyway.'

He took the back stairs route down through the building and out into the car park. Kerr was already waiting. He opened his passenger door and Jacobson clambered in. At this time of day they had no option but to follow the one-way system around the town centre. It would probably have been quicker to walk, Jacobson thought. But also wetter and colder. There were only three interview rooms at Crowby Central, all in use. So they spoke to Ryan Walsh in the cell of which he was the sole occupant: now that the drunk case had been ferried over to the magistrates' court.

Walsh sat on a narrow bench. But Jacobson and Kerr preferred to stand.

'Yesterday morning, Ryan, you say you left William Blake

House at seven o'clock. Who did you run into on your way out?' Jacobson asked.

'Nobody. It was frigging dark. I want to see a brief.'

'The flat just below you, Ryan. Somebody kicked Dave Carter's head in and then burnt his body. Somebody who could do that once could do it again. Especially if they thought a witness—'

'This is diabolical. I want to see a frigging brief.'

Walsh slid along the bench until he was right in the corner, folded his arms, sunk his head down between his shoulders.

Kerr stared hard at Jacobson, thinking. Apart from the break-in, he hadn't flouted any actual procedures, but he was certainly sailing close to the wind. Matching suspected stolen goods to actual stolen goods was a laborious, time-consuming job. And futile as often as not. Besides which, the presence of a couple of half-inched PlayStations hardly made Walsh into public enemy number one. Even if they *had* some charges to put, the magistrates would only adjourn the case or order it to be dealt with alongside Walsh's other upcoming summonses. Greg Salter – or anyone else who cared to look – would see the stolen goods pretext very clearly for what it was.

Jacobson sat down on the bench, less than a foot away from Walsh. He looked very nearly trim alongside the chubby youth.

'Think about it, Ryan. If you saw somebody, somebody *saw* you. Lots more saw you lifted last night, lots more will see you brought back this morning. They might ask themselves why you got arrested but didn't get *charged*.'

The penny finally clicked for Ryan Evans Walsh: Jacobson had no intention of booking him with anything.

'So that's it, you bastards! This is diabolical—'

But his face had gone from pasty to pure white, and when Jacobson gave him the card with his contact details, Walsh thrust it deep into the baggy pocket of his jeans.

Kerr drove Jacobson back in the direction of the Divisional

building. Jacobson got out in Silver Street; he'd needed a taxi to get in to work this morning and now he wanted to move his car back over to the police car park before it got clamped. There was a newsagent's near by. Jacobson bought a copy of the *Guardian* and two hot samosas, one lamb and one vegetable. Wednesday meant that it was the Society supplement – he liked to keep his eye on whatever unworkable crime initiatives the think tanks and government advisers were coming up with – and the samosas would be a bloody sight tastier than anything the police canteen could offer by way of elevenses. He got in and drove off, mildly surprised that the car had survived the night unscathed in body and free of a parking ticket.

Maybe still prompted by the vision of Eileen Carter's comatose figure, drip-fed and wired to half a dozen sci-fi monitors, Jacobson took the *stairs* up to the fourth floor of the Divi where – along the back corridor – the scene-of-crime labs were located. He found Webster, the chief SOCO, in his 'office', which was really no more than a partitioned cubicle at the far end of the second, smaller laboratory. Webster was engaged in the vital first task of the day for a large percentage of the force's employees: getting his paperwork done.

Jacobson sat down uninvited, carefully holding the newspaper and the brown paper bag of samosas over his right knee and well away from any nearby surfaces. Webster's professional need to move carefully, fastidiously, around a crime scene had spilled over neurotically into the rest of his life. You could drive his blood pressure up just by sneezing. The kind of bloke, it was said, who'd fold his clothes before sex: and wear rubber gloves as well as a condom.

'Not your case any more, Chief Inspector,' Webster said, scarcely glancing up from a stack of overtime claim forms.

'No indeed, old son. But I was just interested in a general sort of way as to what kind of progress you might be making. Call it professional curiosity.'

Webster clicked his pen shut, clipped it neatly into the chest pocket of his freshly pressed white shirt. The RCS team were premier division but they weren't likely to become a permanent feature in his working life. Unlike Jacobson.

'Dabs, Frank. A fair old cluster in the lounge – which you'll recall was by far the least damaged room. It's this morning's top priority job for my fingerprint officers.'

It could be something or nothing, Jacobson thought. A flat in the Woodlands, any casual visitor or acquaintance could show up in the NAFIS database without having the slightest connection to the killing.

'And you'll let me know?'

Webster picked up the pile of overtime forms then let them fall, thudding, back onto his desk.

'The gang rape on New Year's Eve. My team gave up their entire New Year's Day with their friends and families. They covered every single millimetre of the crime scene. An impeccable job, Frank. Over the odds. Only now upstairs are saying sorry, no overtime, regrettably we're overbudget for the period.'

Jacobson took it as a yes.

Kerr drove along the winding road that led to the car park in the woodland clearing at the foot of Crow Hill. There was a course appraisal form waiting for him back on his desk. Complete fully and return within forty-eight hours of any training event. That was the rule. Expectations, experience gained, learning outcomes, skills checklist, contacts made, quality of the tuition, overall evaluation. All that pen-pushing for something nobody would ever actually read. Fortunately, Jacobson had suggested an alternative activity.

The car park was a lovers' lane after dark. But – the occasional dog-exerciser apart – at this time of year it stood empty for most of the hours of daylight. Kerr turned in under the height barrier and pulled up next to the only other vehicle there. A scruffy white van with an exotically ancient registration plate. It had been parked as far away from the entrance as possible; 'Wash Me Dot Com' had been finger-written in the dirt across the rear doors. Kerr got out of his car and into the van on the passenger side.

'Geordie,' he said, sliding the door shut.

'Mr Kerr.'

George McCulloch, ex-Glaswegian, ex-user, ex-burglar, had been clean for the best part of two years, was now more or less gainfully employed as a window cleaner. Though you would've thought it might have been basic PR to turn up in clean transport. But he still lived on the Woodlands, still got in the Poets on occasion, still had his ear to the ground. He wasn't an officially registered grass. Kerr wasn't his handler. He was just someone Kerr could call on if he needed an insight into the Son of the Bronx. Money changed hands, of course, if the information was useful. But there was more to it than that: Kerr and McCulloch went back. To Kerr's early years in CID. To the death from bad gear of Geordie's wife, Sylvie. To Geordie finding the body in the Roger Harvey case. A bond of sorts. Something undefined by the cash nexus.

'Dave Carter,' Kerr said. 'You've heard the news?'

'Aye. But two versions. Burnt tae a crisp, according to the papers and the telly. Murdered according tae your boss.'

'Somebody beat him to death and then torched the place. He was dealing, right?'

McCulloch lifted his pouch of Golden Virginia off the dashboard and rolled himself a miserly cigarette, his fingers bony and sharp angled. There was a bit of colour in his face these days but he still looked junk thin.

'Him and Terry Shields, the bar manager. Mainly tae the casual crowd. Still, that can be very good money, Mr Kerr.'

Kerr told him the theory about the Birmingham dealership.

'It's a possibility. Mibbe a punishment beating that went too far.'

'You couldn't put a name to anyone on that scene, could you?'

McCulloch put the tobacco pouch back on the dash, picked up a cheap-looking black lighter.

'The Birmingham connection? Ah'm sorry, Mr Kerr. But that's way out of my league.'

'What about the Woodlands angle, then? They might've franchised the beating out to a local, kept themselves nicely at a distance. If that's the case then you can bet that somebody saw something – or knows something. And they won't keep it buttoned for ever. Not once they're pissed or stoned anyway.'

'You know me, Mr Kerr. Ah ken the players oan the estate all right. But ah've heard nothing.'

'But if you *did* hear—'

McCulloch lit the roll-up. The lighter flared up like a blow torch.

'We're talking murder here. Nutters. Head cases. Ah'd need a lot more than the normal consideration.'

Kerr nodded.

'Just a name, Geordie. That's all it takes.'

McCulloch lifted the roll-up to his bottom lip. He turned his head and stared out of the grubby side window. At the edge of the car park, a path sloped up into the tree line. A way-marked trail led you into the woods or you could stay on the path and climb to the summit of the hill. Barely fifteen yards or so away, a grey squirrel was digging ferociously among the mulched leaves at the start of the path. McCulloch took a drag, then pointed.

'Global warming, Mr Kerr. It seems the winters are too mild now fur them tae hibernate properly.'

Kerr found a minute in his life to watch the squirrel biting restlessly through a dead acorn.

Stephen Adams started his working day an hour or so later than usual as a concession to the night before. He finally climbed behind the wheel of his Mondeo at ten past ten, made two phone calls en route. He checked the day's itineraries with Colin Paterson. Col was already on his way over to Wynarth itself: the granny who might be in need of Sky Sports. The rest of the guys were on reinspects. Linda in the office next. No new enquiries so far, she told him.

'No worries, Linda. The *Argus* doesn't hit the streets till lunchtime anyway.'

Once the punters read about the Family of the Year, he thought, willing it to be true, they'll be phoning up in droves, placing orders all over the shop.

The Wynarth Road was over on the other side of Crowby from the Bartons. He decided to use the bypass as far as the North Crowby junction and then head out past the Bovis estate into the half-countryside beyond. Anything was better than crawling into the town centre and out again. Marion had put the local radio on over breakfast. They'd got a mention on the news admittedly. But nobody listened with their full attention first thing in the morning, did they? No, it would be the spread in the *Argus* which would do the trick. No worries. The radio was just background noise. But the paper was something you *read*. You'd look at it in your lunch break then take it home and the missus would do the same. Even if you forgot at the time, you'd see the story again the next day or the next week. When you were taking out the rubbish or lining the rabbit cage.

He switched on the CD player. Though not too loudly on account of his throbbing head. The long hot shower had helped a little. And the ammies. He hardly ever took them during the day. He really didn't. But just this once. Involuntarily, his fingers tapped the steering wheel: Frank Sinatra – the CD Marion had slipped into his Christmas stocking. He'd thought it was a load of old rubbish – this kind of music – when he'd been a teenager. But what did you know when you were sixteen or seventeen? At that kind of age you knew precisely nothing about anything. Luckily, you grew up, moved on, learned better.

The two properties were nearer Crowby than Wynarth. But the location was still nicely rural. The Chief Constable lived out here somewhere, Steve had been told. In another one of the large, imposing houses; each set well back from the public road, their extensive, secluded grounds prickly with security cameras and intruder alarms.

Even the development work was being carried out discreetly. No large hoardings. The nightwatchman's hut at the site entrance tucked out of any direct view from the roadway. Steve parked between a Range Rover and a Toyota pick-up and walked towards the site office. Nobody challenged him. You could go anywhere in this country, he reckoned, provided you possessed a decent suit, a smart haircut and a confident manner. Bill Elliot had phoned yesterday when he was driving back after football practice: the directors from the property company would be taking the grand tour this morning, checking up on the work.

The party wasn't hard to locate. Four suits in hard hats following Elliot and the site manager through the mud. Steve lingered outside the office, waiting. It was a cold morning and the sky was a foul grey colour. But at least it had stopped raining for now. He phoned Linda again. Still no new enquirers. Oh, and Colin Paterson had called to say that the old lady in Wynarth wasn't interested any more. Her son had told her she'd be better off with a digibox, just plug it into her old set and Bob's her uncle. Steve ran two fingers in behind his shirt collar, straightened his tie. Bob was her fucking uncle all right.

They were coming back now. The site manager leading the way, red faced, squat and burly. Bill Elliot behind him and not much taller. Finally the directors: one woman and three tall, thin rich men. It was very nearly a tableau-in-motion of the English class system. Steve stood to one side and then followed them into the Portakabin. Elliot gave him a gruff introduction and Steve made his pitch. If they already had arrangements in place, he was sure he could match any tender, meet any spec. They listened politely but they didn't smile much, didn't ask any questions.

'I'm sorry, Mr Adams – Steve,' the tallest man said finally. 'But we always work with TeleSys. From Birmingham? An ongoing, rolling contract, you see. It's not something we're planning to renegotiate currently.'

'But local firms – like Bill's here – we're on the spot, immediately available. That's an advantage, surely. Especially when it comes to adjustments or upgrades that need doing later,' Steve countered.

The man said nothing, just held out his hand.

'Thanks for your time anyway,' Steve said, trying to sound bright, offering his business card.

Walking back to his car, he glared unwitnessed through the Portakabin window. Bill Elliot and the site manager re-engrossed in building diagrams. The woman unzipping her laptop from its case. The man who'd taken his card binning it with an expression that looked very like distaste.

# Chapter Fourteen

The day passed uneventfully. For the sake of thoroughness, Emma Smith and DC Williams spent two hours trying to match the goods found in Ryan Walsh's front room to the stolen property lists without getting anywhere. After which they had no option but to return to their existing cases. Barber and Hume were out of the picture also. The Birmingham trial was dragging on. They hadn't been called as witnesses yesterday; they'd been instructed to make themselves available again today – just in case. Kerr drove back to the Divisional building. He'd wanted to fill in his course evaluation, get the damned thing over with. Except that Jacobson sent him out again – on a tour of grungy bedsits over in Longtown. Some idiot had pulled a knife during the student night mêlée at Club Zoo and his victim's condition had deteriorated badly in the last few hours. The plods had already taken half a dozen witness statements; but if the charges went to manslaughter – or worse – it would be as well to make sure that CID had chased each one up properly while memories were still fresh.

By four o'clock, Chief Inspector Jacobson, mooching in his fifth floor office, was the sole member of Crowby's ad hoc murder squad who was less than gainfully or routinely employed. His mobile rang. He picked it up from his desk before he answered, noticed that the caller's number had been withheld. *All coppers are bastards. Burr. Click.* It was the third nuisance call in a hour. Hopefully, he thought, it was a game that would rapidly turn boring for the participants. Likewise the obscene text messages. So far, no one had phoned in with any information about Dave Carter's killer or killers. He yawned fiercely, last night still catching up with him. He couldn't decide, he realised, which was the least attractive option. Boiling up some water on his clandestine kettle and making a cup of instant – or risking the theoretically fresh-ground coffee in the police canteen, which by now would have benefited from several hours' stewing time. He'd started on a mental list of positives and negatives – positive: not having to go out of the room, not running into some bugger I'd sooner not see – when his internal extension rang. Greg Salter. *Meeting in my office. Now.*

Harry Fields had already nabbed the low, cushioned chair in front of Salter's desk so Jacobson had to make do with oafish red plastic, unpadded and uncomfortable. As did the one other officer present: Evesham, the Regional Crime Squad DI. Jacobson sat down and said nothing. Evesham had a solid wedge of paperwork balanced across his knee. He looked barely thirty – the RCS was heavily into accelerated promotion – and he was dressed in the casual sportswear endemically favoured by the younger generation of CID. As far as Jacobson was aware, Supercop hadn't left the Divisional building so far, had spent most of the day snooping into Crowby's localised database of current and recent investigations with the help of Steve Horton, the civilian computer officer. Apparently it had been left to the subordinates – the two detective sergeants – to actually get out and about in the Woodlands. Mostly, so Jacobson had heard, they'd just trudged their way up and down William Blake House, repeating the calls that Emma Smith and DC Williams had made the previous day.

Greg Salter leant forward in his Parker-Knoll-of-office.

'I'll come straight to the point, Frank. One: I've just had the *Argus* on the phone. Could I confirm that the fire death out at the Woodlands is actually a case of murder? Two: DI Evesham's officers have been told that there was a police visit to the estate pub last night during which sensitive facts in the case were publicly discussed.'

'The case was mine until this morning, sir. I handled it as I saw fit,' Jacobson replied, avoiding any specifics.

Salter's thin bottom lip quivered before he spoke again. He could do *looking* angry but somehow his voice never seemed to find a convincing matching register.

'But this isn't that kind of case, is it? You can't just go your own way when there's three forces involved. When there's undercover officers in the supply chain, every one of them sticking their necks out.'

You'd know all about taking risks, sir, Jacobson thought. Not.

'So the RCS strategy is to investigate a murder without letting on that there's been one?'

Salter didn't reply, was maybe still concentrating on at least keeping his facial expression credible. Harry Fields looked across at Evesham. A visual nudge.

'We usually like to play our cards as close to our chest as we can,' Evesham said neutrally.

'But as soon as Robinson gets Dave Carter's dental records and makes the formal ID, there's got to be an inquest regardless,' Jacobson countered. 'The facts will *have* to come out then anyway. Unless we're bypassing the law of the land completely.'

'There was a *window* there, Frank. And now there isn't,' Salter said.

Jacobson lifted his right leg, rested the ankle jauntily on his left knee. Salter was winding himself up to the max as per usual. But there was Sweet Fanny Adams he could do about it without flagging up his own managerial incompetence. Salter *should* have explicitly taken Jacobson off the case as of their teatime meeting yesterday. Implicitly, that's what he'd *meant* to happen. But implicitly just wasn't good enough to ensnare an old hand like Jacobson in any kind of disciplinary procedure. *End of*. Clean Harry definitely knew it. Supercop Evesham – to judge by his non-committal tone – probably knew it. The only issue was whether Salter knew it too.

He flexed his ankle, giving his foot a gentle stretch. He wondered if word had got back as well about the mobile phone stunt. On balance, he reckoned not. Though so long as it wasn't being officially mentioned, it didn't really matter either way. He watched Salter glowering at him, the lip still quivering. But it was Harry Fields, purveyor of Christian charity, even to careerist detective chief supers, who spoke next.

'The thing that matters surely, Greg, is how we move on from here.'

Evesham looked up from his paperwork, nodding enthusiastic agreement. Jacobson grasped suddenly that something pre-rehearsed was about to be rolled out.

'One of our undercover guys has sent a message to HQ,' Evesham said. 'It seems the big firm *did* hire local labour for a punishment job. But not for a murder. So now they've washed their hands of the subcontractors. Our guy can't find out who, unfortunately – since there's no reason from his cover role why he should even be interested.'

The confirmation of the theory was news to Jacobson. More pertinently – he guessed – it was news to G. Salter, Esquire.

'So it looks like a more open approach could be fruitful after all,' Clean Harry explained. 'The Birmingham crew will stay relaxed in any case – as long as it's clear none of their own are in the frame. It's not impossible they might even throw us a name just to get rid.'

Salter fingered his executive toy, setting the tiny chrome cubes on a collision course.

'What exactly are you suggesting, Harry?' he asked finally.

Fields nodded across to Evesham a second time. Evesham coughed, clearing his throat, then dropped his carpet bomb.

'The RCS view now, sir, is that Inspector Jacobson takes the case back. We'd like to put one of my detective sergeants on his team. A temporary secondment. Act as liaison. But basically it's over to the Crowby side again.'

Jacobson tried hard to measure the astonishment on Greg Salter's face. But he was far too astonished himself to get very far with it.

Marion Adams collected Anne-Marie and Sarah from the school gates and drove them home. Anne-Marie phoned her mum to say that she'd got there safely. She had to speak to her on Candice's mobile – the lady who lived downstairs – since her mum had run out of top-up cards. Even though it was cold and already turning dark, Anne-Marie and Sarah wanted to play in the back garden. *All right*, Sarah's mum said, *but make sure you wrap up warm. We don't want Annie-Marie going home with a cold, now, do we?*

Anne-Marie loved Sarah's garden. It seemed huge and endless. Like a secret world. There was a statue of a Greek lady with a water jug behind the greenhouse. And a pond with real fish in; even a frog when she'd been here in the summer. Sarah had her own swing at the bottom of the lawn and they took turns at pushing each other. Backwards and forwards. Higher and higher. Then they played their game where they were hiding from Orcs. Sarah hadn't read Toll Keen but she'd seen *The Fellowship of the Ring* on DVD so she knew what an Orc was and how frightening they were. They hid behind the greenhouse but an Orc scout crept up on them and they had to run off to get away. Boris, Sarah's very old dog, tried – panting – to keep up with them.

'Quiet, Boris,' Sarah scolded, 'or the Orcs will hear you.'

'Yes, sssh, Boris,' Anne-Marie said, putting a finger to her lips, 'or we'll all be boiled in oil.'

What Anne-Marie really wanted to do was to play in the tree house. Which really would be like being in a little world all of your own. It was the single thing she envied Sarah more than any other. But her dad hadn't finished building it yet, Sarah had told her earlier. Until it was finished, it wasn't safe. They definitely had to leave it alone before then. *Definitely, definitely*, Sarah had said.

Anne-Marie bent down and patted Boris on the top of his head. She did so gingerly even though he was very ancient.

'What if Boris is an Orc in disguise?' she asked in a whisper.

And then they were running across the lawn again, pretending to scream.

# Chapter Fifteen

Charlie and Florida Boy called over at Lisa's place again. But took the bus this time. FB spent the afternoon in front of the telly while Lisa and Charlie went upstairs. Charlie's idea was to hide out until it got dark. Then they'd nick a motor and get the hell out of Crowby as far and as fast as they could. Around five o'clock, they were all three sat in Lisa's kitchen, sharing a joint and drinking Nescafé.

'Best make a move soon. Before Lisa's mum gets back,' Charlie said.

Florida Boy passed the joint across the table to Lisa.

'Places to go, people to see, old boy,' he said.

They'd packed a hold-all each, had left them sitting in the hall. Charlie had told Lisa he had to leave town for a bit. But he hadn't said for how long or why.

Lisa frowned.

'I don't blame you. Getting out of this place. Wish I could.'

She'd got dressed in her navy blue Niké tracksuit, had her chair pulled close to Charlie's. Charlie liked to watch her toke, the joint fat between her fingers.

'Why don'tcha come with us, then?' he asked.

As if it was an impulse. But it was something he'd thought about – had more or less thought through – while they'd been lying in bed. If and when the dibble sussed them for the killing, they'd be looking out for two geezers: not a threesome. And there were all sorts of possible scenarios where a lass might come in useful. Strangers trusted women more easily than they did blokes, assumed you must be all right yourself if you had a bird in tow. Everybody knew that.

'D'you mean it, Charlie?'

Handing him the joint, her voice squeaky with unexpected excitement.

'I wouldn't ask otherwise. Just pack a few things. Maybe some cash?'

Charlie and FB had less than fifty quid between them. Which was something of an impediment, Charlie thought.

'After me for my money, is it?' she asked.

'Something like that. Nowt round here for you anyway, is there?'

She kissed him on the back of the neck as she stood up. A hot, slobbery kiss that very nearly turned into a bite. Charlie gave Florida Boy a reassuring wink as she did so – even though the twat was so zonked he'd most probably have agreed to any change of plan. Stick your thick head into the deep fat fryer, FB. There. That's a good mate. Cheers.

Lisa was ready by twenty past. Charlie hurried her up, thought they were cutting it a bit fine. He got her to write a note and leave it on the kitchen table. She put that she was going to visit somebody she used to work with for a few days; a nurse who was living down in London now. Lisa was eighteen, could do what the fuck she liked. But Charlie didn't want her mum or her old man reporting her to the police as a missing person and all that.

'Let's roll, old bean. Exit stage left,' Florida Boy said, bringing the hold-alls through from the hall.

They left by the back door and cut quietly across a couple of gardens, emerging on to the street where Charlie had left the Rover the day before. But not at the same point. There was an Astra – a P reg again – parked outside a couple of houses that were both handily in darkness. Thirty seconds and Charlie had done the locks. Three minutes and Charlie was revving the engine gently to life. Ten minutes and the Astra was safely off the Beech Park Estate and headed out towards the bypass.

Lisa fiddled with the radio, channel-hopping between the music stations. Charlie clocked FB in the mirror, sprawled out on the back seat, leaving the decisions to somebody frigging else as usual. It took nearly an hour to get onto the motorway, crawling through the rush hour as the drones made their nightly way home. Dinner. TV. Shag the wife. Repeat until dead. He pulled in at the Crowby motorway services. FB wanted a piss and Charlie wanted Lisa to clean out her cash card at the hole in the wall. It coughed up eighty quid before it told them to fuck off. She'd brought fifteen with her in her purse which meant they had a hundred and forty-odd nicker all told. It was bog-all really but it was enough to see them on their way. The Astra's petrol gauge was on half so Charlie filled the tank up before they drove off. He sent Lisa into the shop to pay for the fuel, thinking it best to keep his appearances on the forecourt security cameras to an absolute minimum. She came back with a big bag of sweets for Florida Boy and a couple of magazines for herself. Charlie adjusted his seat to a better driving position and started the car. The perfect family outing, he thought. Except that Mummy was a half-mad slag and Sonny Boy was a murderer.

Jacobson left his office at six o'clock on the dot, decided just for once not to put in even a second's unpaid, extra, over-the-odds effort. For one thing, Webster, the chief SOCO, had let him down. Or more precisely NAFIS had let Webster's fingerprint officers down. NAFIS was the National Automated Fingerprint Identification System. For any marks lifted from a crime scene, the NAFIS computer could run an electronic comparison against the five and a half million or so print sets stored in its records, automatically find the fifteen closest fits. It was still a matter of the fingerprint expert's skill to determine the most convincing match. But it was a task that could take less than an hour instead of the weeks or months needed in the past. Except that yesterday and today there'd been technical problems. The entire NAFIS network was experiencing down time, apparently: whatever the fuck down time was. The upshot was that the results which Webster had promised him this morning were now delayed – optimistically – until some time tomorrow. The real danger with computers, Jacobson thought, wasn't that they'd take over the world. Much worse was that they'd get fed up with their mindless, algorithmic tasks, switch themselves off, take a holiday, leave the planet totally in the lurch.

He didn't bother with a swift one in the Brewer's Rest either. He just found his car in the police car park and drove – or crawled – back to his flat in Wellington Drive through the rush-hour traffic and the kind of wet, irksome drizzle that you couldn't decide whether it was worth using the wipers for or not. For another thing, Greg Salter's meeting hadn't gone entirely Jacobson's way. He had the Dave Carter case back, yes. But the investigation was now officially classified as low-resource only. *No excessive overtime claims, Frank. Please. No exotic forensic tests that can't be one hundred and ten per cent justified.* The reasons being all too obvious, Jacobson hadn't troubled to ask why.

There'd been media interest in the fire and in the speculation that murder had been involved. But as soon as Salter tipped the press the wink that Carter had been a culpable low-life scumbag involved in drug dealing, the story would be swiftly relegated to the news-in-brief columns. Police resources these days were as rationed as healthcare or education. If you planned on getting murdered – and wanted a high-priority police operation to catch your killer or killers – then there were four boxes you needed to tick. White. Middle-class. No criminal record. No associates with a criminal record. The killing of a solid respectable citizen meant the media would be breathing down the neck of the Chief Constable, who would breathe down the neck of the Detective Chief Superintendent, who would breathe down the rest of CID's neck to get the case solved. Even ticking the subsidiary boxes – 'child' or 'female' – wouldn't necessarily help if you couldn't score at least three out of the big four. Dave Carter's corpse had been doing fine up until now under a negative additional clause: ensuring that enquiries wouldn't impact badly on ongoing Regional Crime Squad investigations. But now that the RCS had effectively dropped their interest – other than leaving a DS behind to make sure that Jacobson didn't get up to too much mischief – Carter's death was becoming an object of strictly limited curiosity. A technical matter for the gloomy, unsexy specialists.

He stopped at the Chinese takeaway on the corner, a hundred yards or so from home, picked up a beef kung po with egg fried rice. He'd leave his mobile switched on just in case, he decided. But otherwise there were no pressing leads to follow. Nothing that wouldn't keep till the morning. Plus he had some lagers in the fridge and a stack of unread or unfinished books. Jacobson didn't share the general prejudice that some killings were worse than others, that victims could be classified as deserving or undeserving. But just because he suffered from a superior understanding of society, law and ethics, he didn't feel that he wasn't fully entitled to a proper night off now and again.

Kerr was home early too. Rachel had left a message on his mobile earlier in the day to say that she was going over to Birmingham tonight with her friend Kate. Some art house movie or other they wanted to see at the Electric Cinema. Right now his evening at home was at that early, ambiguous stage where it could go either way. Cathy was cooking a meal, had seemed pleased enough to see him. Susanne was engrossed in a crayoning book and Sam was showing Daddy that he was a policeman too. He was wearing his plastic helmet and swinging his plastic handcuffs, had already corralled his Action Man into a makeshift jail at the far end of the sofa. The helmet and the cuffs had been an unthinking Christmas gift from some neighbour or other, one that Kerr had been less than happy about. Like most police, he thought it was the last job you wanted for your children. He watched them playing. Twins. Nearly four now. Seeming to grow bigger by the day. Until mealtime was over and the kids had been bathed and put to bed, there was no telling what kind of mood Cathy was really in. She didn't know about Rachel, obviously – the sky would fall in the day she ever found out – and her sulks and her resentments were all about the job. Kerr's long, unpredictable hours away from home. His absorption in a world she didn't know anything about, didn't *want* to know anything about.

Susanne brought her book over, showed him what she'd been colouring. But sometimes – maybe tonight – Cathy seemed to mind less, just seemed glad to be with him. They'd crack open a bottle of wine once the twins were upstairs, maybe watch a video. And for an hour or so he'd never want to see Rachel again. Until the next time.

# Chapter Sixteen

Charlie had thought maybe Bristol. Across to the M42 then straight down the M5. A fair old distance away. Right out of the area. And he knew a guy down there. A decent sort. They'd looked out for each other the last stretch he'd done. Winson Green. His first stay in an adult prison. The guy had all kinds of rackets going, all kinds of connections. He'd sort them out with something.

Ms Dynamite was on the radio. Lisa had her feet up on the dash, rolling a new spliff.

'Slow down a minute, Charlie. I'm gonna end up dropping all this.'

Charlie cut down from ninety to seventy-five, moved over to the slow lane. He waited for her to finish then gunned the accelerator, ready to pick up speed again.

Nothing. Worse than nothing. A truck that had seemed miles behind suddenly looming up in the rear-view. He switched the radio off, knew at once that the engine was dead.

'Fuck,' he said, steering deftly onto the hard shoulder.

The truck roared past them into the night, the twat behind the wheel pumping his horn for all it was worth.

'A problem, old bean?' Florida Boy chipped in from his stretched-out vantage point in the back seat. Charlie ignored him, found the catch for the engine compartment. Handily, there was a torch in the boot. He got Lisa to help him, to hold the torch and shiver next to him. Charlie had nicked his first motor at twelve, had been on half a dozen motor skills courses. The ones that were supposed to wean you off nicking by showing you what was under the bonnet, getting you involved. He'd even tried a garage apprenticeship at one time. But the regular hours hadn't suited him. Or the joke wages.

'Fuck,' he repeated.

He banged the bonnet back down, kicked the radiator grille for good measure, got back inside.

It was the alternator, he explained to Lisa and FB. Dead as a fucking dodo. Fixable if you had a replacement. Which unfortunately they hadn't. Without one the car was completely, utterly and totally useless.

'See us the joint, Leez,' he said, starting to assess the problem.

He wasn't entirely sure where they were. That was point fucking one. Still somewhere on the M42. South of the NEC, he reckoned, but couldn't be more precise. He searched in the glove compartment but couldn't find anything useful like an AA or an RAC card. He'd done that a couple of times, got the patrol out to a broken-down stolen. But it was a risky game. Probably too risky for the circumstances even if he *had* found a card. Which left two possibilities. Leg it along the hard shoulder till they reached the next services or try their luck off the motorway altogether.

He took a deep toke, passed the joint back to Lisa. The attraction of a services area was gaining access to a replacement vehicle, obviously. Or maybe they could even hitch a lift for a bit, travel legit. The downside was distance. Depending on precisely *where* they were, the next services could be two miles or twenty miles away. He got out of the car and climbed up the grassy embankment. The torch lit up only a few feet on the other side of the barrier. But it was enough to suggest that he was looking at the side of a field. The countryside and all that. Vaguely, and at some distance, he thought he could make out a few street lamps. There must be some poxy village or other over that way, he reckoned. A good chance there'd be some transport as well, then. It looked like a long trudge. But at least it had a definite, finite goal. And at least they'd be off the motorway. Out of the way of the traffic cops, at any rate.

He went back to the car and told them it was their only option. Neither of them looked delighted. But neither of them had a better suggestion. Charlie took the torch with them. Before they left the Astra, he took another look in the boot. There was some kind of waterproof jacket and a hideous tartan rug, the kind that a nine-to-five mug would take on some bollocky family picnic. He passed the torch to FB, stuck the rug into his hold-all and offered the jacket to Lisa.

'Keep you dry if the rain turns heavy, Leez,' he said.

'Blinking great,' she answered, shivering again. 'Blinking flippin' great.'

Marion Adams fitted the last of the washing up into the dishwasher and poured herself a third glass of Chardonnay. Boris padded slowly through from the hall and settled himself into his basket. Sarah and her ill-suited school friend were up in Sarah's room. Both the lads were out since Wednesday was their youth club night. She sat down at the kitchen table and glanced at the first few pages of today's *Daily Mail*. But it was Steve she was thinking about really. He was through in the lounge now, gawping at one of the sports channels. He'd barely said a word at dinner. Not even when Mark had talked about how some of the older lads at school were getting the hire of a minibus together, were planning to go all the way to Manchester or Liverpool at the weekend – some special clubbing event. *Clubbing at your age? Not bloody likely*: the kind of thing he'd usually say. Only tonight it was as if he wasn't really listening, almost like he wasn't really there.

She knew he was worried about the business, whatever impression he gave to the contrary. He used to be open – boastful really – about how things were going. His conversation would be endlessly about new orders, done deals, expansion. Now he tried to keep it all to himself. *No problems, Marion, no worries* was about as much as she could get out of him. Behind his back, Marion had taken to phoning Linda over at the industrial estate to find out what was really going on. She'd phoned her exactly for that reason this afternoon. So far, Linda had said, the Family of the Year publicity hadn't made a blind bit of difference. Not one single, solitary new order had come in.

She polished off the Chardonnay and rinsed the glass under the tap. The girl, Anne-Marie, was sweet enough really. But scum like her mother probably thought that somebody like herself had just had everything in life handed to her on a plate. A nice house. A proper family. Money. What that lot – idle, feckless – didn't understand was that they'd *worked* for everything they'd achieved. Her and Steve: they'd got off their arses and built something up. That was what you did – if you were normal, decent. Even if being married didn't stay the way it started out, you stuck at it, muddled along, kept everything together.

She walked through the hall, paused at the door to the lounge but didn't look in. What she'd do next, she decided, was to check on Sarah and her friend. It would be their bedtime soon. Sarah's anyway. God knows when her friend was allowed to stay up to or what sights she saw of an evening. Once they were settled, she thought, she'd come back downstairs, see if she couldn't get somewhere with Steve. At least get him to share some of his worries with her, not keep it all bottled up the way he'd been doing.

Sarah's bedroom door was half open. Marion paused outside. They were absorbed, didn't seem to notice her. Sarah had a pink bookcase next to her bed. A clutter of books and comics usually. But with Anne-Marie's help, she seemed to be organising it into some kind of tidy order. They were working away quietly together. Then Anne-Marie spoke.

'What do you think heaven will be like?'

The sort of question you might well ask, Marion thought. If an unknown man had been burnt to death in your mother's bed.

'Angels,' Sarah said. 'And big fluffy clouds.'

'But do you think everyone will go there?' Anne-Marie asked.

'Everyone. Unless they're really, really bad – like Oliver Cromwell,' Sarah replied gravely, arranging her Harry Potter story tapes into the correct chronological order.

Marion Adams stepped into the room.

'Time to be getting ready for bed, young ladies,' she said.

'Oh, but Mum,' Sarah protested, 'we've nearly done it now.'

Mrs Adams smiled at her daughter. But a little sternly.

'Good. So if you get a good night's sleep you can finish up in the morning before school.'

Anne-Marie looked up from Sarah's *The Worst Witch* book.

'Well, I'm very sleepy anyway,' she announced politely.

# Chapter Seventeen

Jacobson had gone to bed early, hadn't had all that much to drink beforehand. He'd slept like a log and awoken unusually refreshed. By 9 am, he'd not only been at his desk for an hour, he'd cleared a backlog of paperwork and drawn up his plans for the day's enquiries. He listened to the cheery sound of the kettle as it bubbled up to the boiling point then clicked itself off. He'd even brought a fresh carton of milk in from home. He tipped a little of it into one of his chipped red mugs, added a spoonful of instant coffee then poured on the water. He glanced idly down the latest incident sheet as he waited for his drink to cool. Car thefts were top of the list as they frequently were. Followed by burglaries and half a dozen domestics. But nothing out of the ordinary: nothing that looked remotely likely to illuminate his murder case. Mobile phone thefts barely figured, he noticed. They hadn't usually these past few months. Unless it was a seriously top-of-the-range model, a stolen mobile was increasingly worth fuck all to sell on. And so was decreasingly an object of criminal desire. Which no doubt was why – driving in – he'd heard the Home Secretary on the *Today* programme, talking up what he called a *raft* of measures on the issue. As completely in touch with reality as the next senior politician, Jacobson thought. Still it had a nice management buzz word ring to it, that had. *Raft*. He bet himself a fiver he'd hear the usage weaselling between Greg Salter's pursed lips before the week was out.

He tried his first sip of instant coffee. It was just about cool enough to drink if you blew across it first. He was conscious of not taking a B and H out of the packet, of not lighting one up. For something to do with his spare minutes as much as anything, he phoned the hospital and then Chief SOCO Webster. Mrs Eileen Carter was still clinging on to life but still in a coma. There was still no joy from the NAFIS computer. Webster said he'd let him know just as soon as.

His mobile had clocked up half a dozen text messages overnight. *I shagged yr mum up hr bum* was the least obscene. Jacobson deleted all of them in turn, wondered whether giving out his number to the Poets' hard-core miscreants had really been such a clever move after all. He took a second, fuller sip. Once he finished the coffee, he'd get going.

Since the inquiry was so low-resourced that it didn't even rate a proper incident room of its own, he'd arranged to rendezvous with his team over at the Woodlands itself. Unless or until Webster's prints officers came up with a useful fingerprint match, there wasn't really that much they could do, of course: except repeat for a third day what had already been done twice. Talk again to the inhabitants of William Blake House. Especially Ryan Walsh, if he hadn't legged it off the estate since his release yesterday morning. Have another crack at Terry Shields. If you shoved your head hard enough and long enough against a brick wall, Jacobson believed, something would always start to crumble in the end.

Sheryl took Lucy to school via the usual two buses. Both of them turned up late, set off late, made Sheryl late. She just had enough time to see Lucy safely into the school assembly before it had finished and before she had to dash away again to catch her second bus on its return journey into town. She'd wanted to have a quick word with Anne-Marie while she was there but now it would have to keep to the afternoon. She had a personal appointment at the social this time, couldn't afford to miss it. It was scheduled for ten past ten. Maybe for once she wouldn't have to wait in the endless frigging queue. And Grant, the young advice centre worker, had arranged to go in with her, make sure she got what she was entitled to. Once they were done there, it would be over to the housing department at the council offices. There was a chance, Grant had told her yesterday, of picking up the keys to her new place today. After that, he'd said, they could call in at the Community Furniture Project, see what could be done in the way of basics: a cooker, beds, something for them to sit on.

The social's offices were in a grey concrete block on the other side of the shopping centre. Sheryl took the moving staircase that led directly from the Flowers Street bus station up into the middle of the main shopping arcade. The rain had gone overnight but the cold, biting wind hadn't. Even if you had no cash to spend in John Lewis or Debenham's, you took the undercover route whenever you could: avoiding the wind tunnel streets outside, the dust and litter that blew straight into your face. Grant met her in the grubby Starbucks that had replaced the old Wimpy Bar across from the entrance to the indoor market, treated her to a latte. The Crowby Starbucks was as far removed from Central Perk as the branch on Alpha Centauri, but Sheryl was still glad of the break, still glad of the chance for a hot drink and a ciggy.

Grant was doubtful about the social. Sheryl still had ninety quid unpaid from her last crisis loan and – strictly – the regulations prevented any further loan while there was any existing debt outstanding.

'They're allowed to exert leeway in a genuine emergency, Sheryl,' he said. 'Which this clearly is. So long as there's no suggestion that you're culpable in any way. Which again there isn't.'

His mobile rang but he switched it off without answering, wanted her to know that she was totally the focus of his concentration. The social could cancel what she owed them, he told her. Issue her with a fresh loan. But he wasn't hopeful. He'd been a Social Security clerical officer himself before he'd gone over to the other side. *Dropped out*, as his parents and his former bosses saw it. His inside knowledge stood his clients in good stead. But his status as a deserter could go against them too. Especially if the case got handled by the kind of CO who was on a mission to defend the taxpayers' cash from the greedy fingers of the underclass.

Once Sheryl had finished her coffee and the first of the four Superkings Candice had spared her from her own depleted packet, they left Starbucks and took the nearest flight of exit stairs out of the shopping centre. They needn't have hurried after all. Even for those with an appointment, the social was running as late as usual. It was a quarter to eleven before Sheryl and Grant squeezed into the private interview booth. Above their heads, malfunctioning strip lighting buzzed, one of the omnipresent security cameras blinked. Everything the tiny square room contained – the desk, the three meagre-arsed chairs – was quite literally nailed to the floor. Whether to prevent thieving or to discourage the taking of a chair leg to the vulnerable head of some overly smug or zealous apparatchik wasn't entirely clear. The clerk stepped into the room, a bulky manilla folder under his right arm. He looked about the same age as Grant, Sheryl thought. But whereas Grant had a neat number-one haircut and a clean, smooth face, the clerk's hair was old-fashionedly long and very nearly as greasy as his complexion. He sat down behind the desk, avoided eye contact when he spoke.

'Sheryl Hope?'

'No it frigging isn't. It's Sheryl Holmes. H-O-L-M-E-S,' Sheryl said, exasperated, correcting the bureaucratic error for the third time in as many days.

Pauline Harrison, Anne-Marie Holmes' and Sarah Adams'

teacher, was also the school's deputy head. A role which meant not much extra cash, a lot more extra work and responsibility. Today was a case in point. The actual head teacher was attending an LEA day conference. Which meant that Pauline had to teach *and* deal with anything executively pressing. She hadn't paid much initial attention to the fact that both Sarah and Anne-Marie were absent this morning. So were four other kids in her class. It was February, after all, the very middle of the colds and influenza season. At break time, she checked her pigeon-hole in the staffroom, fully expecting the usual message slips from the school secretary. *Sarah Adams' mother phoned to say, etc*. But there was nothing regarding her two best pupils. She grabbed a cup of tea and headed for the school office where, in any case, one of her extra tasks was to check with the school secretary that the morning's fresh absences had been correctly notified. There'd definitely been no word about either girl, the secretary told her. She brought up the contact details on her computer screen. She found one number for Sheryl Holmes – a mobile – and two numbers for Marion Adams – a mobile plus a land line. She tried all three. She got an answerphone response each time and left a message on each.

A tiny girl knocked timidly on the door, even though it was wide open to the corridor anyway. Her face was flushed and she looked on the verge of tears. Pauline recognised her: Lucy, Anne-Marie's little sister.

'I can't find my sister,' the girl said in a quiet voice. 'I asked Sophie Norman but she said she'd been sent home for being smelly.'

Patiently, Pauline got the story from Lucy. Anne-Marie had stayed at Sarah's last night. But Lucy couldn't find Sarah either. She gave them another mobile number to call, fishing it from her pocket in a messy, crumpled note. Her mum was out of top-up cards, she said. Candice was her mum's friend. The secretary tried the number, shook her head: Candice wasn't answering either.

'I could try Mr Adams' business number, Pauline, if you think—'

Good idea, Pauline thought. She picked up the Yellow Pages, found the number herself. The secretary dialled again, shook her head again. He hadn't called into the office yet, the receptionist at Adams Installations told her. It was unusual but she supposed he was probably out chasing up an order somewhere. She could give them his mobile if they wanted it? That would be useful, the secretary said. But when she tried the number she only got one more answerphone greeting.

Pauline took a deep breath. There would be a simple explanation, surely. She asked the secretary to take Lucy back to her class for now. And to ask the teaching assistant to cover her own class for the next little while. She'd try the telephone numbers again herself. And then she'd think about what else to do. Two ten-year-old girls were missing from the school, last seen in each other's company; no responsible adult was immediately contactable. And then she'd try not to panic.

Most of the houses on the Bartons were less than ten years old. Custom built, upmarket. There were half a dozen basic templates available. According to the building prospectus, the purchaser could mix and match from a whole range of style features, derive a satisfyingly individual solution that would still be within the overall design motifs of the development. The street names reflected floral and natural themes. Willow Court was where the Adams family lived. Number eight. Detached, five bedrooms, ample gardens front and back, private driveway, garage with automatic doors.

'All right for some,' PC Barry Sheldon said, drawing the patrol car up none too neatly. PC Ogden, unbuckling his seat belt, didn't bother to reply. Like Sheldon, he reckoned the call-out was probably a complete and utter waste of time. A couple of ten-year-olds bunking off school who'd never bunked off before. As if there wasn't a first time for everything. Just another school overreacting, covering its back. Ogden clicked his radio to stand-by. But at least it was something harmless to be doing. They'd been in the area anyway. Plus it would kill some of the time remaining before their mid-shift meal break.

'Bloody schoolteachers,' Sheldon persisted, flinging the driver's door open, never knowingly fazed by anybody's lack of response. 'Always poking their noses in where they're not wanted.'

Jacobson's team assembled in the street outside William Blake House. Jacobson had a ludicrous, fleeting image of himself as some kind of evangelist, a Jehovah's Witness maybe, geeing his troops up to spread the good news, bring salvation to the damned. He designated Mick Hume and DC Barber to doorstep inside the block again. Emma Smith and DC Williams, who'd already done their stint at that unenviable task, he sent over to speak to Dave Carter's neighbours in Tennyson Court. He had precious little hope that any of them would be in possession of any relevant information. Even less that they'd be prepared to share it with Crowby CID. But this was how real policework got done: thankless, plodding spadework on hostile, unforgiving ground. Hours, days and even weeks of it. Until somewhere along the line, if you were lucky, you at last struck through to the deep, rich soil underneath – the layer where the truth lay. He reminded Hume and Barber that Ryan Walsh was the priority tenant. Then he was climbing into the passenger seat of Kerr's latest Peugeot, glad at least to be out of the cold.

It was very nearly the Poets' opening time. Terry Shields was unlocking the main doors as Kerr pulled into the pub car park. Jacobson and Kerr followed him inside and through to the lounge. DS Renbourn was with them, the secondee from the Regional Crime Squad.

'Sergeant Renbourn here is something of an expert on the war against drugs, Terry. Since he was in the area, he thought he'd take a look around,' Jacobson said.

Shields opened the cash register, setting up for the day.

'Got a warrant, has he?'

Jacobson showed him the warrant, duly signed. Also the standard leaflet, approved by the Plain English Society, which now had to be handed out whenever an official search took place: *Police Searches: Your Rights and Responsibilities.* Shields grunted, starting filling the change from a couple of money bags into the till: twenty pees, fifties, pound coins. The two barmaids from Tuesday night were sitting at a table, finishing off cigarettes and mugs of tea. There was an older woman in kitchen whites with them. The lunchtime cook, apparently. Renbourn wasn't ecstatic about the idea of any of them witnessing the search but Shields turned down the offer when Jacobson made it anyway. Renbourn and Kerr went behind the bar and disappeared into the kitchen, intent on giving the back room the once-over first of all.

'When precisely did you last see Dave Carter, Terry?' Jacobson asked.

Shields wiped a breakfast remnant, something tomato coloured, from the side of his mouth.

'Sunday night, about ten. This place wasn't doing much business. So I said I'd cover the last hour on my own. Let Dave off early, like.'

'He left with the lass, then? Sheryl Holmes?'

'No, he didn't. Sheryl had been in earlier but she'd left on her own a while before. Fly bugger, Carter – as it turns out.'

Jacobson kept the motions of question-and-answer going while Renbourn and Kerr carried out the motions of the search. Not that Shields told him anything useful. Not that

Jacobson expected him to. Shields hadn't seen any new or unusual faces around the pub recently. Nobody had seemed to be taking any kind of unusual interest in either himself or Dave Carter. There was such a thing as harassment, mate. Such a thing as interfering with a legitimate business.

'Save it for somebody who gives a fuck,' Jacobson advised him.

Renbourn and Kerr took a look down in the cellar then came back into the lounge. 'Nothing, guv,' Renbourn said, addressing Jacobson. 'I expect if we did a full forensic search though—'

'I dare say, old son. What do you say, Terry?'

'You've got it all wrong,' Shields answered. 'I only sell beer.'

Jacobson grinned, shook his head.

'Bin Laden, Terry,' he said, alluding to the T-shirt that Shields had been wearing the other day, which he was wearing again now. Though it didn't smell much like he'd washed it between times. 'You do know where most gear on sale in the UK comes from, I take it?'

Shields didn't answer, had started polishing a badly washed beer glass. Like most professional toerags, he knew when to keep his mouth shut. You didn't rub the Old Bill too far up the wrong way – there was no mileage in that – but you didn't incriminate yourself either.

'Any reason Dave Carter took the beating and not you?' Kerr asked, wiping cellar dust off his jacket.

Shields put the glass down, picked up another one, still saying nothing.

Jacobson drummed the bar counter rhythmically with the fingers of his right hand. Like a customer impatient for service, gasping for a pint. He already knew why, he thought. Professionals like the Birmingham crew would always pre-assess any action. Something about Carter's routine had just made him a simpler, easier target than Shields. His habit of grabbing a lie-in while the young lass, Sheryl, took her kiddies to school maybe. Whatever: they'd stopped the trade for the time being evidently, would expect Shields to be ready and willing when they felt safe to start up again. By which time, the interloping suppliers would simply have given up, would be trying their luck elsewhere. Most probably, Renbourn had intimated, they were just some small-scale local outfit anyway – cowboys chancing their arm.

'Never mind, Ian,' Jacobson said, bringing his hand to a rest. 'There's a parallel universe where Terry's the one get's his arse burnt off.'

It was a throw-away line only. But Jacobson's mobile rang the next second. So that the remark came to be logged in his mind alongside the other data that spoke of where he'd been, what he'd been doing, when he'd first heard the news. Shields' food-stained T-shirt. The stale smell of last night's beer. Etched in his memory, carved in. For a long time. For years.

# Chapter Eighteen

Renbourn's remit was restricted to the Dave Carter case. So Kerr dropped him off outside William Blake House before he drove himself and Jacobson back into Crowby and then out towards the Bartons area. There were two patrol cars, the scene-of-crime van and an ambulance outside in the street when he reached the location in Willow Court. He cut the engine and both of them got out. Barry Sheldon and young PC Ogden were leaning strangely over the bonnet of the first patrol car. As if for support. As if they could no longer trust their legs. Ogden's face was whiter than a sheet and Sheldon, in defiance of half a dozen regulations for a plod in uniform, was puffing at a cigarette which he was holding clumsily between trembling fingers. Seeing them, and especially a macho nutter like Sheldon, Jacobson knew at once that something unquestionably bad had happened here. Something whose nature hadn't been fully captured by the contents of the curt, business like message he'd received from the control room: the police code for suspicious death plus the map reference and the address.

Webster, the chief SOCO, was standing in the front porch. He seemed to be holding up better than Sheldon and Ogden. But only just.

'No need for an incompetent police surgeon on this one, Frank. I've put a call straight through to Robinson at the mortuary. He's on his way.'

Webster was in full protective clothing kit. So was the other

SOCO who emerged from the house and handed a kit each to Jacobson and Kerr.

'What's the score, old son?' Jacobson asked Webster.

Webster, untypically, avoided a straight answer.

'We'll take a look when you're ready.'

Jacobson struggled into the protective suit. Also known as a Durex, Extra Large. But nobody seemed to be making that or any of the other standard jokes today.

Webster showed the way. His team were standing at the foot of the stairs. That was all. Just standing there. They must have had a good twenty minutes' start on him, Jacobson reckoned, should all have been busy dusting, filming, sampling. But all they were bloody doing was bloody standing there.

'What the fuck—' he started to say.

Webster shook his head – meaning don't say anything yet – not till you've *seen*. He clasped Jacobson's shoulder, pointed upwards with his other hand to the top of the stairwell. Jacobson looked up, *saw*. A sturdy wooden balustrade over which a rope had been slung and snugly knotted. An adult male dangling by the neck from the end of the rope. The head lolling, lopsided. Two dead eyes bulging in a face like a fright mask.

'This isn't everything, Frank,' Webster said quietly.

They put their own masks on and he led them upstairs.

The first bedroom was teenage, male. Posters on the wall. Beckham. Eminem. An impossibly big-breasted model draped over a sports car. Also blood splatters in classic textbook patterns. Also a naked boy sprawled on the floor. Dead. Bloody and beaten around the head and face. His right arm – still raised across his forehead as if to ward off a blow – was badly bruised below the wrist, looked smashed, broken. The second bedroom replayed the first with minor variations. A group poster of Man U next to a Premier League wall chart. The results and goal-scorers had been penned on neatly for the first few matches of the season but had ceased to be recorded some time well before Christmas. A kid losing interest in a project, the way they did. Jacobson, Kerr and Webster crowded in, gaping. The second lad had met the same kind of death as the first. But maybe more quickly. He was still in bed, still under his duvet. Above his bashed-in face, his blood had drenched his pillow.

'How many?' Jacobson asked through the mask.

Webster ushered them out and along the corridor. He didn't speak, held up his right hand for an answer: five fingers. On a basic level, Jacobson would think later, the woman and the girl were easier to cope with: neither had been beaten, neither had obvious injuries. If you'd never seen a corpse before, you might have thought for a foolish moment that they were only sleeping, only pale. But Jacobson could no longer count the dead bodies his profession had brought him to. He knew – even from the doorway to each bedroom – that both of them were stone dead.

Slowly over the next half-hour the scene came back to a semblance of life for those still alive. The SOCOs steeled themselves and got painstakingly down to work. Plod reinforcements arrived and began to unpack the tent-like sheets which, once erected, would screen off the garden and the front of the house from idle eyes. Robinson the pathologist speedily joined the forensic effort. Jacobson and Kerr retreated to the porch and then to the row of slabs that veered off at a right angle to the front path and gave access to the lawn and a seasonally empty flower bed. Jacobson organised his team on his mobile. Mick Hume and Renbourn could hold the fort on the Woodlands, he needed the rest of them here five minutes ago. Out in the street, beyond the hastily erected line of police tape, curious neighbours had started to gather. The MIU, the mobile incident unit, hove into view around the corner: computers, fax machines, secure initial storage for forensic evidence.

It was always like this at the start of something major,

Jacobson reminded himself, willing his mind into police mode, trying to ignore his emotions. Enforced idleness: until the SOCOs and the pathologist had done their preliminary recce there was essentially bog all for CID to do. Except to stand and wait. Drink a cuppa if there was one going. Smoke a fag.

He fingered his B and H packet. But whereas there were non-smokers all around him lighting up to combat their distress, Jacobson realised that for once he couldn't bear his habit. The girl was no more than ten, Robinson reckoned. He could hardly bear to breathe. He felt like a thief just to have a beating heart.

# Chapter Nineteen

There *was* something Jacobson's team could do while they waited for an initial assessment from the SOCOs and Robinson: check the immediately available records, verify who was supposed to live at the address – names, ages, occupations. Emma Smith and DC Williams did the bulk of the work from the second of the MIU's two linked portakabins. Phoning the council, surfing the Police National Computer. Kerr and DC Barber took Sheldon and Ogden to one side, quizzed them slowly through the sequence of events. Arriving at the house. Not getting an answer despite the two vehicles parked in the driveway. Suspicious about the three pints of milk left unattended behind the unlocked porch door, the pile of letters visible on the floor behind the main door – a white blur through the stained-glass panel. Sheldon had his uses, Kerr thought. The newer breed of street police would have thought twice, would at least have radioed a shift supervisor for advice. But Sheldon liked the thud of his own boot and any opportunity to apply his Shotokan techniques. He'd aimed two kicks at the lock, had bust the door open with the second.

Jacobson spoke to Pauline Harrison on his mobile. Yes, there were two girls missing from the school. The other girl, the one who didn't live on the Bartons, was Anne-Marie Holmes; the school still hadn't been able to contact her mother. It wasn't until the teacher read out the address that Jacobson made the unexpected connection to his Woodlands inquiry. Pauline Harrison wanted to know what was going on, whether her pupils had been found safe and well. Jacobson spoke as matter-of-factly as he could. They were still looking into it. Leave it with them. It was probably best if as few people as possible were involved at her end for the time being. He'd be in touch again soon. That was a promise. Jacobson ended the call, redialled: Mick Hume at William Blake House.

'Mick, old son. We need to get in touch with the young lass, Sheryl Holmes. If she's not on the premises, find out where's she gone. Forget everything else for the time being. This is urgent – I'll explain why later. Phone me back as soon as you know where she is.'

It was better for now, Jacobson thought, for as few as possible to know what was up. Even inside the force. Even inside the murder squad.

He wanted to see the back garden. The only way round, without going through the house itself, was along a narrow path which was jammed in between the side of the garage and the low wall that bounded the neighbouring property. There were eight sizeable houses in Willow Court, all detached. But each pair of neighbouring houses rubbed close together almost claustrophobically at the sides. It was simple arithmetic for the developers, Jacobson thought. Save ten feet here, a couple of square yards there, and, overall, you might squeeze sixty houses onto your land area instead of fifty-five. There was a kitchen extension and then a patio directly behind the house. A row of wispy perennials in shiny blue ceramic pots marked the way out to the greenhouse and the long, flat lawn. His first guess was the father: kill the wife and kids then top yourself. It wasn't a common crime. But it happened regularly enough for the criminologists to have stuck their oar in, to have computed probabilities, to have propounded evidential patterns.

Beyond the lawn was a long-established beech tree that must have survived from the meadowland the development had usurped. Jacobson walked down the neatly paved path at the side, knew better than to go anywhere near the soggy grass. If it wasn't the paterfamilias scenario, if evil had come knocking uninvited, then there could be the fragment of an imprint of a sole on there, something dropped unnoticed from a pocket. The detective's instinct was always to rush in, to get the case moving. But Jacobson had finally learned to let the SOCOs do their job properly first.

There was some kind of structure built around the tree. He'd noticed it from the top of the garden. Now, close up, he could see what it was. A tree house. Six feet in the air. It looked three-quarters built only. Plastic sheets – customised bags for gravel or cement maybe – crudely pinned to the spaces for which proper windows might eventually be planned. There was a ladder at the foot of the tree. How you got up and down while you were working on it, Jacobson supposed. It was the angle it had been lying at, he reasoned later, that had given him the impulse. Something exact about it, something purposeful. He only had to climb two or three rungs anyway to have his head level with the unfinished entrance, to see all the way inside.

'Are you Sarah or Anne-Marie?' he asked as gently as he could, peering at the girl huddled in the corner, clutching a torch and a book in her arms, her expression silently beyond hysterics.

# Part Two

Part Two

# Chapter Twenty

EVENING ARGUS\*\*\*

Estd. 1901    Thursday February 20    thirty pence    **LATE FINAL**

**Neighbours tell of grief and shock as police seal off house of horrors**

# Five found dead in 'Perfect Family' slaying  by our Staff Reporter

A major police investigation is under way in Crowby after a family of five were found dead earlier today at an address in the residential Bartons area. A police spokesperson confirmed this afternoon that the dead are believed to include Stephen and Marion Adams of 8 Willow Court and their children Matthew (12), Mark (14) and Sarah (10). A Home Office pathologist and the Coroner had been informed of the deaths and post-mortems were being scheduled at Crowby General Hospital. Asked about the cause of the deaths, Detective Chief Superintendent Greg Salter refused to speculate but said that he was '**ruling nothing out**' for the time being. Mr Salter also declined to comment on whether the tragedy was being treated as a **murder** case or not.

As the grim drama unfolded, uniformed police guarded the

property while CID detectives and forensic officers examined the scene. On Tuesday night, Mr and Mrs Adams and their family had been honoured by the **ARGUS** as the local 'Family of the year'. Today shocked neighbours told **ARGUS** reporters of their horror and anguish as they witnessed the intensive police operation – continued page two

flashback to night of celebration – turn to page three

police baffled in search for motive – turn to page four

Jacobson took a long, hot shower, dried himself and then shaved, squinting at the reflection of his face in the steamed-up bathroom mirror. In the kitchen, he fixed himself a cup of strong, proper coffee, even though instant would have been quicker, and flicked through the rumpled, beer-soaked copy of the *Argus* while he drank. He'd picked the paper up on his way out of the Brewer's Rest last night. New brooms like Greg Salter read the *Argus* religiously, obsessed with the force's public image. But Jacobson followed the newspaper coverage of his cases from a resolutely old-fashioned motivation: every now and again – although not on this occasion – the hacks would stumble over a fact the police had somehow missed.

All in all, his head didn't feel too bad, he thought, after a night that had ended up, for the second time this week, needing a taxi to get home. But at least his car had been left safely in the police car park this time. His entire team had wound up down the pub, had all stayed on until well after closing. Even the ones with wives and lovers, available shoulders to cry on. It was how the job went sometimes. Things you saw, experienced, that you couldn't expect an outsider to cope with. Emotions that only made sense if you'd felt them yourself. He hadn't planned it that way. Nobody had really. But it had probably been just what was wanted. They'd vented their feelings. Now they could get on with the tasks at hand.

He followed the coffee with toast. Two determined slices with modest layers of sunflower margarine and marmalade.

After a lifetime of consumption, he'd finally persuaded himself away from butter. He even drank a glass of orange juice before the second coffee and the essential, kick-start B and H. But one only: and stubbed out well before he reached the tip.

He left his breakfast dishes unwashed, his uninviting-looking post unopened, called a CrowbyCab taxi to drive him into town. Whether by coincidence or design, the driver from the other morning turned up again. A taciturn Asian about his own age who mercifully spared Jacobson his views on the state of the roads or on the world in general. Jacobson climbed into the back seat, checked his mobile for calls or messages: nothing. The hangover was just a dull thud really. He'd felt far worse on less. Far worse. The driver was listening to the World Service. The way some of that generation did. A habit acquired years ago on a different continent. At 8.30 though, with the clogged-up Flowers Street junction in sight, he switched over to Crowby FM, caught the local headlines. The story was nearly word-for-word with the *Argus* report. Shocked neighbours and school friends. The family-of-the-year angle. DCS Greg Salter quoted as keeping an open mind. Jacobson sunk his head back on the seat, resigned to the final traffic crawl to the Divisional building. Open-minded Greg Salter, he thought. It had the makings of a decent party game. Soft-hearted Adolf Hitler. Frivolous Søren Kierkegaard.

His daughter Sally had disappeared once when she'd been around that age. Ten or eleven. A hot summer's day during the school holidays. Her and her friend Becky. They'd gone off to the swimming baths and turned up hours later than they were supposed to. It turned out they'd gone off into town with a couple of older lads who should have known better. On an impulse. And mainly innocent. Burgers in a café, loitering in the games arcades. Three hours she'd been thought missing. A hundred and eighty ticking minutes. It was every dad's bad dream. It would have been hard, Jacobson thought, to imagine anything worse: until yesterday.

He checked his mobile a needless second time. Anything not to replay again the image of the little dead face. Anything to lessen the chance that the driver would break his silence, offer a comment on the case. Killing your daughter, your wife, your sons. Familicide. DIY slaughter. By contrast, whoever had beaten Dave Carter to death, and then burnt his body, seemed almost ordinary. Almost one of us.

The cab pulled up outside the NCP car park, the nearest vehicle point of access to the Divi unless you were in an official police vehicle. Jacobson paid his fare and hurried across the road. The wind caught his tie, sent it flapping. So that once up the steps and through the revolving doors at the main entrance, he had to stop for a moment, shove it back into place. He treated himself to a calming breath before he took the slow, uncertain lift to the fourth floor.

The incident room filled up quickly. Jacobson's usual murder squad minus Mick Hume but plus a mixed-dozen crate of extra officers – CID and uniformeds – who'd been made available for the day. Despite the gravity of what had occurred, a day, Jacobson thought grimly, might be all it would take to turn emergent theory into established fact. His team had been nine hours at the Bartons yesterday before they'd finally hit the Brewer's Rest. They'd talked to neighbour after neighbour. They'd visited the school, the church, the local shops, the pub. Jacobson himself had visited Adams Installations, had talked to the engineers, to Linda in the office. Everywhere they'd gone, they'd heard the same words and phrases. Normal. A decent bloke. Such a nice family. Over and over: like a litany. Today they'd be talking again – reaching some they'd missed the day before or revisiting those whose testimony had seemed the most useful. He walked across the room to the whiteboard while the last arrivals found themselves a seat or the edge of a

the frigging radio. Some daft old cow moaning about the buses or wanting to swap an ironing board for a hairdryer. Something normal and boring and ordinary. The way things had been before Monday. Before the fire. Before she'd been daft enough to think that a house in the Bartons would be a safe place for her little sweetheart to spend the night. Sheryl gazed at her daughter. She'd turned away on her side as if she might be sleeping. Yet when Sheryl leant across to see, Anne-Marie's eyes were staring ahead of her. Blue and wide open. But scarcely blinking.

Ten am. The majority of Jacobson's team en route to the Bartons. Jacobson and DS Kerr en route beforehand to Crowby General Hospital in Kerr's Peugeot. Jacobson three-quarter smoked his second B and H of the day, rolled the window down fractionally as a sop. Neither of them spoke. Peter Robinson was waiting for them in Professor Merchant's office. He looked tired and drawn. He told them he'd just this minute spoken to Chief SOCO Webster on the phone.

'Developments, old son?' Jacobson asked, sitting down.

Crowby's assistant pathologist shook his head.

'Nothing that alters the initial picture, Frank.'

Jacobson noticed that Merchant's Cona machine was coffee-less. Robinson, he decided, had probably been too busy to brew up. Kerr paced to the window, enjoyed the view of a ventilation duct and a grey concrete wall.

'A bloke wakes up in the middle of the night, sticks his pillow over his wife's head and suffocates her to death,' he said, a questioning tone in his voice. 'Then he goes next door, does the same to his daughter. He *wants* to do the same to his sons – only it doesn't go so smoothly. So he has to *batter* them to death.'

Robinson nodded this time.

'It's the only scenario that fits the facts, Ian. Stomach contents, rectal temperatures, comparative degrees of lividity.

All the indices point to the father being alive anything up to two hours *after* the other family members. Webster's adamant that there's no sign of a break-in or an intruder. He's also convinced about the MO in the case of the two boys.'

'Still the kid's baseball bat, you mean?' asked Kerr.

'Precisely. Think of it like an escalation. The wife and the daughter he kills fairly easily. Mrs Adams had put away a fair old bit to drink before going to bed – and she's taken by surprise. In the case of the daughter, there's the overwhelming difference in strength. What seems likely is that Adams killed both of them with his own pillow, took it with him when he went into the younger boy's room. Only the boy woke up, put up a fight. So Adams abandoned the pillow and used the nearest available weapon.'

'We've been through all this already, Ian,' Jacobson said, wanting to move things on. 'Or did you sleep through the briefing?'

Kerr looked back from the window. There were times when he wondered where it was that Jacobson stowed his feelings during working hours. And whether he ever let them out in his spare time.

'I've got two kids and a wife at home, Frank. I'm just trying to get my head round this, that's all.'

Jacobson let it go. A bad case provoked every kind of reaction, he thought. Even the spectacle of Kerr playing the family-man card.

There was silence.

'Anyway, the other probability is that the older boy heard his brother struggling in the next room and also woke up. That's why he was the only victim attacked out of bed.'

'And you're confident the science can confirm the sequence of events?' Jacobson asked.

Robinson rubbed his eyes, willing tiredness out of them.

'We're repeating some of the post-mortem tests today, Frank. Just to be doubly certain. And Webster's got half a dozen FSS experts booked in via the Birmingham HQ. There's hardly a methodology they *won't* be using at the crime scene. Besides, it's a matter of common sense as much as anything else. If Adams didn't kill his family then we'd have to believe that he invited someone else in to do it for him. Then waited around a couple of hours before permitting this unknown person to hang him from his banister.'

Despite the session down the pub, Kerr had woken up in the middle of the night. Bolt upright. Sweating beer. His head swimming in the memory of Stephen Adams' corpse, a Halfords tow rope wrapped clumsily round the neck.

'But his face, Peter,' he said. 'Gouge marks underneath both cheeks. Like he'd been trying to save himself, trying to work his fingers under the rope.'

'Put it down to pure instinct. The body automatically fights to stay alive regardless of the state of the mind. And you need to keep your hands free if you're planning to hang yourself, after all.'

Robinson paused, bit a nail inelegantly.

'Also the hanging looks to have been as amateur as the suffocations and the beatings. There was a whole art to it in the days of the hangman, don't forget. Careful weight calculations. An expert noose under the left ear. Measuring the drop. All designed to snap the neck quickly enough for an instantaneous death. Adams on the other hand could have taken anything up to half an hour to die. He'd have been conscious for some of that time at least – even with the booze and the tricyclic overdose.'

Kerr was looking out of the window again, spoke with his back to both of them.

'Two hours. Jesus. Just there on his own. And then the bastard hangs himself.'

Jacobson had other questions he wanted to ask. Where would DNA get them in a context like this, for instance. But he decided to wait for a moment. To let the memory of his nightmare recede a little. Twice in the night it had disturbed him. Once at three o'clock and then again at four. Jacobson grabbing Janice by the throat. Sally screaming futilely at him to stop. Even though, with the illogic of a dream, he'd already sliced his daughter's throat wide open.

# Chapter Twenty-One

The paediatrics department was also in the new wing of the general hospital. But on the ground floor and at the other end of the building. Sheryl and Anne-Marie were sat in a brightly painted room that had been got up to look like a nursery or an open-plan classroom. Sheryl had only agreed to it when Candice had promised faithfully to keep Lucy with her, not to let her out of her sight for a single minute. The police cow from the other night, DC Smith or whatever she called herself, had driven them over from the Woodlands, would drive them back afterwards – or anywhere else Sheryl wanted dropping off. Nice as pie to your face. Trying to bond with you or something. Win your frigging trust. Yet still with her piggy antennae twitching.

There was a shelf full of books behind them. Anne-Marie, though, hadn't even glanced in their direction. The woman sat on the other side of the low oval table. She'd come all the way from Birmingham. Some kind of specialist. According to the police cow, they didn't have the expertise locally. Sheryl thought she looked around thirty, thin like a drink of water.

'Mum says you're doing well at school, Anne-Marie,' the woman said. 'And so does your teacher. Mrs Harrison, isn't it?'

Anne-Marie, staring straight ahead, didn't say anything.

'Sometimes when we've seen something really bad happen, Anne-Marie, we feel that we can't tell anybody about it.

Maybe not telling is a way of pretending that it never happened. Like a nasty dream.'

Anne-Marie pulled the hood of her jacket tight over her head then folded her arms. The woman brought a box of cards out of her bag and placed it on the table. The ink-blot test. Sheryl knew it from when she was fourteen and pregnant. 'Sent for assessment,' they'd called it, wanting to judge if you were a fit mother or not.

'Just look at the shape and see if it reminds you of anything, Anne-Marie. Anything at all. Anything that comes into your head.'

It was hard to tell if Anne-Marie even saw the woman placing the cards in front of her. She'd put out one card, wait a moment or two, then cover it over with the next one. After five minutes she gave up, put the cards back in the box.

'Mrs Harrison says you and Sarah were such good friends. Really close. It's good to have friends, isn't it?'

There was a play area on the other side of the room, set out for younger children and toddlers. Anne-Marie slid off her chair and walked towards a big wicker basket filled with Lego pieces. Without the slightest sound coming from her mouth, she tipped the basket sideways and rummaged the pieces out.

She dragged the empty basket into a corner. Squatting down, she hunched herself in between the two walls. She held the basket in front of her until she could hardly be seen. Hiding behind it. Building herself a fortress.

# Chapter Twenty-Two

The sunken whirlpool bath was a novelty for Charlie. Definitely and distinctly. With his back resting comfortably against the side, he stretched his right arm out behind himself and picked up the Veuve Clicquot. Between his legs, Lisa's wet head bobbed enthusiastically up and down. He took a long, deep swig and finished the bottle.

'We're out of champers, Leez,' he said.

Pushing her head back with his hands. Forcing it out of the water. Off of him. Lisa eyed him sulkily for a second. Then she was climbing out of the bath, drying herself on the big white towel, finding a matching bathrobe.

'Chop, chop, girl,' he said, deciding to make a bit of an effort.

He watched her padding towards the door. Master and slave-girl. That was today's daft game. Tomorrow she'd probably want it the other way round. Or some new, unthought-of variation. Idly, he stretched himself out until he was submerged in pleasantly warm water right up to his chin. He'd call a halt after the next bottle, he thought. Maybe take a cold shower, get his brain in gear, take stock. It was a bit like an unexpected win on the horses all this. But they couldn't afford to get carried away. Not under the circumstances and all that.

There had been two bottles in the fridge when they'd let themselves in. Perfectly chilled. And another case down in the wine cellar. The Old Rectory, the place called itself.

Right on the edge of one of those pig-shit little villages you got out this way. Where they'd chucked out the peasants to make way for the big-money yuppies. It was the kind of gaff you saw on the telly. Up in the main bedroom, you opened what looked like an antique wardrobe door and instead you found a spiral steel staircase that led you down to the indoor swimming pool and mini-gym. The whole thing must've cost a fortune to put together, would be worth even more if you were selling it on. *It's like blinkin' Hello! magazine,* Lisa had said when they'd taken in the extent of the place come daylight yesterday morning. The night before in the dark, all that had mattered to them, wet, exhausted and cold, was that it had looked invitingly empty. No cars in the drive. No lights, no drawn curtains. And a week-old local paper sticking out of the mail box next to the front gate. As good as placing an advert in Blaggers' News.

Charlie had told Lisa and FB to wait, had gone in solo over a side wall. A place like this you didn't stint on home security. But even though he'd set off the intruder lighting a couple of times as he'd crept across the garden, Charlie hadn't panicked. Probably happened all the time, he'd told himself. What with foxes, badgers, all that. He'd scouted round with the torch, picked on one of the kitchen windows. Thank fuck there'd been nothing unusually clever with locks or hinges, something that would have necessitated any noisy smashing of glass.

Lisa had found a tray somewhere. Solid silver, she reckoned. Like you'd be able to tell, Leez, he thought. And a couple of glasses. She brought the champagne over, knelt on the tiles beside his head, popped the cork.

The window was wired, of course, and the frigging alarm had gone off. But Charlie knew he could have found the control panel blindfolded – in the hall cupboard near the front door, where they always were. Among the other useful bits and bobs of knowledge he'd acquired inside, Charlie had memorised six codes that had been traded around his wing of Winson Green: the manufacturers' overrides for the six most popular domestic systems. They wouldn't do the job every time, he'd been warned. But in this case – the only one that bothered him right now – the very first sequence he'd tried had worked perfectly. Twenty seconds max: if the system *was* externally monitored, which it definitely would have been if Charlie had owned a gaff like this one, Charlie still reckoned he'd cut the signal well within the safety margin.

Lisa handed him one of the glasses. The answerphone message on the hall telephone was what had really tickled Charlie, though. *You're through to Tim and Nichola. I'm afraid we're in Antigua until the twenty-seventh. Use Tim's mobile for anything really urgent. Otherwise leave a message and we'll get back to you later. Ciao.* He felt Lisa's breath warm on his ear. *Does Sir require anything further?* He sipped the champagne, tried to think of something lewd enough even for her.

# Chapter Twenty-Three

Alan Jones, a chartered accountant whose customers – like Stephen Adams – typically ran small or medium-sized local businesses, worked from home, had dispensed with the additional cost of an office somewhere in town that he didn't really need. Mostly he'd meet his clients on their premises, mostly he'd take their books back here to get them sorted. He supplied Jacobson and Kerr with this unasked-for information as he showed them into the lounge of his house in Chestnut Avenue, barely ten minutes' walk, Jacobson estimated, from the Adams residence. Jacobson had spoken to him briefly by telephone last night. But now he needed to get at the facts in more detail.

On the ground floor at 8 Willow Court, just along from the kitchen, there had been a small room which Stephen Adams had evidently used as a home office. A couple of filing cabinets. A fax machine and a computer. A neat pile of paperwork sitting in the absolute centre of the beech-wood desk. The nearest thing to a suicide note that they might be likely to find, he'd said to Kerr at the time. That had been yesterday afternoon. When the forensic team had reluctantly let Jacobson's officers explore the house. Strictly under sufferance: every one of them suited up in protective clothing. The pile of tax returns, accounts, bank statements, mortgage deeds and all the rest hadn't just been neat to the eye. It had been set out with an impeccable, narrative logic. Even a financial dunderhead like Jacobson had been able to follow the main story more or less straight off. The digested read: Adams Installations was headed for bankruptcy and was set to take the Adams family lifestyle with it. Stephen Adams' hadn't just committed nearly every single penny of their personal finances to his failed attempt to keep his business afloat; he'd even remortgaged the family home. And not just once. But a second time and then a third time.

Jacobson declined Jones' offer of tea without consulting Kerr on the matter, fidgeted with his watch strap while Jones ran through the standard, banal expressions of shock and incredulity about the killings. Stephen Adams wasn't just a client, he told them, he was more or less a friend. He was a bloke he'd known at school; they'd both been in the football team together. They'd lost touch later on, of course. Steve had left at sixteen. Jones had stayed on for A-levels then uni. It hadn't been till he'd moved out to the Bartons that he'd run into him again. He just couldn't believe it, couldn't take it in. They were just an ordinary, decent, everyday family.

Jacobson passed him a transcript of the papers that had been left out so conspicuously on Stephen Adams' desk. Kerr cast his eye around the room. It was comfortably furnished in a modern, nondescript style. The kind of room that gave nothing much away about its owner. Assuming, of course, there *was* anything to give away. There were some framed holiday photographs on a shelf, a themed collection of bronze ornaments on a coffee table. The photos: Jones off somewhere sunny, an ordinary-looking woman – near enough plain – along with him. His wife presumably. She was an assistant manager at the NatWest in the High Street, Jones had already told them. Unlike himself, he'd said, she still had to *go in* to work – more unsolicited information. The ornaments: cannons, tanks, a battleship. As far as Kerr could tell, they were the kind of thing for which the major selling points were the authenticity of the design, the accuracy of the scale.

Jones put on a pair of rimless reading glasses to look through the paperwork, took them off again when he'd finished.

'It's worse than I thought, Inspector,' he said. 'Far worse. These extra loans on the house – he must have lied his head off to get them. Collectively, they're hugely in excess of the equity on the property.'

'So I'm correct to think that he was looking at repossession of his house as well as the collapse of his business?' Jacobson asked.

'No question about that. Maybe even an investigation for fraud if one of the lenders decided to get stroppy.'

Kerr could have done with the cup of tea. Or at least a glass of water. He'd been regretting the previous night's piss-up ever since he'd crawled out of bed only just on time not to be late for work.

'You're the Adams Installations accountant, Mr Jones. But you didn't know about this extra borrowing?' he asked.

Jones put his specs down on the broad arm of a modish pink sofa.

'No offence, Sergeant, but I'm an accountant, not a policeman. I can only go on the facts and figures the client gives me. My first guess would be that he must've filtered the extra money through his books as bogus orders. Orders – or even customers – that never actually existed. What a mess,' – he tapped the pile of photocopies with an emphatic finger – 'I expect I could follow the paper trail if I cross-referenced this little lot against the certified accounts.'

Jacobson interrupted, tried to keep the irritation out of his voice. He needed detail. But he wasn't sure he needed this level of it. Whether Adams' financial practices had been less than kosher and whether Jones had a hand in any malpractice was all just a matter of *process*. What Jacobson needed to know, needed to be certain of, was *outcome*. The end result. The bottom line.

'But even filtering in the extra dosh wasn't enough to save the business from bankruptcy, then?' he asked.

Jones looked healthy enough for a man in his mid-thirties. Ten minutes into the conversation, there was still a thin band of sweat on his forehead. He'd answered the door in his tracksuit, had been working out on his weights, he'd told them: another unasked-for explanation.

'Steve's set-up was going straight down the pan, Inspector. I told him just precisely that on Tuesday afternoon. Not that it was news. The writing's been on the wall for months.'

'And Mr Adams *knew* for months?' Kerr asked.

'Oh yes, Steve knew all right. But I don't think he was really facing up to it. Took his family off to Cuba for Christmas, refused to cut his director's salary or lay off any staff,' – Jones tapped the photocopies again – 'I just didn't realise the endgame was so close.'

Jacobson left the irritation in this time:

'Could you be more precise, Mr Jones?'

'The main thing is the personal bank statements. His and Marion's – Mrs Adams. Unless there's another source of cash hidden somewhere that I don't know about, it looks to me like they had no more than a couple of thousand quid left – most of it in Marion's current account—'

Jones wiped a teardrop of sweat from his eyelid.

'That wouldn't have kept them going very much longer. Not with a mountain of personal debts as well as business ones. Credit cards, mortgage arrears, council tax, car loan repayments – you name it.'

'How long would you say before it all went pear shaped?' Kerr asked.

'When I spoke to him on Tuesday, Sergeant, I told him six months. But if he'd shown me all this? More like a matter of weeks.'

Walking down Alan Jones' sharply angled garden path in the direction of the front gate, Jacobson took a call from

Mick Hume. Ryan Walsh had eluded Hume and Renbourn yesterday but now Hume said they had a possible angle on his current location. Jacobson told him to check it out. The call reminded him that he still hadn't got the results of the fingerprint analysis from the burnt-out flat. He made a mental note to check with Webster when he got a moment. Optimistically, the NAFIS computer was back up and someone on Webster's team had made a useful match. Pessimistically, which was to say *actually*, the big forensic effort at the Adams house would have temporarily sidelined everything else the SOCOs were working on.

Kerr misinterpreted a couple of culs-de-sac for the main drag before they reached their next destination: the Bartons health centre at the far end of Barton Avenue, less than half a mile from Sarah Adams' primary school. Dr Rochester, the Adams family GP, turned out to be female. A seemingly brusque woman in an elegant white suit who might have Botoxed the furrows out of her unlined face. Still attractive. But almost certainly older than she looked. There was a cuddly toy corner for her youngest patients, supermarket daffodils on a shelf, Radio 3 playing quietly in the background. Even so Jacobson sat himself down uneasily. Despite the flowers, the room smelt indefinably medical. People walked in here of their own accord, complaining of some minor ailment, and never got well again. Rooms like this were staging posts, intermediaries, between the solid, complicated world of the living and whatever rubbish came next. Most probably bog all; just the final flickering moment between existence and non-existence. He slung his right ankle across his left knee, did his comforting trick of placing his right hand on his right knee, the other hand around the crossed-over ankle. He wasn't here for that kind of trouble, he reminded himself; he was here strictly on other business.

Dr Rochester had a spread of case notes in front of her.

Her computer screen was swivelled so that neither Jacobson or Kerr could read it properly.

'I'm afraid Mr and Mrs Adams have only been on my list for the last year and a half,' she said.

'The kids too?' Kerr asked.

She nodded.

'Yes. The whole family. Although actually it's mainly the kids I've seen. Colds. Chickenpox. The oldest lad worrying about his acne. Nothing out of the ordinary. Before that they were all Dr Lamont's patients. He retired the summer before last – which was when I joined the practice.'

'It's really Mr Adams that we're interested in immediately,' Jacobson said.

Dr Rochester looked down at her records. Her fingernails, brushing her forehead, were carefully painted; some kind of pearly silver colour. Her hair was a defiantly non-natural blonde. She was the new breed of older woman, Jacobson thought. Fifty going on thirty. His ex-wife, Janice, was another. He mentally rehearsed the three relevant sections of the General Medical Council's guidelines in case there was about to be a problem. He knew them practically off by heart, even knew the paragraph numbers: 37(C), 41(A) and 44. What they amounted to was that the public interest overrode patient confidentiality, provided disclosure was to a proper authority and relevant to the detection of a serious crime. Five dead bodies in a leafy suburb where bad things weren't supposed to happen probably fitted the bill, he thought. But it was always the doctor's prerogative to tell you to get stuffed: to insist on a court order or to make you wait until the coroner's hearing.

'It said on the radio that the police mightn't be look-ing outside the family,' she said finally, lifting her head again.

Jacobson hesitated. Confidentiality could cut both ways. Then:

'We're considering the scenario that Mr Adams killed his family and then hung himself. But that's not for public consumption. Not yet anyway.'

'And you're wondering whether there's anything relevant in his medical history?' she asked.

'Apparently he'd recently consumed a significant quantity of a prescription tranquilliser. We're still waiting for the full post-mortem report,' Jacobson answered.

'The empty packaging was found in the bathroom. Amitryptyline,' Kerr offered.

Dr Rochester smiled distantly. Jacobson guessed she was going to cooperate. At least to a minimal extent.

'Amitryptyline 50 mg, I expect, Sergeant,' she said. 'I put him on a three-month programme – it can take that long to be fully effective. He collected a repeat prescription earlier this week, as a matter of fact. Monday, I think. Plus he was due for review next week: Thursday at six o'clock. The appointment's still in my schedule.'

'So he was suffering from, eh, clinical depression?' Jacobson asked.

'Clinical depression? Not in my opinion. If I'd thought that was a possible diagnosis I'd have referred him on to a specialist. No, stress, Inspector. The universal catch-all term for the problems of modern life.'

'His business worries, I take it?'

'Precisely. He came to me complaining about feelings of anxiety, inability to sleep, loss of appetite. The usual symptoms. I *did* suggest counselling. But Mr Adams wasn't keen on the idea, claimed he didn't have the time,' – she looked at her notes again – 'said he just needed something to help him to cope, till he got it sorted. *Getting it sorted* – those were his exact words if I remember correctly.'

Jacobson formed his question as politely as he could. Thinking: the coroner isn't going to let you off so lightly.

'So why a tricyclic, if you don't mind me asking?'

You picked up all kinds of esoteric knowledge in detective work, especially when you hung around the mortuary. Jacobson was well aware of the decline in popularity of the older-style tricyclic anti-depressants – like amitryptyline – and the rise of the newer SSRIs, of which the best known was fluoxetine, aka Prozac. One of the reasons ammies had gone out of medical fashion was that in the right quantity and washed down with booze they offered a simple, attested and reliable method of topping yourself.

If Dr Rochester caught the sub-text, her face didn't show it.

'I started him off on Prozac but he came back to me about side effects. Night sweats, loss of libido. It's not a wonder drug in every case, I'm afraid. Also he'd had another depressive period four – no five – years ago. Dr Lamont had prescribed amitryptyline then and Mr Adams indicated to me that he'd got along all right with it.'

'So he had a history of depression?' Kerr asked.

Dr Rochester allowed herself another patronising, professional smile.

'I'd hardly call two episodes a *history*. Life is rough on all of us these days.'

'So in your opinion, Mr Adams was "normal"?' Kerr persisted.

'There's nothing remotely out of the ordinary in the symptoms he presented or in the causative life events.'

Jacobson changed legs – left ankle to right knee – but for some reason it never felt as comfortable.

'If our scenario fits the facts, there'll be a full coroner's inquest. The question's going to be *why* a normal guy, even if mildly depressed, would—'

'Most of the world's horrors are committed by ordinary *guys*, Mr Jacobson. And I'm afraid medical science is still a few discoveries short of clairvoyance at the present moment.'

Jacobson pretended not to understand the feminist jibe.

'So you'd say Mr Adams was mentally stable within any normal measurements. And he gave you no reason to suppose he was a danger to himself or anyone else?'

Dr Rochester bundled her case notes together.

'That's exactly my view,' she said. 'He was worried about losing his business, about the effect on his family. I can't see how it gets much more "normal" than that, can you?'

Jacobson thanked her for her time, added that he thought she could probably expect a visit from the coroner's officer in due course. He followed Kerr out of the surgery, down a flight of stairs and through the crowded waiting room. There were twenty or so customers waiting for the three doctors on consulting duty. Twenty or so opportunities for Jacobson to catch some damned bug or other. He practically shoved Kerr through the main doors. Outside, a streak of weak wintry sun broke through the clouds over the car park. But only for a moment.

Jacobson's next appointment was back in town. Kerr started up the engine.

'Hard-nosed cow, wouldn't you say, Frank?' he asked. 'Hardly a trace of emotion.'

Jacobson took out a B and H that he planned on smoking all the way down to the tip this time.

'Be fair, Ian, they're trained the same as us to keep their feelings out of it. Plus which she's probably mainly preoccupied with covering her not unappealing arse. Nobody wants to be the doctor who failed to spot the dangerous loony when they had the chance.'

He lit up the cigarette.

'When you get a minute, though, give the receptionist a ring. See if you can find out where old Doc Lamont's got to in his retirement. If he's not off sunning himself somewhere exotic, he just might be worth a quick visit.'

# Chapter Twenty-Four

The Coroner's Office was housed in an annexe behind the town hall, a temporary arrangement in theory that had so far persisted in fact for a dozen years. The inquest into the deaths at Willow Court was quickly convened and just as swiftly adjourned – pending the outcome of the police investigation. Greg Salter, resplendent in one his best suits, read a prepared statement to the assembled press and other media afterwards. The national dailies were taking an interest now. The BBC, Sky, ITN likewise. Open minds were still a feature but now Salter emphasised that the focus of the inquiry was mainly *within* the deceased family, came close to admitting that no living suspects were being sought. Jacobson didn't linger. He walked back to the Divisional building via the hushed corridors of the town hall, the soles of his shoes echoing on the marble floors. Jacobson liked it there. The impression of old-fashioned solidity. The sense of something built to last, built to survive the builders. If only the same could have been said about its neighbours. The Divi. The library cum multi-storey. The shopping centre, the back arse of which mooned yobbishly across from the other side of the pedestrianised town square. The thing he liked best of all, maybe, was coming out of the main entrance and seeing the staunch row of oak trees lined up in front. A stately outcrop of nature that even the 1960s planners had left unmolested.

He took the Divisional building lift to the fourth floor, where the Adams incident room was now fully operational.

Sergeant Ince was busy with the database. He'd wangled himself out of his regular control room duties, the way he always seemed to do whenever something major was afoot.

'I've just heard from Peter Robinson, guv. Expects to fax us the preliminary pm report within the hour,' he said, looking up from a computer workstation.

Jacobson told him to run off multiple copies just as soon it turned up. He found himself the corner of an empty desk near the window and phoned round his A team. Emma Smith and DC Williams had just left the Bartons primary school, were headed towards the Simon de Montfort, the comp where Mark and Matthew Adams had been pupils. In both cases, their delicate task was establishing whether anybody at either school – child or adult – had heard whispers of strangeness in Willow Court. So far, so normal, Emma Smith told him. Kerr had tracked down Dr Lamont. It turned out that the retired GP was still local after all; Kerr was already on his way to the address. Jacobson phoned DC Barber last. He'd given him the role of coordinating the big door-to-door effort. Barber had a promotions board in the offing and it would be something else for him to stick on his CV. Duly filed under task management, organisational ability, people skills – or whatever other weaselly categories the selection process currently favoured. There were now twenty officers involved all told. CID and plod. The aim was to knock on every door on the Bartons estate and to keep on knocking until four potential questions were definitively answered. Did you know any of the Adams family? If so, when did you last see him, her or them? If so, was there anything unusual in his, her or their general demeanour? What were your own precise whereabouts on Wednesday night?

'Nothing out of the ordinary so far, guv. Anybody that knew them liked them, reckoned they were all happy as Larry,' Barber reported, 'and everybody we speak to says

164

they were personally tucked up in bed with their teddy bear well before midnight the night before last.'

'Exactly as predicted, old son. But stay with it anyway,' Jacobson said, ending the call.

Through the window, he watched the clock hands on the town hall's art deco white tower poised towards twelve noon. Behind him, one of Ince's phone lines rang: the child psychologist from Birmingham. Jacobson picked the receiver back up and Ince did whatever it was you did to transfer a caller. She had an hour before she caught her train, she told him, offered to speak to him informally about Anne-Marie Holmes. Jacobson agreed to the arrangement even though he guessed from her tone of voice that she'd made exactly as much progress as his own officers had done. Aka sod all.

But at least Claire Burke, PhD, fellow of the British Psychological Society, turned out to be an aficionado of a decent curry. Her only question about Jacobson's invitation to Mr Behar's was whether the grub would be up to Brummie standards. Jacobson just said diplomatically that it was, kept to himself his devout belief that Behar could beat anything in the city hands down. He met her at the Divi's reception and they walked the five-minute walk to his favourite curry house.

Jacobson underwent a moment of epiphany halfway along the High Street. He'd needed a skinful of booze to get him through last night's bad dreams. He'd barely been able to face a parsimonious breakfast this morning. He hadn't really enjoyed any of the three cigarettes he'd had so far today. Now he noticed, as if suddenly for the first time, that the sky, although grey, wasn't raining anything at him. The air might have been cold but it was also wonderfully sharp; deep and satisfying even in his smoker's lungs. Above all he was absolutely, totally and completely famished. Simultaneously with experiencing it, Jacobson knew his state of being for exactly what it was: the elation that came with the awful, selfish realisation that whatever might have happened to someone else, to five someone elses in this case – six, if you factored in Dave Carter – *you* were still alive: still moving around, thinking, blinking, feeling. It was why, someone had told him once, you had a better chance of a shag at a funeral than in the average nightclub.

Dr Burke ordered mixed pakora as a starter. Her main course was a lamb rogan josh with mushroom rice, a garlic nan *and* a serving of ladies fingers on the side. For all this – plus the (large) bottle of Cobra – she looked as thin as a rake. And dressed as if Charles the Second had never defeated the Puritans. Short black boots, black trousers, black jersey. Black hair in a severe, black bob. No make-up. A black trench coat slung over the spare chair. If she'd ever taken fashion tips from the same sources as Dr Rochester, it had only been to put them bloodily to the sword. Nevertheless, Jacobson thought, she was still a looker. Undeniably. Indisputably. He matched her course for course. Onion bhajees, chicken pathia, special pilau rice, his favourite nan – peshwari – and a side dish of sag aloo. Finally he ordered a pint of draught Kingfisher and a preliminary round of poppadams with the pickle tray for both of them.

'Still the silent witness, then?' he asked, after Behar's younger son had retreated from the table with their order.

'I'm afraid so. I'm hoping to arrange some further sessions if the mother will agree to it.'

Jacobson lit up a tentative cigarette, was more than impressed that the psychologist, far from objecting, cadged a light off him for one of her own Superkings.

'Thanks,' she said. 'I'm always losing lighters and boxes of matches.'

On the way over from the Divi, she'd mentioned the possibility in the case of something called traumatic mutism. Jacobson put his lighter back in his pocket, asked her to elaborate.

'It's an easy enough condition to diagnose,' she said. 'But a lot harder to treat.'

Behar Jr cleared a space in the centre of the table, brought over the beers, poppadums and pickles. Dr Burke dropped the topic until he'd gone again.

'A seven-year-old girl is the classic case in the textbooks. She was standing at her school bus stop with her mother when a car came by at speed and ran another child over. An instant killing. The girl watched the victim tossed into the air right before her eyes.'

'And couldn't speak about it afterwards?' Jacobson asked.

'Couldn't speak full stop, Inspector. Quite literally struck dumb with terror.'

Jacobson drained an inch off his beer. Uncharacteristically, he told her that his first name was Frank, that he'd be pleased if she used it. Then:

'And you think something similar's happened to Anne-Marie Holmes?'

Dr Burke nodded.

'There's a more common condition known as elective mutism associated with children who have low self-esteem or the more usual kind of speech problems. Stammering, for instance. They can find communicating – making themselves heard – so difficult that eventually they just clam up altogether.'

She took a deep draw, exhaled, topped up her glass from the bottle.

'But I can't see any of that here. An academically able child and a loving mother. Sheryl Holmes might be on the breadline but she's got good parent stamped all over her forehead.'

'This, eh, mutism, is it likely to be long-term?' Jacobson asked.

'Elective mutism can recur for years. With good intervention, you'd expect traumatic mutism to resolve less slowly. But it's impossible to generalise. She could start talking again tomorrow or next week – or next month – or six months.'

Jacobson watched her slug the beer down and follow it with a poppadum and half the contents of the lime pickle dish. She continued her explanation between mouthfuls.

'Another possibility is that she recovers her speech in general but never refers to the incident of trauma.'

'You mean just blank it out of her memory?'

'Not exactly, Frank. Think of it what you might call *transactionally*. Not speaking about what's she's seen – being left alone with it – might be her *condition* for rejoining a conversation with the rest of the world.'

Jacobson drank another inch of Kingfisher. It was virtually certain that the girl had witnessed something at 8 Willow Court. Yet what Dr Burke was telling him was that she might keep whatever it was locked inside her memory for ever.

'But you'll keep on working with her?'

'As long as her mum agrees. I need to think about the best way forward, obviously. Psychodynamic, behavioural, drugs. Or multimodal. Which basically means everything – all three approaches, the kitchen sink included.'

Jacobson allowed himself a wary grimace. Multimodal: you could probably *sell* a needless obfuscation of that calibre to Greg Salter. Probably for good money.

'Drugs?' he asked

Dr Burke tipped her ash. Her long fingers ended in long but unadorned fingernails.

'Some of the serotonin inhibitors have had beneficial results according to the literature,' she said. 'But I tend to see them as a weapon of last resort personally.'

Jacobson said he was glad to hear it: a lot of good Prozac had done Stephen Adams, for instance.

They stopped talking again while Mr Behar himself served the starters. Anne-Marie might have seen the killer, Jacobson thought, might have been lucky to get away with her own

168

life. Or she might have been a clever little girl from a council flat who couldn't resist the idea of a fairy-tale night in a tree house; who'd crept back indoors some time in the early hours to find her school friend dead and Stephen Adams dangling from the end of a rope. Either way the experience would certainly have been frightening enough to cause the syndrome Dr Burke had diagnosed.

'Dr Bateman,' Jacobson said when they were alone again. 'I don't suppose you know him?'

Bateman was the forensic psychologist Jacobson had spoken to by telephone yesterday; the expert who'd propounded the 'family annihilator' theory.

'Not personally. But I do know his reputation – and I think I attended one of his seminars when I was a postgrad.'

'You'd rate him, then?'

'Oh yes. Definitely. He's a serious researcher. Not one of your showbiz *Cracker* types.'

Jacobson laughed. He'd encountered just that kind of bullshitter more than once – the sort who saw advising the police as a short cut to the chat-show circuit.

'He reckoned familicide is more common than we tend to think.'

Dr Burke forked half a chicken pakora into her mouth and ate it before she answered.

'It's not really my area, Frank. But he's right, of course. I checked the stats last night. There's at least half a dozen cases each year nationally. They don't all make the headlines.'

'Like murders in general,' Jacobson replied. 'The media usually like an angle otherwise they're not interested. Unfortunately Family of the Year Brackets Deceased Close Brackets is an angle and a half.'

Dr Claire Burke smiled knowingly at the comment and Jacobson found himself smiling back. He drank another inch of beer, warned himself not to be silly. She couldn't be much older than his daughter Sally, mightn't even be *as* old. Just because she liked a beer and a smoke and ate her food with relish. Just because she spent her evenings working.

Dr Ronald Lamont, retired, lived in a converted coach house on the outskirts of Wynarth. He had the kind of kitchen that seemed to be compulsory out this way. Whitewashed walls. An Aga. Sturdy wooden furniture that Kerr failed to recognise as an original Shaker design. He didn't recognise *Winterreise* either. But it was hard to ignore, blaring out at the kind of *über* volume you usually associated with gangsta rap and half a dozen waste-of-space youths disturbing the peace in a souped-up death trap. Whatever it was, it was a gloomy choice for a February lunchtime, Kerr thought. Music to cut your throat by. Or top the wife and kids.

Lamont offered Kerr a seat at a big oak table. The surface was a sprawl of books, magazines, newspapers. From somewhere under the pile, Lamont found his hi-fi remote and turned down the decibels to something that was merely loud. He was a thin, frail man with a bald head the precise colour of tinned salmon. He was also, Kerr realised, rat-arsed. Thanks presumably to the bottle of Bell's which sat on the centre of the table next to a copy of yesterday's *Argus*. The newspaper was spread open at page three, where the *Argus* had rerun some of its photographs from Tuesday night. Vice-Chancellor Croucher shaking Stephen Adams by the hand. Stephen Adams kissing Marion Adams. Mark, Matthew and Sarah Adams waving their Family of the Year scrolls.

'Dram, no?' Lamont said, answering his own question.

He took a swig from a blue china mug.

'Fischer-Dieskau sings fucked-up Franz, Sergeant. The journey into the abyss. Marvellous—'

He fumbled with the remote again.

'But not why you're here.'

This time he turned the volume to very nearly off.

'You remember the family, then?' Kerr asked.

'Thirty years in general practice. You learn techniques, mental cue cards. Plus a quick look in the docket before the next malingerer shuffles in. Tea, then?'

Kerr nodded yes to the idea. Especially if Lamont was going to have one himself.

'So you remember the family?' he repeated.

Lamont quarter-filled a kettle, banged it clumsily onto the front plate of the Aga.

'Mr Stephen Adams. One of the low on whom assurance sits like a silk hat on a Bradford millionaire.'

Kerr looked at him blankly.

'Thomas Stearns Eliot, Sergeant. *The Waste Land*,' Lamont said.

He turned back to the table, took another swig of whisky. Then another.

'Oh, fuck, my apologies. The fact of the matter is I buried my wife a month ago. I'm still not quite bearing up to it. To say the damned least.'

He slumped into the nearest chair. The kettle began to whistle.

'I'm sorry to hear that. I could brew up – if you like,' Kerr said.

'Decent of you,' Lamont said quietly.

Kerr made the tea, found a couple of clean cups, milk, sugar. Ronald Lamont moved his mug of whisky resolutely to one side.

'I could have done without this into the bargain,' he said, indicating the *Argus*.

Kerr stirred his tea. Sometimes you didn't ask anything really, just waited for someone to talk.

'According to the radio, the police – you – aren't looking outside the family.'

'The theory is Mr Adams might've killed his wife and children and then himself,' Kerr replied.

171

Lamont clasped his teacup in both hands but didn't lift it from the table.

'Three years before I retired – so call it five years ago – he came to see me about what he called his nerves.'

'Dr Rochester told us you prescribed a course of anti-depressants.'

'That's right. He had business worries, said he couldn't sleep. The usual detached, suburban story. Mild, reactive depression – or so I thought at first.'

'At first?' Kerr asked.

'I think I put him on a three-month course, something like that. I'd have to see the notes again to be certain.'

Lamont looked wistfully at his whisky mug but left it untouched. Kerr said nothing.

'Anyway, the last time he came to see me he seemed worse than ever. To be honest, he'd never seemed *very* depressed before – he'd always had a rather unpleasant fucking cockiness, to my way of thinking. As if it was my job to dole out the magic pills and let him get on with it.'

'But not this time?'

'No. Not this time.'

Lamont stared at the pages of the *Argus*.

'He told me he'd been seeing a light in the middle of the night. A light he didn't think was real. Sometimes, he told me, he didn't think he was real himself.'

Kerr frowned.

'Delusional, don't you see, Sergeant? An early warning signal. Something way beyond a mild depression. Something that should have been acted on.'

'So what did you—'

'I made a referral to the psychiatric clinic. Two referrals actually. But he never showed at the hospital. Never came back to see me either.'

Lamont gulped down some tea.

'And you didn't pursue it?' Kerr asked

'With hindsight I'd've had the bugger sectioned. But at the time, I didn't give it a second damned thought. Never thought of him again in fact until this popped onto the mat,' – Dr Lamont pointed his palm towards the *Argus* – 'do *you* right every wrong that comes your way, Sergeant Kerr?'

Kerr told him that he didn't, nothing like.

'You married?' Lamont asked.

Kerr nodded, finishing his tea.

'Take my tip. Drink like a fucking fish and smoke like a factory chimney. Make bloody sure you're the first one to go.'

He shut the door after the policeman left, watched him buggering off down the path. Glad to get away, he expected. Especially when I'm acting like a total prat. He poured the rest of his tea into the china mug, mixing it with the whisky and then pouring in more from the bottle. The word alcohol had an Arabic root that meant something like clarity of vision. But you had to drink so damned much to reach it. He turned the CD back up in the middle of a piano interlude, the chords crisp as a frozen cavern. Marilyn, his wife, had been the culture vulture really. Poetry. The theatre. Opera. All that damned shit. It was a habit he'd acquired from her against his better judgement. What had got humanity down from the trees had been *science*, he'd always told her. Dealing with the practicalities of life: engineering, chemistry, medicine. Yet now it was a way of keeping her with him. The books she'd liked. The music. He turned the volume up as loud as it would go.

> *Every stream finds the sea*
> *and every sorrow its grave.*

And the practicalities could go straight to hell.

Kerr phoned Rachel then drove on into Wynarth. She was helping out – Rachel's phrase – in the Looking East Gallery, told him she was just about to take her lunch break anyway. Working there was the kind of thing she usually did when she hadn't sold a painting for months or when there were no current takers for her interior design and *feng shui* 'consultancy'. She'd been helping out in the Dragon's Lair when Kerr had first met her. A tiny shop, behind the wine bar, specialising in imported Chinese kites, job-lot carved Buddhas, over-priced, over-scented incense. He parked a couple of streets away, set off on foot. Not only from adulterous paranoia but because Rachel's flat was in Thomas Holt Street, just off the market square. With the Friday market still well under way, there were cars and vans double-parked right along it.

She was already undressed, not wasting time; sitting naked on the edge of her bed when he let himself in with the spare key she'd given him. London had been an infrequent luxury. Two entire evenings together: time to talk, dine out, share a quiet drink in a pub. As important, maybe more important, than the nights that had followed. He took off his own clothes, boots and socks first. Four years or five? He wasn't sure any more without thinking about it, counting it out. But this was how most of their time had been spent. An hour snatched here, half an afternoon grabbed there. A week once when Cathy's mother had been ill in Lancashire and Cathy had gone up to stay, taking the twins with her. If we could share even an entire month, Rachel liked to say, I'd have time to get sick of you, end it, send you away on your fascist police bicycle.

He dumped his clothes on the wicker chair she'd placed near the window where – Rachel's notion – it caught the sunlight, Van Gogh style. He left his mobile on top of the pile, never took the risk of switching it off. He sat down next to her. He knew she'd tried other men. Single men. Unattached, compatible. One – an architect – she'd lived with for a year. She'd gone off on some kind of world tour with him. India, Thailand, Australia. But none of it had stopped them, none of

174

it had stopped this. He pressed her body down onto the sheets. Quickly, not gently. Maybe searching her eyes for the shadow of her thoughts, maybe pretending to search. You cared and you didn't care. You only wanted to fuck her. You didn't only want to fuck her.

# Chapter Twenty-Five

Jacobson pulled his desk lamp in close against the gloom of the afternoon. Barely a quarter to three and already the daylight had a fading, temporary quality. His lunch appointment had overrun. Dr Claire Burke had caught her scheduled train, the one o'clock. But only because it was twenty-five minutes late and only because Jacobson had called a minicab for her. She was just one of those rare people who were easy to talk to. Or – to be more precise – that Jacobson found easy to talk to. Her topics of conversation, even when they'd stepped outside of their professional remit, had been interesting, stimulating, intelligent. Not the stupid, idle, gossiping small talk that he loathed, that caused his attention to wander, that could make him – if he was in a pig enough of a mood – such a definite non-hit at the few civilian or force parties he ever bothered to attend. The living human brain was the most complex structure in the universe, beyond stars and suns. Yet mainly it was used to process garbage about car prices or loft extensions or the property market. Like playing nursery rhymes on a Stradivarius. No, worse than that, Jacobson thought. Like chopping one up for firewood.

He'd grabbed a copy of Robertson's preliminary post-mortem report from the incident room on his return. He'd skim-read it and then traced his way back through again from page one, making his own notes and studying certain sections in detail. All they really amounted to, of course, was the usual grim reckoning of death into its constituent biological and chemical components. Only quintuply so in this case: five dead bodies, the youngest ten, the oldest – Stephen Adams himself – barely thirty-seven. In each case Robinson's report followed the normal, approved structure. *External Examination. Internal Examination. Other Remarks. Histology. Cause of Death.* Jacobson had become an initiate to the major arcana of the pathologist's art over the years, no longer had to turn to the dictionary for a translation of *meninges, ecchymoses, extravasation, petechiae* – and all the rest. Even so, he'd spent very nearly an hour absorbing the report. And still he felt that he hadn't given it enough time.

He made himself a cup of instant coffee, reread the near-to-plain English notes he'd made for himself. Marion Adams and her daughter had been suffocated. Both her sons had sustained fatal skull fracturing. Marion Adams hadn't had sex on the day or night she'd died. She had a possibly benign but apparently undiagnosed mammarian tumour. In the six hours before her death, she'd ingested a volume of alcohol equivalent to consuming the contents of two ordinary-sized bottles of wine. There was no evidence that her daughter had been sexually molested either then or previously. Mark Adams had been a regular user of cannabinoids. There had been a trace presence of semen on his body. Under *Other Remarks* Robinson had noted – and Jacobson had transcribed – *it is anticipated that this will test as subject's own.*

He turned the page of his notebook. He'd made his notes about Stephen Adams last, had felt impelled for some reason to give them their own page; as if he had to keep them separate, even segregated.

<u>Stephen Adams:</u>

Killed by self-hanging. Robinson: "DEEP IMPRESSIONS AROUND NECK". "Vital changes locally and in the tissues underneath as a consequence of prolonged constriction". <u>PROLONGED</u> – there's the rub. Rob. suggests death by slow strangulation lasting approx up to 30 minutes. High level of booze (8 times d/driv limit) and amitryptyline (4,010mg). Rob. says this amount near to total 28 day prescription supply. Rob. says O/D deaths have been reported at levels as low as 750mg. Tho fatal doses are usually from 5,750 mg and upwards (Rob. notes 7,000mg invariably fatal). Speculates (rare for Rob.) that <u>SA</u> could have been in <u>HYPNAGOGIC</u> state for some time before own death. Confirms <u>SA</u> time of death as min. Of 2hrs <u>AFTER</u> other killings (estimates other deaths in "time window" from 1am to 2am). Rob. appends note re Hypnagogic (sometimes hypnogogic, alt sp.) viz a dream-like state often experienced on verge of sleep or on partial reawakening. Vivid hallucinations are symptomatic. Physiological basis not fully understood.

Jacobson sipped his coffee, which had just about become cool enough to drink. Robinson had done his standard, impeccable job. Once the laboratory analyses came in – and if they came in as anticipated – the investigation would be very nearly done and dusted. The coroner's office would get a nice, fat report which would include the recommendation that no further police action was necessary. The pillowcase, the baseball bat and Stephen Adams' clothes were the crucial items. Adams had been found hanging wearing only a dressing gown and a pair of Calvin Klein underpants. The dressing gown had been blood splattered. For the 'family annihilator' theory to hold, the blood couldn't just be his own: it had to be Matthew Adams' and Mark Adams' too. Both boys were group B, which was a helpful start; the same as their mother but different from their father. But the crux would be the results from DNA testing. Not just the samples lifted from Adams' clothes but from the pillowcase and – especially – from the bat. Jacobson swigged his coffee, tried not to replay the memory in too much detail. Even to the naked eye, the bat had *stuff* sticking to it: hair, skin, something that looked like bone. Comparisons for difference within a family group were intricate but eminently achievable. As Robinson had pointed out this morning, only identical twins had completely identical DNA bands. The upshot was the expectation that there would be nothing incriminating on the bat that wasn't forensically traceable either to Stephen Adams or to his sons.

Jacobson closed his notebook, paced to the window with his chipped red mug in his hand. Greg Salter had asked to see him at three o'clock. Only he'd phrased the request – the order, really – in best, full-on Greg-speak: *Let's touch base on developments, Frank.* Jacobson shook his head and snorted audibly even though he was standing there alone. Maybe not *every* single living brain out-complicated a black hole or a crab nebula.

# Chapter Twenty-Six

Mick Hume cruised the unmarked Corsa twice up and down the length of Mill Street. In the passenger seat, DS Neville Renbourn, the secondee from the Regional Crime Squad, clocked faces, failed to find the one they were looking for. Hume reckoned he was OK – probably. He was a smoothie, obviously, that went without saying – exactly the type that DC Barber tried so hard to be like. But while somehow Barber never convinced, or never convinced Hume anyway, Renbourn was the genuine, high-flying article. Yet he hadn't tried to pull rank, had insisted on first names, had essentially let Hume get on with it.

'Fuck this, Nev,' Hume said. 'If he *is* here, he's not obliging us by going walkies.'

Hume did one more circuit and then turned left, opposite the Bricklayer's Arms, into Hayle Close. They got out of the car and Hume locked it.

'Nice area,' Renbourn said, glancing up at the crumbling row of condemned properties and then at the overgrown waste ground beyond.

'Tell me about it,' Hume replied. 'Every year the council say knock it down. Every year it's still here.'

He double-checked the car alarm and they started walking along what was left of the pavement. Ryan Walsh, he was thinking, had become a right little effing pest. And an embarrassing one at that. He'd given them the slip for more than twenty-four hours now. He wasn't at his mother's gaff or at any one of the half-dozen addresses on the Woodlands that had been suggested to them – mainly by untrustworthy little toerags who lied on instinct. The latest, mendacious little bastard in that line was Jason Whitmore. Hume still had to do the paperwork on Whitmore's joyriding and vehicle-trashing spree. He'd reminded Whitmore of the fact when they'd persuaded his brain-dead mother to turf her little angel out of bed at the ungentlemanly and early hour of 11 am. Whitmore had sworn deaf, dumb and blind that Walsh was stopping over at his – Whitmore's – cousin's on Wordsworth Avenue. *Like fuck he is, Jayce*, Hume had told him a wasted hour and a half later when they'd run him to ground in the games arcade at the bottom end of the Lower High Street. *He was there, Mr Hume, I swear. But he was talking about roughing it for a night or two – maybe down the Close, he said. I swear he did.* Hume had resisted the impulse to slap him one when no one except Renbourn was looking. It would have been a modern, progressive, rehabilitative not-bloody-hard-enough slap. But he knew that Inspector Jacobson would still have gone spare if word had got back. Instead he'd rammed a coin into the Golden Jackpot machine, his fingers stabbing the buttons. *We don't find him, we'll be right back, Jayce.*

Renbourn sidestepped a fresh, unhealthy-looking dog turd.

'Think our luck's in this time?' he asked.

'Everyone has to be somewhere, Nev,' Hume answered, trying to sound optimistic.

They reached what had once been the front door of 2 Hayle Close. There had been forty neat, terraced houses here in the Close's Late Victorian heyday. Artisans' dwellings. Men going off to work. Women scrubbing the doorsteps, keeping the whitewashed edges pristine and brilliant. Even the anti-poll-tax squatters back in the 1980s had taken some kind of care; fixing windows, applying the odd lick of paint, tapping ingeniously into the power supply from Hudson's scrapyard for heat and light. But the squatters were long gone and old man Hudson had finally closed up his yard a couple of years back. Nowadays Hayle Close was strictly derelict city. Winos, druggies, runaways. The unspoken reason why the council hadn't bulldozed it yet was that it kept them out of the way in a place the ratepayers didn't venture. Hume leant his hand against the boarded-up doorway.

'Here's as good as any. But let's try the back way.'

Renbourn followed him around the side, scuffing his Timberlands on broken bricks and hefty pieces of rubble. In the rear yard, the remains of a door had been half-heartedly placed against a glassless, paneless window. Hume's foresight meant he'd brought a torch. He pulled the door clear, shone the beam into the gloom of the interior.

'After you, Nev.'

Renbourn clambered in. Hume passed him the torch and then climbed in himself. The room was less filthy than he'd expected but it was still a toilet. There was a manky-looking sleeping bag in the corner and a few smelly belongings. As far as they could be sexed at all, the clothes looked male. On a makeshift table – a plank of plywood set on three bricks at either end – there was a broken alarm clock and a dog-eared, crumpled paperback. Howard Marks: *Mr Nice*. Renbourn shone the torch around the sleeping bag and then around the foot of the plank and the bricks. He looked at Hume and Hume nodded back. Drug detritus. Spoons and a kitchen knife, the surfaces tarnished by heat. Lighters. A plastic Coke bottle with a tiny hole melted into the side into which a bright pink Ronald McDonald party straw had been inserted. One of the spoons was a St Christopher, protector of all who journeyed in faith. All over the shop: crushed-up balls of silver foil the size of thumbnails. If you unfolded one, you'd see the telltale user's stripe along its length, burnt between brown and black. Hume and Renbourn didn't need to bother. Instead, they took the door out into the unlit hall. Renbourn followed Hume, holding the torch. He pointed the beam ahead so that Hume could watch where he was putting his feet.

The next two rooms told the same story. Empty but for a handful of wretched clothes and Class A residues. Hume led the way upstairs, taking it a stair at a time, testing his weight. Finally they found six human figures in a room at the back. Living – in some sense of the word. Three lying on the floor across a couple of dank mattresses. Two sprawled over an ancient, busted sofa. One sitting in the armchair which once upon a time might have matched it, might have sat next to it in a house that had electricity and running water. What heat there was came from a battered Calor gas stove. Five of them were drugged up and zombied out of it, sleeping the cosmic sleep. Only the girl in the armchair was something like awake. The windows were boarded up but the light from a candle jammed into a wine bottle cast a flickering light on her face.

'Is it for business?' she asked despite herself, despite knowing them instantly for who they were without so much as the flash of an ID.

'No, you're all right,' Hume said, 'I don't need the clap this week.'

Renbourn told her who they were after. When she looked blank at the name, he gave her a physical description. Nineteen but looking younger. Podgy. Last seen in a blue Tommy Hilfilger jacket and matching cap.

'There'll be a drink in it,' Hume added.

The girl was about that age herself, he reckoned. Thin to the point of malnutrition. A short skirt that you'd only wear in a frozen dump like this in the middle of February if you were either about to go out whoring or just back from a spell.

'Fifty,' she said.

'I said a drink. Not a lottery win.' Hume took a note out of his wallet. 'A tenner. Take it or leave it.'

The girl swivelled off the chair, pulled her puffa jacket tight around her shoulders.

She held out her hand for the cash. But Hume said no, they'd want taking first.

They followed her downstairs and then back out into the yard via the window they'd come in by. She started to lead them down the block, through what had once been tended back gardens where diligent, hopeful men had kept pigeons or dug potatoes.

'Anybody who's not permanent. They're down this way. That's the rule,' she said.

'You've seen him yourself, then?' Hume asked.

'I've seen a fat-arse kid all right. Sounds like the same one,' the girl answered without looking back.

She squeezed through a gap in what had once been a garden wall but it was too narrow a space for either Hume or Renbourn who both had to take the long way up and over. Hume reckoned they were now approximately mid-terrace. The girl stopped in her tracks and turned towards them.

'He'll be in here if he's anywhere,' she said.

She'd lowered her voice to a whisper and she was holding her hand out again.

It was ridiculous really, Hume thought. A tenner of his own cash and no guarantee that he wasn't being played for a mug. On the other hand, a tenner was only a tenner. And if the little bugger *was* here. He re-took the note out of his wallet, handed it to her, watched her disappear back the way they'd come.

There was a doorway this time. But no door. Hume went in first. Renbourn followed with the torch. A rat, brown and twitchy, scurried out the way of the beam. They passed through what had once been a cramped kitchen and into the hall: two ground-floor rooms on their left, the precarious staircase up to the first floor on their right. The stench was compounded of tomcat spray, urine and – somewhere indefinably near their feet – newly-dropped human excrement. The nearest room was empty. But there was the sound of voices from the other room, the one at the front. And the glimmer of torches other than their own.

Hume spoke from outside the doorway before they went in.

'Police! No stress. We only want a word with Ryan Evans Walsh if he's on the premises.'

Just the two of you in a gaff like this, you established your credentials straight off. It was no deterrence against an out-and-out headbanger, could even have the opposite effect. But it usually calmed the average toerag. Like bears in the woods, mainly they just wanted to be left alone.

There was a card game under way by intermittent torchlight. Maybe eight players altogether. Hume never succeeded in counting them all. An old wino known locally as Prince Albert seemed to be the banker. The rest looked to be youths, high on weed and cider. Hume sniffed the air, willing the hash sweetness to override the lingering smells from the hall. It was the kind of situation that could turn ugly in seconds. Somebody winning too much, losing too much or getting it into their head that Albert was a soft touch for robbery. But none of that was pertinent. All that mattered to Hume was the sight of Ryan Walsh dropping his cards and sloping off into the shadows. Nothing like quickly enough.

'A word, Ryan,' Hume repeated, 'here or in the car.'

His arm disappeared into the darkness like a conjuror's and retrieved firstly Walsh's flabby left bicep and secondly the sweating rest of him.

He opted for the car. They took him out to it and stuck him in the back seat. The others had gone straight back to their card game, not giving a toss about Walsh, just mildly glad the CID hadn't been after *their* arse – on this occasion. Surreptitiously Hume clicked the central locking shut just in case he tried to bolt. They ran him through his story once, twice, three times. When had he really left William Blake House on Monday morning? Who had he seen on his way out?

What was being said on the Woodlands about Dave Carter? What the fuck was he doing down the Close when he could be back at home with his nicked PlayStations? Walsh avoided eye contact, played with his fingers, never varied his replies: *he'd left at seven, he hadn't seen anybody, he hadn't heard anything, he hadn't nicked anything.* Hume shot Renbourn a silent glance, knew that Renbourn understood it – if the kid still wasn't daft enough to talk then they were back precisely where they started.

'Can I go now?' Walsh asked, lifting his gaze at last and risking a smirk. 'This is flaming diabolical.'

Hume leant back from the driver's seat and stared hard at him. Another face in need of a slap that was about to go unslapped. Hume could cope with the loss but he needed Walsh to know that he was the beneficiary of a moral choice in the matter. Or if not entirely that then at least of a professional one. He was still staring when Renbourn answered the call from DCI Jacobson, watched the nascent smile vanish from Walsh's pasty-white face.

# Chapter Twenty-Seven

Jacobson had phoned Hume though it had been Renbourn who'd answered. Thereafter he called Emma Smith and DS Kerr. When he'd finished the calls, which he'd made after receiving a call himself – from Chief SOCO Webster – he switched off his desk lamp, drained his coffee and took the lift up to Greg Salter's office on the eighth floor. He knew he'd have been better off and less stressed using the stairs. But post-Behar, his body wasn't in an exercise-friendly mood.

For three o'clock in the afternoon, Salter looked suspiciously smooth chinned, was more than likely the type prepared to shave every two or three hours – putting up with whatever inconvenience it took to preserve his executive image. Admittedly Jacobson kept a set of shaving gear in his *own* desk drawer. Plus a hand towel, a toothbrush and toothpaste. But that was because sometimes he'd work a case round the clock if he had to. Or at least not get home inside twenty-four hours. It was how he also justified to himself the illicit kettle, coffee jar and litre bottle of Glenlivet that lived behind the back numbers of the *Police Gazette* in the bottom drawer of his filing cabinet.

He updated Salter on both of his current investigations. The familicide theory was still holding up for the events at Willow Court, he told him. Plus the classic warning signs had been there – if someone had been in a position to notice all of them sufficiently. On the other hand, they were no nearer to a suspect or suspects with regard to Dave Carter. Although something had just come in that might change that situation drastically in their favour.

Predictably Salter didn't comment on the Woodlands inquiry and didn't ask for details. The press and media focus had switched overwhelmingly to the Adams family killings. And where the press went, DCS Salter followed, taking his ever-shifting PR agenda with him.

'A grim case, Frank. None grimmer,' he intoned, possibly rehearsing for some pre-arranged TV or radio slot. 'A whole family taken out, a wife, children. But at least no dirt attaching to the force. None whatsoever. You'll do a thorough job, make your report to the coroner – and that will be that as far as we're concerned.'

As far as *you're* concerned anyway, you bald, pompous, managerialist dwarf, Jacobson thought, relishing his political incorrectness on all fronts. At the ground level, you got a daily bellyful of human nature at its worst. A lot of civilians wondered why coppers kept to themselves, often had few mates outside the force. The truth was that it was hard to deal with everyday people when you saw what they were capable of once the mask of normality slipped. But fast-track cowboys like Salter – a bare two years on the beat, a minimum of CID foot slogging, a maximum of paper-shuffling and committee-chairing – delegated the messy stuff to others, slept untroubled by bad dreams, might as well have been running a chain of supermarkets as a police unit. Jacobson left him to it as quickly as he could. Although at least Salter wasn't trying to interfere operationally this time. Not today anyway.

Since he had gravity on his side, he took the stairs back down to the fifth floor. His mobile rang just as he was opening his office door: Emma Smith. Smith and Williams had just arrived outside William Blake House. Assuming both Ryan Walsh's mother and Sheryl Holmes were on the premises, they should be able to give him the confirmation he needed one way or another more or less straight away. Jacobson reminded them to take a break when they were done if they hadn't had one earlier. Then they could resume their interrupted Adams inquiry tasks. He relayed the news to Hume and Renbourn then checked his watch. Give them quarter of an hour to drive over here, half an hour for processing and booking out an interview room. Call it four o'clock basically. He closed his office door behind him. He was tempted by the idea of a quick cat nap but rejected it. Instead he did a general phone around: Barber, Ince downstairs, Robinson. Lastly he phoned Webster – in order to make doubly certain of his basic premise. At least that was a solid fact – even if the rest *did* turn out to be just the product of his case-hardened, overly devious mind.

Kerr pulled in to the car park of the Harvester more or less on schedule. His mobile had stayed silent while he'd been with Rachel. He'd stayed only an hour. And you were entitled to a lunch break – even on a murder case. But walking back to his car, he'd still rehearsed a cover story: Doc Lamont was several sheets to the wind, the interview had dragged on. One of these days he might have to carry the can for playing away on police time. The least he could do was to protect Jacobson from any of the flak – even if meant being economical with the truth in his direction every now and then. Fortunately there'd been no need on this occasion. Jacobson hadn't phoned until Kerr was in his car, turning the ignition. He'd asked only how the visit to the retired GP had gone and then suggested setting up the meeting over here. As usual, Jacobson was preoccupied with *results*, paid as little attention as possible to what the hierarchy liked to call *monitoring the process*. A new bullshit jargon, as far as Kerr could see, for wanting to know exactly what you were up to every single minute of the day.

His mobile was ringing now, though, just as he was getting out of the car. *Cathy.* Sam had taken a tumble down the stairs pretending to be Spiderman. No real damage, she thought, more shaken than anything. But she was still going to take him over to Lynne's just in case. Lynne lived on the other side of their street on the Bovis estate, was a fully qualified SRN. Cathy was in the habit of using her as an arbiter of whether either of the twins needed medical attention. Kerr said fine. He asked to speak to his son and told him to be a big, brave boy. Somewhere in the background he heard Susie trying her best to sound like a scolding, bossy adult. Cathy came back on the line and he told her he'd try to get home at a reasonable time – *but you know how it is*. Only of course you don't, he thought, putting his mobile away. Not at all, love. Not remotely.

The Harvester was modern, less than two years old, and proudly, energetically, bland. A non-pub on the edge of the Waitrose complex. Family friendly. A forlorn, unseasonal bouncy castle outside. A Beefeater restaurant attached. Kerr ordered a half of Grolsch at the bar and cast his eye around. The bar had less than ten customers, most of them clustered near the tent-sized TV screen showing NFL highlights from one of the American satellite sports channels. Henry Pelling and his colleague, by contrast, were sitting on their own at a table near the far window.

For most of the years of its existence, the offices of the *Evening Argus* had been inside a spacious Victorian building opposite the railway station. But a takeover and a related property deal had led inexorably to relocation. These days, apart from a modest shopfront in the High Street where you could place a classified ad or buy a photo of the school sports day, the *Argus* lived in purpose-built premises which looked out across the Toyota dealership towards Toys R Us and PC World. *TFS* the hacks called their new home: *That Fucking Shed*. Pelling was the Senior Crime Reporter. Kerr paid for his drink, walked over and joined them. The woman with Pelling, Beth Mosley, was the paper's Features Editor, the brains behind the Family of the Year campaign.

'Cheers,' Pelling said, sinking his mouth around a pint of Guinness and evidently pleased to be out of the office.

'Cheers,' Kerr replied.

Pelling had brokered the meeting but it was Mosley, whom he'd not met before, that Kerr needed to talk to.

'You were actually with the family on Tuesday night?' he asked her.

'That's right. At the reception anyway. One of the junior reporters came over with them in the limo.'

'And your impressions?'

Beth Mosley was probably about Rachel's age, he thought. Small. Not unsexy. Blonde hair tied back for the working day.

'Exactly as the first time I met them, Sergeant. One hundred per cent ordinary and normal. I thought maybe Stephen Adams was a touch too self-confident. But you'd have to be, wouldn't you? To put yourself forward for something like that.'

Kerr sipped some beer. Then:

'So Adams put *himself* forward for the award?'

'Strictly speaking no,' Beth Mosley answered. 'You need to be nominated by four names on the voters' roll. But if I remember correctly all the Adams signatures were employees at his firm. So yes in a way—'

'And that wasn't a problem for you?' Kerr asked.

Pelling looked up rotundly from his Guinness. He was probably only fifty but he looked a lot older. Any day the *Argus* dropped him he had a future with the Health Council advertising department. Get down the gym, don't drink, don't over-eat, don't smoke – OR THIS IS YOU.

'It's only a sales booster, Ian,' he said. 'And maybe a bit of fun. Beth checked them out, of course. I don't think there were any criminal records involved, for instance – not that *we've* any way of getting at the raw data naturally.'

Kerr ignored the joke or the boast or whatever else Pelling

thought his sub-text amounted to. If the *Argus* didn't have a backhander route into the PNC, at least some of the time, then the Dalai Lama wasn't a Tibetan Buddhist.

Beth Mosley toyed with what looked like a Red Bull and vodka.

'Henry's right, I'm afraid. It's all about marketing really. From the nominations we got in, Mr and Mrs Adams were the best match to our audience profile. Coming from what used to be called a working-class background. But affluent, aspirational and consumer oriented. Parents with no higher education yet wanting it for their kids.'

'Sounds like me and my wife,' Kerr commented, instinctively watching her lift the drink to her mouth and clocking the tiny smear of red her lips left behind on the glass.

'Exactly, Ian,' Pelling said. 'Just some ordinary Joe until he flips out. There was a similar story I covered down south – Essex, I think – when I was working on the nationals.'

Kerr kept his smile to himself. Sooner or later, usually sooner, any conversation with Pelling necessitated some mention of his Fleet Street glory days.

'This meeting's off the record, Henry. Inspector Jacobson wouldn't want to see that comparison in print.'

Pelling held his hands up in an exaggerated gesture.

''Course not, mate. But I take it that *is* the score – topping the wife and kids?'

Kerr nodded.

'So it seems. That's why we wondered if Adams had struck any of you as – well, *odd*.'

Beth Mosley said again that he hadn't:

'Before we made the final decision, I spoke to the head teachers at both the kids' schools. And some of the other dads who helped out with the football team. Pretty much all I got was Stephen Adams, Decent Bloke.'

'They do say Hitler was kind to animals,' Pelling commented.

He may not have been alluding to the dead spaniel sprawled in its basket across Marion Adams' terracotta kitchen tiles. But before he finished his beer and left, Kerr reminded him that there was a definite police embargo against any reporting of that specific fact.

In Candice's kitchen, Sheryl had her hands in a sink full of dirty plates and pans. It had been decent of Candice to put them up. So a bit of cleaning and tidying had seemed the least she could do in return. After the police cow had gone again, Candice had nipped out to the Poets to be on time for the grocery women. Lucy was through in the lounge watching *A Bug's Life*, one of the few suitable videos from Liam's collection. Liam was theoretically at school but might just have been hanging around somewhere on the estate. Anne-Marie sat listlessly at the kitchen table. Sheryl had bought her a magazine of *Lord of the Rings* stickers and puzzles in town. But she'd barely seemed to look at it.

The grocery women, two ageing sisters, specialised in butchery theft and resale. Chops, minced steak, burgers, anything in that line. It was frigging Friday, Candice had said. Between them they could cook up something decent for tea, have a couple of drinks afterwards, try and unwind a bit. Sheryl hadn't argued. Life had to go on somehow, hadn't it? No matter frigging what. Anne-Marie got up from the table. Sheryl watched her walking out into the hall, heard her go into the bathroom. The council had offered them a place at last anyway. Over at Byron House. It was up on the eighth floor but at least they'd still be living in the part of the estate they knew. Sheryl's biggest worry had been that they'd end up shunted over to somewhere like Shelley Road. *Smelly Shelley*: right on the farthest edge of the Woodlands – miles from the shops and the bus route – the place where they were dumping all the asylum seekers.

She finished up the last pan, rinsed it under the cold tap

to get the suds off, stacked it on the draining board. Grant could have arranged it so that they moved in today, would have sorted out the furniture and everything. But she'd talked it over with Candice: Monday would be better, they'd decided. It was probably best for Anne-Marie to have as much company around her in the meantime as possible, keep her used to being with normal people. She dried her hands on the dish towel and gazed out of the kitchen window. Mainly what you saw was the neighbouring block staring back at you or the litter-strewn tarmac in between. Although, if you looked upwards, you could watch the sky turn dark and cloudy, like a final slap in the face.

Candice had treated her to a packet of Silk Cut, knowing things were tight. Not even Grant had been able to chisel a crisis loan out of the social. *You're being rehoused and domestic essentials are being made available from local charitable sources*, the spotty clerk had told them: frigging, sodding end of. She decided she'd tackle the cooker next, sweep the floor. And then she'd sit down with a cup of coffee and a fag. She put the dish towel back on the sticky-backed plastic peg that Candice had fixed at a skewed angle to the side of the fridge. Anne-Marie seemed to be taking her time. Sheryl went into the hall, called her gently by name – no reply. She knocked on the bathroom door and then tried the handle – snibbed from the inside.

'Anne-Marie,' she called again.

Urgently this time, stridently.

'Anne-Marie!'

She tried shouldering the door but only succeeded in banging her arm. She knew that Candice kept a hammer in her bedroom. *Just in case*, she always said. Sheryl found it, wedged between the bed and the bedside cabinet. Lucy was in the hall when she came back, pushing uselessly at the door. Sheryl shooed her out of the way. She swung the hammer, aiming just above the handle. The first time she missed, took a chunk out of the door jamb. Somehow, not really sure how she did it, she finally smashed the door open.

There was never enough drying space when you had kids. Candice had strung a green plastic washing line across her bath, used it for Liam's pants, socks, things that could drip-dry over night. Anne-Marie was standing on the edge of the bath, precariously balanced. She'd tied one end of the clothes line to the metal arm that opened the tiny bathroom window. The other end she'd wrapped half a dozen times tightly around her neck.

Sheryl just held her there for a moment, her heart pounding. Lucy clambered up on to the cistern but her fingers were too small or too weak to untie the knot. Sheryl nearly panicked, nearly freaked. But then she lifted her daughter up in her arms and set her down again farther along the edge of the bath at a point where the clothes line started to have some slack in it. She held her close with one hand, untangled the plastic rope from her neck with the other. Anne-Marie coughed and spluttered. Then she was hugging her mum and wordlessly sobbing.

# Chapter Twenty-Eight

Jacobson brought Kerr up to speed in Kerr's cramped, shared office and then they took the lift together down to the custody area. The custody sergeant led them along the low-ceilinged corridor and stopped outside interview room B. Ryan Walsh and the duty solicitor were already ensconced inside. According to Mick Hume, Walsh had gone as white as a sheet when they'd told him what was what. But for all that he'd still declined to make any kind of comment other than to demand a brief.

Jacobson and Kerr sat themselves down.

'What it is, Ryan,' Jacobson said, 'you've been arrested on suspicion of illegal trespass and theft on a date – or a series of dates – yet to be specified.'

He coughed. Then:

'Do you understand what that means?'

Ryan Walsh nodded. But still didn't speak.

'Mr Walsh has nodded assent,' Kerr volunteered for the benefit of the tape recorder.

Jacobson continued:

'Specifically, forensic officers have identified a set of fingerprints obtained from the premises of 41A William Blake House as *your* fingerprints, Ryan. The legal occupier of those premises has given a statement to my officers to the effect that she is unaware of any occasion on which you were ever invited into her house. She has also identified certain items removed from your bedroom, Ryan, as her belongings.'

Walsh's face turned beetroot red.

'If there's an innocent explanation, Ryan, now would be a good time to air it,' the duty solicitor said.

Kerr dumped the transparent evidence bag on the table. Three soiled pairs of black lace panties removed from Walsh's mother's flat in the past hour by DCs Smith and Williams. When she'd got through with requesting them to sod off and leave her alone, Sheryl Holmes had said they were probably hers, they certainly looked like hers, what the hell had that fat slug upstairs been doing with them? How the hell had he got hold of them? All of that had been after Chief SOCO Webster's fingerprint officers had finally got a response from the NAFIS computer. The database had held a match for only one set of prints from the burnt-out flat: Ryan Evans Walsh's.

'I was shagging her, wasn't I?' Walsh muttered indistinctly.

Jacobson asked him to repeat what he'd said.

'I was shagging her,' he said, barely more audibly.

Kerr cracked up, couldn't *not* laugh; the duty solicitor looked away, trying to keep his face straight.

'In your dreams,' Jacobson said superfluously.

He lit up a B and H, offered one to Walsh, lit it for him with his silver lighter.

'Now listen, Ryan, this would be a serious charge if it proceeded to court. You could end up on the sex offenders register. But that's only the half of it. You've already admitted you were out and about in William Blake House first thing Monday. And now your prints turn up in the flat where Dave Carter was beaten to death and where his body was set on fire.'

Walsh puffed on the cigarette as if his life depended on it. His big reddened face dissolved back into white. Jacobson took a deep drag himself. He had nothing really. Only the balance of the equation in Walsh's toerag brain between fear and embarrassment. He didn't see him for the killing and the fire in a million years. It was pure serendipity that his prints had survived the fire and no one else's. Or no one else's that matched an entry in the NAFIS database anyway. Plus the panty theft probably wasn't worth the necessary paperwork even if Jacobson *had* been serious about it. Walsh didn't know that, of course.

The two smokers carried on smoking. Kerr moved his chair as far out of the trajectory of the smoke trails as he could. The duty solicitor crossed then uncrossed his legs, straightened his tie. Kerr hadn't seen him before. He was from Alan Slingsby's firm apparently. A new recruit to Slingsby's ever-expanding empire.

Walsh held his fag over the scuffed ashtray.

'It was weeks ago, I swear. It weren't deliberate. I didn't break in or nothing. The daft cow hadn't locked her door properly. That was all. In a rush taking her kiddies to school, I expect. I even shut it right for her afterwards.'

'It sounds just about plausible, old son,' Jacobson said. 'But why should I go out of my way to believe you?'

Walsh lifted his free hand to his face, scratched at an ugly yellow spot on the left side of his nose.

'What if I did have a name? For Monday morning, like.'

'You know the score, Ryan,' Jacobson said, keeping his voice matter-of-fact, even. 'No promises. But I can put a word in if you're being cooperative about a bigger case.'

Kerr moved his chair forward again, despite the smoke.

'Sex offences, Ryan. Not recommended if you're living on the Woodlands. And even if it doesn't go to that, just think about all your mates knowing.'

Walsh avoided eye contact, stared at the ashtray when he spoke.

'But this name – what if it's, like, a nutter, somebody who might—'

Jacobson finished his cigarette, stubbed it out.

'Sooner we've a name, sooner they're inside, Ryan. Out of harm's way,' he said.

He knew he could be setting the lad up for something much worse than ridicule or a thumping from the Woodlands anti-sex-pest posse. But you did what the job needed you to do. Or you found another occupation.

Charlie stepped out of the en suite shower, dried himself, got properly dressed. Lisa was fast asleep in the middle of the big oval bed. Tired out at last from the sex and the champagne. He walked over and covered her up with the sheet. She was making a gentle, grunting kind of noise as she dozed; louder than just breathing but not quite snoring. He checked the time. Four fifteen. He decided to let her sleep on while he sorted things out with FB. It had been all very well hanging out here for a couple of days. But it wasn't the plan he'd had in mind. Disappearing out of the area for the duration, not taking stupid risks, not playing silly buggers. This was nothing like that at all.

At least he wasn't going to have to look very hard for Florida Boy's whereabouts; the moment he stepped outside the bedroom he could hear the surround speakers blaring out from downstairs. Fuck: he'd already warned the stupid cunt to keep the noise down. The gaff was in its own grounds and it was maybe a quarter of a mile to the next place. But there was still a footpath and a B road outside. And the village not that far off. They liked the outdoors, the rich twats who lived out this way. And they probably all knew each other as well. From fox-hunting. Or from wife-swapping parties. All that. For Christ's sake – it only took one nosy parker out walking the dog to see or hear something unusual, to start poking their nose in.

FB had spread himself out along the length of a sofa in the room that had been kitted out as a home cinema. He had a fat joint in one hand, the remote control in the other. Bruce Lee was up on the screen, giving it his usual wellie. The hall of mirrors showdown from *Enter the Dragon* it looked like.

'Charles, old bean,' Florida Boy said, glancing up. 'Taking a short break from fornication, no doubt.'

Charlie found the plug for the DVD player, pulled it out from the mains socket.

'Stow it, Brian. I already said about the fucking volume.'

'Take it easy, old bean,' Florida boy said, dopily, proffering the joint.

'No. No thanks. That's just the point,' Charlie said, sitting down on the opposite sofa. 'We're not on holiday, we're on the frigging run.'

Florida Boy swung his legs slowly to the left, sat up, propping a yellow cushion behind his head.

'Bandits and vagabonds. Living outside the unjust law.'

Charlie took the joint anyway, as much to cool his temper as anything. FB looked a right mess. They'd been here two days and he hadn't bothered to shave or sort out his clothes. That was FB for you. Obsessively neat on one high, an untidy gobshite on the next. Plus the joint was for pure show only. What was really going on behind his pin-head irises was still frigging pills. Uppers, downers, last night even some microdot. Which he'd talked Lisa into as well. Like her brain wasn't wired up weirdly enough to begin with.

'Listen, Bri,' he said, trying to sound reasonable. 'You killed a bloke on Monday that didn't need killing. It's not the same as joyriding. And don't forget that kid who clocked us on the way in. The one you said you knew. We need to get right away, keep our heads down for a bit.'

FB adjusted the cushion, sat up farther, as if he were making an effort to concentrate.

'Fat Ryan? The young man has more sense than to indulge in loose talk.'

'Maybe, maybe not,' Charlie said.

He dug an empty hand into his trouser pocket, pulled out a wad of notes.

'Anyway, look. Six hundred quid, mate. Just sitting in a drawer in the kitchen. Pin money for emergencies, isn't it?'

He drew on the spliff. Then:

'First thing tomorrow, I'll borrow some wheels and we'll fuck off. Take the back road into Coventry and make for the railway station. Three legit tickets: Bristol via Birmingham.'

'Touring the West Country and what not,' FB commented.

Charlie passed the joint back silently. He realised all at once that he couldn't really tell any more if he was getting through to Bilston or not. And that maybe it didn't matter anyway.

# Chapter Twenty-Nine

Steve Horton, the civilian computer officer, pulled up everything associated with the name from the Police National Computer, even cross-referenced the data with Crowby's own localised database in the interests of accuracy. DS Renbourn telephoned the Regional Crime Squad, ran the name past his bosses, got the precise result that Jacobson needed: Brian "Florida Boy" Bilston was a local toerag only, he had no known connection to the RCS three-county drugs operation; *if the Crowby side could nick him for something, they were welcome to him – with their good wishes.*

Jacobson arranged to meet Clean Harry Fields in the police canteen, brought Kerr, Mick Hume and Renbourn along with him. Fields turned up with a morose-looking detective constable called Watts. Classic drug squad in appearance: nylon bomber jacket, running shoes, number-one haircut scraped right in to the wood. Watts was Field's area guy for the Woodlands, had the helpful advantage of knowing Bilston instantly by sight. Renbourn displayed outsider's courtesy, picked up the tab at the till. Two coffees. Three teas. A sausage roll but nothing to drink for Clean Harry, whose teetotalism extended to the exclusion of caffeine and tannins.

'No problem with meat products, then, Harry?' Jacobson asked him when they'd found a table.

'*Every moving thing that liveth shall be meat for you*, Frank,' Fields replied imperturbably, wiping the first crumbs from his mouth, 'Genesis, nine, three.'

Jacobson dimly recalled a counter-quote, something about the lion and the lamb. But he decided against the wisdom of playing at biblical hermeneutics with an expert.

He was mildly surprised that Fields had offered his personal assistance in any case. As drug squad supremo, he was supposed to park his arse next to a nice warm Divisional building radiator and let his goons do the running around. But it wasn't easy to give up real policing, exchange it for committee work or wine-and-nibble evenings with Dud Bentham and his entourage of assistant chiefs and superintendents. Not if you were a real copper, anyway. Jacobson understood that fact more than anyone. Once – years ago, when he'd still been in uniform – he'd nicked an anarchist on some street demo or other. The way the day had gone, they'd had to wait around for an hour together before Jacobson could process him into custody. Like any two young men whose paths had crossed accidentally, they'd ended up talking: beer, women, life. Why do leaders always disappoint their followers, always betray them and let them down? the anarchist had asked him. And then answered his own question. Because, he'd said, anyone who *wants* to be a leader, who *wants* get to the top, is automatically psychologically and morally unfit to lead. This was the fatal flaw, the anarchist had argued, in all hierarchical societies. It was an argument that Jacobson still remembered from time to time. Usually when he was kicking his heels or biting his tongue up on the eighth floor.

They took two cars when they were ready. Jacobson and Fields, driven by Kerr, headed for the Mill Street area. If – and it was a big if – the PNC and the local data were up to date, Bilston was off the Woodlands and living in a bedsit. Renbourn and Watts, driven by Hume, would tour the estate itself, check out Bilston's known hang-outs and associates. Jacobson phoned the rest of his team – Smith, Williams and DC Barber – en route. It was up to them to keep the Adams inquiry moving forward in his absence, he told them. Anything major, contact him direct. Anything else, log it with Sergeant Ince back at the incident room.

Bilston's gaff was a typical DSS piss-hole. A rambling Edwardian villa, one of half a dozen, in a little crescent-shaped street not far from the old grain store. The street and the houses had both fallen on hard times. Then the hard times had fallen on hard times. It was useful, though, that it had a live-in landlord, a theoretically-reformed heavy by the name of Pete Bradley. Bradley's business empire also extended to a share in a minicab firm and the running of the kind of door security organisation that started more fights than it ever circumvented. Fields intimated that his officers had recently spoken to Bradley in relation to Section 8 of the Misuse of Drugs Act. *Knowing and Permitting*, the drug squad called it – turning a blind eye to using or dealing on the premises.

Kerr locked the car and stood on the pavement. In a minute or two, he'd sneak round the back of the building and stay there till they were finished. Just in case. Jacobson and Fields made their way up the unneat path to the front door. Jacobson rang the dangerous-looking main bell, wishing he'd come equipped for the purpose with insulated rubber gloves. He rang it another four times until finally somebody answered the door. But only after they'd latched the security chain. Jacobson squeezed his ID into the gap and a red-haired young woman in a dressing gown undid the chain, pulled the door back. Jacobson kept his eyes from lingering on the healthy amount of breast visible under her terry towelling.

'Pete ain't here,' she said.

Jacobson told her it was Brian Bilston they needed to speak to.

'Got a warrant, have you?'

Jacobson told her he didn't need one, Section 17 of the Powers of Search covered him in a case like this, she could have the leaflet if she wanted one.

'No, you're all right,' she said. 'Upstairs, number six.'

She pulled the dressing gown tight as she let them in, ending temptation.

Bradley had evidently reserved the ground floor for his own use. The carpeting, such as it was, vanished the moment you set foot on the noisy, creaking stairs. Dance music thumped out from somewhere further up the building but there was no response from Bilston's door on the first floor. Fields went back downstairs, returned with the redhead, the redhead's name and the master key. You never searched anywhere without a witness; not if you wanted evidence that would stand up in court.

'I'm missing the frigging *Weakest Link*,' she said, unlocking the door.

'Mr Bradley's what, forty?' Harry Fields asked her. 'And you're what, Carol, twenty?'

'The fuck's it to you?'

She had a habit, probably unconscious, of pulling on her left earlobe when she was agitated, playing with her tiny red stud diamond.

'A young girl, your whole life ahead of you,' Fields said, shaking his head sadly. 'Do you ever think of Jesus, of why we're on this earth?'

Fields was a kind of local treasure, Jacobson thought. His missionary faith entirely undimmed by experience. In his own way, he might be the force's biggest, wildest maverick.

She laughed despite herself.

'Who's your weird friend? Blimey.'

She winked at Jacobson and pushed the door wide. Jacobson went in first, his eyes sweeping the room.

Point one: Bilston wasn't there. Point two: it was the neatest rat trap he'd seen in a long time. The few magazines and CDs orderly on a shelf. A row of dishes spick and span next to the tiny sink. Jacobson made sure Carol kept a close watch while they took a look-see. There were a few clothes hanging in the wardrobe, dangling like skeletons from cheap wire hangers, a few pairs of trainers. But that didn't mean that others hadn't gone, packed into a hold-all and scarpered with their owner.

'You've seen him today?' he asked her.

'Not today. Earlier in the week maybe. They're bedsits, it's not frigging bed and breakfast. They got keys, they come and go as they like.'

Fields was rooting around inside the CD cases, not finding anything.

'When exactly in the week?' he asked her. 'It's important we know.'

'Wednesday morning maybe. I heard him going out, he had some mate with him, I think.'

She'd answered without a murmur of complaint. Maybe to avoid another sermon.

'And you didn't see this mate?'

'No, I didn't. It was a bloke, though. You can tell the difference by the steps even if they don't speak.'

Jacobson had done the fridge, the cooker, under the sink, the woodwormed chest of drawers with one missing. All that was left was the bed and the mattress. Fields took the other end of the frame and they tilted it up on to its side.

Point three: a rusted tyre lever stowed carelessly inside a Lidl carrier bag. Not so much hidden as discarded, left behind.

# Chapter Thirty

Six thirty pm. Jacobson called a briefing on both cases for those available. DS Kerr. DCs Barber, Smith and Williams. Sergeant Ince. Harry Fields had clocked off as soon as they'd got back to the Divi. The extra plod and CID who'd spent their shift doorstepping out at the Bartons had likewise filed their reports and gone home. Mick Hume, DS Renbourn and DC Watts were still over in the Woodlands, still trying to track an initial clue as to the whereabouts of Brian Bilston. Ince closed the door of the incident room and Jacobson lit himself a B and H, realised that he'd lost count of his running daily tally.

Barber went first, reported on the door-to-door enquiries. No change from yesterday's results: anybody who'd had any contact with the family only had good words to say about them. Emma Smith and DC Williams told much the same story from the Bartons primary school – where Sarah Adams had been a pupil – and from the Simon de Montfort comp which Matthew Adams and his brother, Mark, had attended. Neither boy had been a teacher's pet like their sister, nor had they shown anything like her academic potential. But for all that, the head teacher had said, they'd been pleasant, ordinary, middle-of-the-road lads. They'd both seemed more interested in sport than school work but they'd been averagely well behaved. They definitely weren't troublemakers or problem cases. Absolutely not. The whole school, he'd said, was in a state of shock.

Kerr recapped on his and Jacobson's meetings with Alan

Jones and with Dr Rochester – and on his own encounters with Dr Lamont and the *Argus* reporters. Jacobson summarised the main findings from Robinson's preliminary report on the dead of Willow Court, reminded them they could read a copy for themselves if they felt in need of the grisly detail. He also announced that the dental records check had been completed. The body in William Blake House was now confirmed to be that of Dave Carter. Then he called up Hume. Sergeant Ince switched the telephone on to broadcast so they could all follow the conversation. So far, Hume told them, they hadn't found a single toerag prepared to say they'd seen Brian Bilston in the past week or to suggest who he might be hanging around with these days. But they'd keep at it: *as long as it took*.

Ince mentioned that he'd circulated other police forces with Bilston's details. He also had a public appeal drafted and ready to go as soon as it was wanted. Jacobson waved his cigarette carelessly, knocked fag ash down the lapel of his jacket.

'Check with me later, old son. If we get nothing definite ourselves, we might as well scare Joe Public and his granny into keeping an eye out,' he said, dabbing at the ash with his free hand. 'Clean Harry's promised me that the rest of the drug squad – not just Watts – will be doing the same.'

'So is Bilston the priority now, guv?' Emma Smith asked.

'Bilston could be a *live* killer, Emma. That makes him a lot more dangerous than Stephen Adams. Ideally we pick the bugger up tonight, get back on with crossing the *t*'s at Willow Court over the rest of the weekend.'

Jacobson coughed, surprised at himself. In his line of work, *ideally* was the kind of weasely, fate-tempting adverb that was best avoided.

He readjourned to the police canteen after the briefing ended, ordered the Friday special of cod and chips. He'd sent Barber over to the Woodlands, to supplement Hume, Renbourn and Watts. Smith and Williams he'd left office bound: cross-referencing two days' worth of interviews and statements in connection with the Adams family. Ince was minding the telephone lines and the computers. Kerr was staying on call for the duration but in the meantime he'd gone home to dinner with his wife and kids. Jacobson sprinkled salt and vinegar, bit into his food. Which left himself – doing what exactly? Not much if the truth be told. The tasks that needed doing had been parcelled out to competent officers who knew what they were about. All he had to do was to stay in touch in case a decision needed to be made or something new and unexpected turned up. Like Kerr, he might just as well have gone home until or unless something *did*.

He finished his meal slowly and then got in everyone's way in the incident room for half an hour. Needlessly, he interrogated the grammar of Ince's public appeal, which had been worded perfectly to begin with. He made Emma Smith a cup of tea she really didn't want, that she only accepted out of politeness. Reluctantly he retreated to his office at last, intent on collecting his coat and finally buggering off to Wellington Drive. Once he had his coat on and buttoned, he lingered futilely between his coat rack and the door. The phone or his mobile could ring at the last minute, the way they always did in films and on TV. But here, in Jacobson's real life, the silence inside the room stayed put, matched by the silence outside in the empty, Friday night corridor. What you never saw on TV were the hours and the days when nothing really happened on an investigation, when all you did was spadework. Or not even that. When you just *waited*.

He turned out the light, locked the door, took the lift down. It was gone 7.30 and the rush-hour traffic had eased. He was home inside fifteen minutes, slinging his coat and jacket, kicking off his shoes. He'd take a shower, maybe even a bath, and settle down with a book. His daughter, Sally, had presented him with a boxed set of P.G. Wodehouse as a Christmas present, had argued that he spent far too many evenings reading about the ancient Sumerians or – his latest enthusiasm – the history of philosophy. *You should lighten up, Dad*, she'd told him, *sometimes I think maybe Mum had a point*. Jacobson had promised half-heartedly to give it a try.

He eased the knot of his tie around his shirt collar, dug one of the Wodehouses out from the bottom of his to-be-read pile in readiness. But in the next second, his mobile, buried on the floor inside his coat pocket, really did ring.

Kerr washed up after tea and got involved in bathtime. After his tumble downstairs, Sam was exempted from a full bath on account of the cuts and bruises on his leg. They'd stopped hurting him but they'd remained a source of fascination. The cuts and the sticking plasters especially. Something you could pick at and fiddle with when your mum wasn't looking. After the twins were put to bed, Cathy gave Michelle, her most reliable babysitter, a ring. Michelle could be over in twenty minutes, she told Kerr. They could take a walk over to the Lonely Ploughboy if they liked – if *he* liked.

'OK. Fine,' Kerr said. 'I can't have more than a couple of pints, though.'

He went upstairs, took a shower, had a shave, put on his new jeans and a clean shirt.

Cathy's jacket was hanging at the back of the wardrobe. The scuffed black leather one that she never wore any more, 'Fuck Off' studded in metal across the back. She'd been wearing it the night he'd first met her; in a grungy pub in Birmingham, Mark E. Smith and the Fall cranking the volume on the beer-soaked stage. She'd worked in an office, even then, only she'd lived for the weekends: gigs and clubbing. She'd have spat on the Lonely Ploughboy in those days, spat on the Bovis estate altogether. But that had been before marriage. Before the kids. Before Kerr had joined the force for reasons he still hadn't fathomed – or still couldn't face.

Michelle had already arrived when he came back down, was making a fuss of the cat in the kitchen while Cathy fixed her a cup of coffee. She was seventeen; a calm, quiet girl studying for her A-levels, who never brought boyfriends around, never seemed to nick the booze. Kerr smiled at her from the doorway, pulling on his own jacket. The kettle clicked off. In the same instant, the phone started to ring. Cathy still had the handset beside her. She picked it up but let it ring on. Six rings. Watching his face for a reaction.

'Yes, he's here,' she said, finally pressing the green button and answering.

She held it out towards him like a pile of dirty washing.

The hospital had phoned Jacobson and Jacobson had phoned Kerr. They drove over there in Kerr's Peugeot. Jacobson spoke to Mick Hume en route. Then to Sergeant Ince. Ince could wait precisely another hour. If there was still no joy by then, he was to set the public appeal in motion. It was the kind of task which even Jacobson conceded had been improved by modern technology. So long as the duty communications supervisor approved the release, Bilston's mug shot could reach the newspapers, radio and TV stations within seconds. The hospital car park was jam packed with peak-time visitors. Kerr squeezed in between a mud-caked D-reg Skoda and a pristine silver Espace, an identical model, it looked like, to the one Stephen and Marion Adams had driven.

Dr Chaudhury was waiting for them, gave them strict instructions.

'You must go easy, Inspector. And no more than ten minutes.'

'So she's going to pull through after all?' Jacobson asked.

'If you were a relative I would say that we must take

things as they come, that we must wait and see – and hope,' Chaudhury answered.

'But since I'm not?'

'The liver is very badly damaged, Mr Jacobson. Very badly. I fear that this will be a temporary rally only.'

'And she remembers about her husband?'

Chaudhury nodded. He led them along the corridor but didn't go in with them. The nurse who'd been at the bedside stepped outside. But she didn't go far. And she left one of the doors open.

Mrs Eileen Carter was still wired to a life support system. But she'd been shunted out of the main intensive care area into a side room. Jacobson and Kerr pulled their chairs in along the same side of the bed. Jacobson sat closest. He held up his ID, told her who they were, why they'd come.

'Filthy to meet you, I'm sure.'

Her voice was somewhere between a lilt and a rasp. There was a sign above the bed. Nil by mouth.

'Dave, Mrs Carter. Do you know who he was trading with?' Jacobson asked. 'Who his associates were?'

'Ice,' she said, her head lolling slightly against the mountain of white pillows.

Kerr stepped outside, had a word with the nurse. There was vein damage in the oesophagus. Apparently it was a common secondary complication, especially when heavy drinking was a factor. It meant that for the moment it wasn't safe for Eileen Carter's mouth to take in liquid from anything other than a carefully measured quantity of ice cubes. He came back with a meagre handful inside a paper cup. Jacobson held the cup to her lips but she took it from him, insisted on holding it weakly herself.

He tried again after a minute.

'Dave, Mrs Carter—'

'The cats. How are the cats?'

'The cats are fine, just fine,' he lied, realising he'd totally forgotten about them, hoping he sounded convincing. 'A young lass in your street. I've slipped her a few bob to keep them fed all right.'

She lifted the cup again, sucked on a cube. The worse thing, Jacobson thought, was the colour of her skin. You dimly associated jaundice with yellow. You didn't realise, never imagined, *how* yellow. Or how it was in the eyes just as much as it was in the hooded, drowsy eyelids. Or just as much as it was in the face.

'Dave,' he persisted.

'Davey boy. Always such plans. Going to make a mint this time, he said. Make a mint and get out of here. Move somewhere decent.'

Her head lolled again.

'But who else was involved? There must have been meetings. Visitors coming round the house.'

The nurse came in, checked the monitors, adjusted one of the drip packs. Kerr watched her watching Jacobson. He's being as gentle as a lamb, he thought. But he doubted if the nurse saw it that way.

Mrs Carter sucked on another cube. Then:

'You think I'd tell you that, do you? Why? Because Davey boy couldn't keep it in his trousers? Because he broke my heart you think I'd talk to you?'

'We're trying to catch whoever killed him, Eileen, that's all. We need to be able to prove a motive,' Jacobson said.

'Davey's dead and that's it. It's what happens to scum like us. And don't tell me *you* give a flying fuck.'

She seemed to be trying to move in the bed, trying to pull herself up.

'You filthy—'

The nurse turned towards them.

'I'm sorry. That's really enough. You need to go now.'

Jacobson didn't argue, just thanked her for putting up with the intrusion. Kerr picked up the chairs they'd used, stacked them neatly in the corner. You did the job and you never saw beyond it – how it looked from the outside, how it barely papered over the cracks, how it could fuck up everybody who went near it.

# Chapter Thirty-One

They only had one of the bedside lamps lit. Charlie flicked the remote through the channels, the TV volume turned low. No drugs, no booze, he'd said earlier on: what they needed was an early night. They'd more or less stuck to it as well. Charlie and Lisa anyway. Christ knows what FB was up to in the guest bedroom he'd made his own. But at least he seemed to be keeping the noise down. The plan was to get up just before dawn. Lisa and FB would clean up: hoovering, wiping down surfaces, putting as much as possible back the way it was. Like they'd never even been here. Charlie would liberate a discreet set of wheels and they'd be ready for the offski.

Lisa nudged him.

'Try BBC One again, Charlie,' she said.

There was a late film she wanted to see, *The Postman Always Rings Twice*. It was one of those ones her old dear was always banging on about. She didn't know shit in Lisa's book, her mother. Except that she did know about movies. Lisa certainly gave her that much. Not that it was all that surprising. Seeing as how, when she wasn't slaving in the paint factory, all the poor cow ever did was gawp at videos and DVDs.

Charlie flicked over.

'It ain't started yet, Leez. It's the news first,' he said, letting the remote drop onto the bed and running his fingers lightly across her tits.

*BBC News in the Midlands. Police have tonight issued a*

*description of a man they want to speak to in connection with the case of suspected murder and arson in Crowby earlier this week . . .*

He took his hand away, sat up.

*Brian Bilston, aged twenty, is described as . . .*

Lisa found herself scrambling for the remote.

*A police spokesman urged Mr Bilston to come forward in order to assist them and to eliminate himself from their enquiries . . .*

It wasn't a great picture of FB, Charlie thought. But you could tell it was him all right.

*A body, believed to be that of a local barman, Mr David Carter, aged thirty-nine, was retrieved from a burning flat on . . .*

She waited until the report had finished, clicked the TV completely off.

'Charlie' – her voice was flat, disbelieving – 'what the fuck have you got me into?'

# Chapter Thirty-Two

*Up early. I like to be up early when there's a need. Don't you? Shower, proper breakfast. Everything sorted and neat. Ready without any fuss, any last-minute rush. I sorted most of the kit last night really. But I always like to check, always like to be thorough. It's what I need, this. Focus on the tasks at hand. Concentrate. Keep it steady. And be with those I can trust. It's what I do, have done for years. Why would today be any different? Even if I let it, made it different in my head – it still wouldn't do any kind of good, would it? It was the right thing to do anyway, whatever way I look at it. No different with a human than with an animal really. Put down. Put to sleep. Put out of misery.*

*There – all done. Packed and checked. Put the kettle on first. Cup of tea while I think about grub. Stick the news on too. Just follow the normal routine. Be at the depot promptly: demonstrate readiness, reliability. Just like any other time. They'll talk about it, of course. That's only natural. And I'll say what they expect me to say, that's all. Shock. Tears. Can't really believe it. It's the kids you feel sorry for the most. Their whole lives snuffed out. I'm better off doing something all the same. They'll understand that. Don't you think? Anyone would understand that.*

*Maybe put on some mushrooms as well as the eggs and bacon. Just toast, though. No fried bread. But a proper fry-up otherwise. It can be a long day at this time of the year. And out in the cold for most of it. Just act like I always act. That's crucial. Anything else, little signs out of the ordinary, that's the way to fuck up. That's the way to draw attention. That's when things can start to fall apart.*

# Chapter Thirty-Three

Charlie left by the kitchen door and took the curling path that bordered the long, rolling lawn. It was just before dawn. Light enough to see, dark enough to hide. Every now and then some bird or other would disturb the peace. Singing out or flapping its wings among the branches. But not too many of them yet. Weird, Charlie thought, that silence was something you could hear, almost like it was a noise itself. But that's how it was in Toff Land, first thing of a morning.

The garden was several gardens in one. Immediately after the lawn came the area that Charlie liked best. Ferns and a series of lily ponds. The occasional glimpse of a goldfish under the dark water. A little Japanese bridge. But no time for any of that now. He made straight for the back wall, down past the greenhouses and the wired-over vegetable patches. The wall was Midlands red brick, solid, high. Someone had taken the time and trouble to top it out with the old concrete and broken glass routine. There was a green-painted wooden door about a third of the way along. Thick bolts on the inside and a decent Yale lock. Charlie undid the bolts and stepped through, pulling the door shut. He had the key in his pocket just in case. Somebody – *Tim* or *Nichola*? – had hung it up on a brass peg inside a neat little antique wall cabinet. A dozen or so pegs, a dozen or so keys. Each one with a helpful, handwritten label attached.

A small, dense woodland ran behind the house. Charlie didn't rush, tried to keep as light on his feet as he could manage. You had to watch yourself the whole time or you'd end up with a twatting branch poking your eye out or thwacking you in the balls. The wood stretched on as far as the next property, a quarter of a mile further up the winding B road if you went along the front way. Charlie had reccied it a couple of times on their first day and then again at daybreak yesterday, sneaking out and back before Lisa even knew he was gone. Security cameras. Lights. Alarms. And definitely under current occupation.

Bastard! He swore despite himself, extricated his foot from underneath the creeper that had tripped him, very nearly twisted his ankle. He hobbled on regardless until the pain eased. Finally he reached his destination – a tall oak that gave a side view of the gaff and the driveway beyond. Trees hadn't really been the thing, growing up on the Woodlands estate. But he'd found out that climbing them wasn't all that frigging difficult. You tested the strength of a branch before you put your weight on it. You picked a route upwards that didn't involve over-stretching your arms or legs. A piece of piss really once you got the hang of it.

When he'd climbed high enough, he wedged himself in, checking his balance and his footing. Yesterday – Friday – would have been better, easier. Hubbie had buggered off in his Beamer by 7.30. Wifey had left on the dot of eight, shunting a couple of young kiddies into the back of the Audi. A Quattro Sport, two point seven: black and sleek enough. Off to school and all that. She hadn't come back in the twenty minutes Charlie had kept watch after she'd gone – which was well more than the kind of window he needed. But there was no point thinking about yesterday's missed opportunities. All that could matter now was what you did today.

He peered out towards the house through the branches. Waiting. The Beamer and the Audi weren't his targets. Especially as they were parked right at the top of the driveway, right outside the frigging front door. What Charlie was after was the other car. The one that wasn't here yet. The pig of it was that there were two vehicles sitting at the ready inside the Rectory's thatched-roof garage. Plus space for a third – the one that dear Tim and darling Nichola must have driven off to the airport in. The problem was what those vehicles *were*: a vintage Jag and some kind of shark-finned sixties Chevy – both in brilliant, immaculate nick. The Chevrolet was the sweetest set of wheels Charlie had ever seen at close range. But it was a complete non-starter when what was necessary to the purpose was something completely tedious and inconspicuous.

He squinted at his cheap imitation Rolex. Seven twenty-three. Any minute now, if yesterday morning was any guide. Mrs Mopp, he thought of her as. A fat, waddling old bag. The housekeeper or the general skivvy. Something like that. She'd even whistled some daft, ancient tune as she'd lumbered her way around the path towards the kitchen door. What was beautiful about her, though, was her parking routine. Identical both days: she drove a light blue Fiesta, old but with a healthy enough sounding engine, parked it at the *side* of the house under a wooden trestle set-up, the roof covered over with ivy or some such. If you went out deliberately to check, you'd notice soon enough if it had gone. But even today there was every chance that nobody would. Not for an hour or so anyway. The couple would have a weekend lie-in. The kiddies would be glued to the box or a computer game. The old dear would be ironing laundry or dusting the china or sneaking herself a quiet cup of tea. Seven twenty-four. And the security lighting would switch itself off as soon as lighting-up time ended.

He rested his head against the tree's thick, comforting bark, his ears pricked for the first sound of an approaching car engine. Any minute now. Drop down over the back wall and go steady. 'Course, he'd be on the security footage when they came to take a look. There was no way round that. But with his hood up and his head down, he'd just be any unknown toerag. Non-distinct. Anonymous. One useful thing he'd noticed was that the driveway sloped away from the house. What he thought he'd try was pushing the Fiesta first off, let it freewheel downhill, get it out onto the road and *then* start it. Seven twenty-five. That could work quite well, that could. Any minute now surely. Any frigging minute now.

# Chapter Thirty-Four

Kerr locked his fingers together behind his neck and stretched back slowly, willing the weariness out of his spine. He straightened up and let out a yawn. The older of the two sofas in the front room, the one that Cathy said needed replacing, was comfy enough for sitting on; for lounging, watching the telly or reading. But it had ceased some time ago to be an adequate support for a good night's sleep. He wandered through to the kitchen, naked but not especially cold under his dressing gown. The cat impeded his progress until his foot gently shunted her out of the way. She loved it when he slept downstairs in the wintertime, when she mainly stayed indoors herself. He'd find her draped across his feet when he woke up or stationed on the arm of the sofa above his head. A jet-black sentry. He filled the kettle, found a clean mug and a tea bag. At least she seemed to have given up on her succubus act at last. Cat's breath on your face in the darkness. Cat's purr in your ears. Cat's weight on your chest. Cat's isotope eyes.

He opened a fresh carton of milk, poured the first of it into her saucer. When the kettle boiled, he made his tea and sat down at the kitchen table. It was the one piece of furniture they still possessed that they'd owned since the first weeks of their marriage. The sagging sofa was a shiny new purchase by comparison. Cathy had found it in a saleroom. An old pine table in poor condition, going cheap. Kerr had sanded down the surfaces and together they'd applied the blue stain.

Ultramarine: dark, he always thought, like the bottom of the sea. He waited for his tea to cool, tried to enjoy the early morning quiet. If you took Rachel out of the equation, who Cathy didn't know about anyway, none of it was his fault. Not this time. The trip to the hospital with Jacobson had used up less than an hour. He'd been back by nine which had still left plenty of time to get over to the Ploughboy. He'd predicted as much before he'd gone. She could easily have asked Michelle to wait on; they could still have enjoyed a couple of hours out. But by then all Cathy had wanted was a shouting match.

The cat brushed against his leg, willing breakfast to follow her milk. When he'd been younger, his life had seemed linear, edging towards goals and purposes. Now mainly what he saw were patterns, binary and limiting. Cathy pissed off, Cathy not pissed off. Wanting to see Rachel. Not wanting to see Rachel. Only the job held surprise, change. New nastiness. New badness. New opportunities to rub your face in shit. He drank his tea then found the Whiskas tin and the white plastic spoon reserved for cat-feeding purposes.

Cathy had her head under the duvet when he snuck his clothes out of the bedroom. Whether asleep or in hiding it was impossible to say. He showered, shaved, dressed. Before he crept back downstairs, he edged the twins' bedroom door open for a moment. Both of them still soundly asleep, the side of Susie's head nudging her teddy bear. He didn't check his mobile until he was out of the house and sitting inside his car on the short driveway. *meet@8 ok? mac.* The text message was half an hour old, the sender's number withheld. He texted back, withholding his own number, started the engine.

George McCulloch's van was parked in virtually the same spot as it had been on Wednesday, still didn't look any cleaner. Kerr pulled up alongside and got out. Above his head, a crow flapped its way towards the tree line. Kerr had suggested more than once that they should vary their meeting places but McCulloch, nervous anyway, hadn't been happy about the idea, maybe had a superstition about sticking with somewhere that had worked out so far. Because the arrangement was unofficial, unlicensed, contact was best carried out in person. Extensive or regular phone calls were out of the question, left too many permanent traces. He slid back the theoretically-white door, climbed in.

'Morning, Geordie,' he said.

'Mornin', Mr Kerr.'

The interior reeked of tobacco and fried food. There was a brown McDonald's paper bag crumpled on the dash and McCulloch was forking at the residue of an Egg McMuffin and hash browns.

'Something hot tae start the day, Mr Kerr. Know what ah mean?'

Kerr, who rarely ate any kind of breakfast on a working day, said that he did.

'So you've got something for me, Geordie?'

McCulloch finished eating. Relit a roll-up. Then:

'Nothing about Dave Carter. Not a whisper. But this other case. The perfect family? Where the papers are saying the father did it?'

'You've heard something about *that*?'

'Not so much heard as seen.'

'Seen?'

McCulloch fished out a copy of yesterday's *Argus* from the compartment under the dash, pointed to the photo of Stephen Adams shaking hands with the mayor.

'An occasional visitor tae the Poets, would you believe?'

McCulloch paused to take a draw, flicked his ash inelegantly onto the floor.

'And ah don't mean the mayor either.'

Kerr's expression entirely failed to mask his surprise.

'Stephen Adams in the Poets?'

'Ah've a habit of calling in there on a Friday afternoon. End of the working week, isn't it? And that's when ah've seen him. Straight up, Mr Kerr. A guy in a business suit in a dump like that. Not exactly inconspicuous.'

Kerr asked for the details. McCulloch said he wasn't sure for how long. Probably more than six months. Probably less than a year. But no more than once in a given month, twice at most.

'You'll be wondering why he was there? Who he was with mibbe?'

'Don't piss me about, Geordie. We're not looking outside the family. We're looking into the background, that's all.'

Kerr rolled the window down a couple of inches, unable to stomach the stench of fried nicotine a second longer. He tapped at his wallet through his jacket.

'The usual consideration – take it or leave it.'

McCulloch had a blue-backed receipt book on the dash next to his Golden Virginia pouch. He tore out a blank, found a grubby biro, scribbled a name and an address.

'A nice enough lassie,' he said, passing the receipt across. 'Not really hard core. More in the way of a gifted amateur.'

# Chapter Thirty-Five

Just to be on the safe side, Charlie stowed the Fiesta in the garage for now. In front of the Jag and the Chevy. He found Lisa in the kitchen, wiping down the surfaces. She'd already done most of what needed doing, she told him. The only problem, she said, was Brian Bilston.

Charlie belted upstairs, flung open the door of the bedroom FB had made his own. He was still in bed. He was still in his useless, fuckwit, lazy bed. Flat on his back and snoring. Charlie pulled the thick duvet off him, shook him by the shoulders, got no real response. He was wasting his time and he knew it. Despite what had been agreed, the twat had evidently trashed himself out of it again. With a little help from the travelling pharmacy stashed at the bottom of his hold-all. Charlie just stood there, staring at the fuckwit face, the dribble of saliva at the corner of the aimless mouth. The worst thing was realising that it was his own fuck-up too. A management failure as much as anything. If you needed associates, you were meant to choose carefully, supposed to separate the wheat from the chaff. That much was elementary, basic, a matter of first principles. Yet Charlie had gone for FB over others, had probably let sentiment and misplaced loyalty cloud his judgement. He'd known Bilston was a pill-head but he hadn't known the extent – he hadn't understood, for instance, that the cunt was up and down more often than a tart's knickers. Down this time evidently. Diazepam. Or even effing methadone. FB's drug habits had gone beyond sensible, had become totally promiscuous, totally non-discriminatory. *Anything to get off your face, old bean:* the kind of fuckwit remark that Charlie had taken to be a joke when bastarding, shit-brained Florida Boy had meant it as a philosophy of life.

He went back downstairs, helped Lisa with the kitchen. The easy option, the obvious one, was just to leg it without him. According to their helpful answerphone message, Tim and Nichola were gone until the twenty-seventh, still a clear five days away. It was a good bet that a housekeeper or some such would turn up before then, get the place nice and welcoming for the dear couple. But that still left FB lying low and undetected for another two or three days – provided he didn't do anything too daft in the way of lights and noise. Lisa and himself would be well away in the meantime. Very well away. That would have to be it, then. Leave the sod to grab his own chances. Charlie was passing unwashed plates to Lisa, who was stacking them into the dishwasher. He'd get caught on his own, of course. Get caught and blab. He didn't have the nous, the gumption or the brains for anything else. But at least I'll have a frigging head start, Charlie thought, gingerly lifting a hefty Clarice Cliff dessert bowl. What the fuck else could he do anyway?

# Chapter Thirty-Six

Jacobson walked into the Divisional building at 8.45 and took the lift four floors up to the incident room. Emma Smith gave him a weary smile as he came through the door. Smith and Williams had cross-referenced approximately half of the Adams case door-to-door statements before they'd called it a night. It would probably take them the best part of Saturday morning to finish the job. On the other side of the room, Sergeant Ince was sitting at a computer workstation alongside Steve Horton, the civilian computer officer. Jacobson had become as proficient as he thought he needed to be at querying the PNC and Crowby's localised crime database. But it turned out that Horton had a new toy, something he called an expert system, a piece of software which, he'd claimed, looked *intelligently* for evidential patterns.

'The last bugger I knew that played around with this kind of thing ended up doing time for GBH,' Jacobson said darkly.

Horton's fingers sped over the keyboard. He was blond and muscular; six foot three when he wasn't hunched over a pc. Jacobson always wondered why he wasn't raking it in elsewhere. Modelling beachwear or acting in an Australian soap.

'What I'm accessing first, Mr Jacobson, is the basic data set.'

'That's to say every scrap of information the system has about Bilston, guv,' Ince added, trying to help.

Jacobson nodded affably enough. He'd phoned Mick Hume

on his way in: still no serious leads to go on. The media appeal had likewise yielded bog-all so far. The least he could do was to give Horton's technofix a chance.

The computer screen scrolled through the official signifiers of Brian Bilston's life. Permanent exclusion from schooling a few days before his fourteenth birthday. Juvenile court appearances. Probation reports. Fines. Community service orders. Bilston had progressed from children's detention centres to stretches in young offenders' institutions, had clocked up in excess of forty convictions before he was old enough for the adult court system. Impressive, Jacobson thought, although it was nothing like the record. Not even locally.

'Another thing we can do is link the search in with the local press archives,' Horton said enthusiastically, double-clicking his mouse and flashing his brilliant teen idol smile.

The *Argus* looked to have clutched Bilston to its fickle bosom even if no one else had. Five or six years ago, like papers elsewhere in the country, it couldn't get enough of 'boys'. Safari Boy. Pyjama Boy. Spider Boy. Balaclava Boy. Rat Boy. Blip Boy. You weren't allowed to name an offender below the prescribed age so you gave him a nickname which related to how he got caught, how he evaded capture or, best of all, how he was 'pampered' at public expense by the do-gooders and social workers.

Jacobson didn't see anything gigantically wrong with trying to encourage a lad in difficult circumstances, still a kid really, showing him there could be more to life than hanging around street corners and nicking cars. If the attempt failed more often than it succeeded, then that only put it on a par with most other human endeavours. But the hacks at the *Argus* did – or affected to. According to the *Argus*, the taxpayers' money had been thrown away on Safari Boy's trip to Kenya and pissed down a veritable drain in the case of Florida Boy's adventure week in the Everglades.

'Now what, old son?' he asked when they'd glanced at the last newspaper entry.

Horton did his best to explain in non-technical terms. Bilston's offences weren't always solo efforts committed in isolation. Even when they were, they'd still taken place at specific times and in specific places where other crimes might have been detected. Plus he wasn't the only kid from Crowby sent into specific custodial settings during specific, verifiable dates.

'It's all about true correlation, Mr Jacobson. What the program can look for is other offenders who link more than randomly to the data on Bilston. Potentially, one of the names it throws up could have been his associate on Monday.'

Jacobson thought he followed the logic. But he remembered something that Kerr, another would-be computer buff, had said to him once: the machine was only as smart as the data that an overworked copper in a hurry had typed into it in the first place.

'Let me know how it goes anyway, Steve,' he said, leaving them to it.

In his fifth floor office, he checked his voicemail and read down the latest incident sheet, the log of police and criminal activity issued every twelve hours. His mobile beeped. The stunt of giving out his number in the lounge bar of the Poets had been unquestionably his daftest for a while. Although the volume of text messages had mercifully eased off since earlier in the week. The last one he could definitely recall had been on Thursday morning. He read the new arrival – *lic my rshole* – and deleted it, wondered idly if there was an academic somewhere in need of a research project: anal obsession and the British underclass, something like that. He read to the end of the incident sheet, which was actually three sheets of yellow A4 stapled together. But there was nothing that looked remotely pertinent. His mobile rang before he got around to stuffing it back into his pocket: DS Kerr. He stood over by the window to take the call and watched a dirty black cloud drape the sky beyond the shopping centre.

Before he grabbed his coat, he turned the photocube on his desk to an angle from which he could see the whole of Sally's photograph and only the edge of his ex-wife Janice's. He'd slept badly again, the scene at Willow Court melding in his dreams with Eileen Carter's hospital room. Peter Robinson had been there too, trying over and over again to infibulate the dissected heart inside Stephen Adams' dangling corpse. Adams was dead yet somehow able to speak. But only one phrase. Over and over. *Get it sorted. Get it Sorted.*

He nipped into Kwik Save in the ten minutes Kerr said it would take him to reach the Divi car park. He glanced through the newspaper rack near the tills, noticed that the national tabloids were still running with the story. The *Express* gave it the biggest coverage: *Slain Family Had Everything To Live For, turn to page five.* Jacobson added a copy to the rest of his purchases, picked the wrong checkout as usual. On this occasion the one with the harassed new assistant, the flustered old lady and the six months' worth of tenpence-off coupons.

Kerr found the place easily enough. Southey House. The sixth of the six ten-storey blocks if you counted William Blake House as the first. Amy Hobbs lived right up on the tenth floor. She wasn't answering her entryphone but Jacobson and Kerr had arrived at the same time as the postman and followed him in anyway. The lift stank but it worked. Kerr recognised Moby behind the scuffed yellow door. Jacobson just heard an electronic thump which he took as a sign to thump harder himself. Eventually the usual business was negotiated. Shuffling behind the door. ID flashed through the letter box. *You'd better come frigging in then.*

Inside, the flat was warm, clean, tidy. From the lounge window, you could just about see over the Woodlands estate towards something that might be countryside. Amy Hobbs was a looker. Blonde, blue eyed, early twenties. She had a toddler with her, a placid little girl sitting on the carpet next to a pile of soft toys.

'Panda,' she said, lifting up her favourite.

'This is Cinnamon, she's three,' Amy Hobbs said. 'Cin, these nasty big men who've come to see Mummy are the horrid filth.'

'Same age as my two,' Kerr said, finding a seat uninvited on a white leather sofa.

'Blimey,' the girl countered, 'the experience made you very nearly human, has it?'

Jacobson plonked himself next to Kerr, watched her point a remote at an upmarket hi-fi, turn the music off. There was a laptop computer on a pine desk near the window, a stack of textbooks, a mug of tea. Jacobson clocked the most prominent titles. Louis Althusser, *For Marx*; Max Weber, *The Protestant Ethic and the Spirit of Capitalism*. She turned the chair outwards from the desk, sat down, picked up the mug between both hands. Jacobson told her why they were there but not how they'd been put on to her.

'The guy who killed his family?' she asked, then took a sip of tea.

'Who *probably* killed his family,' Jacobson corrected her. 'We're looking into the background. Talking to anyone who knew him or the family well, trying to build up a picture.'

She took another sip, didn't reply.

'We don't give a fuck *how* you knew him, eh, Amy,' Kerr said. 'We just need to know what he was like. What kind of a bloke he was in your experience.'

A laugh this time, replacing the mug on the desk, crossing her legs.

'Same as any other. Same as you, I expect. After a shag on the side.'

'He used to meet you in the Poets or so we're told,' Jacobson said. 'Unusual, isn't it?'

235

'He's not the only one. You'd be surprised. There's a fair few that like to meet you somewhere first, pretend they're on a date – that it's not just them paying for it.'

Jacobson had planned on a B and H during the visit. But the room smelt smoke free, even fragrant. And there was the toddler to consider. He contented himself with the thought of lighting one up in the car afterwards. Amy Hobbs took another sip of tea. Then:

'The only thing unusual about it was choosing the Poets. Mostly they prefer somewhere a bit classier. The Riverside Hotel or somewhere like that.'

'So he was a regular. What – once a month? Twice a month?' Jacobson asked.

'About that. Every four weeks or so. Always on a Friday.'

'And you met him how?'

She had a swivel chair, swivelled it to her right, tapped a key on the laptop. The screen saver – Buffy kissing Angel – vanished to reveal another – Willow kissing Tara.

'I started off with one of the escort agencies in town. But then I went online. I suss them out by email first, filter out the head cases and woman haters.'

'I don't suppose you store your emails?' Kerr asked.

'That's right. I don't,' she answered, too quickly for him to know if she was lying.

Jacobson fingered his silver lighter: another compensation.

'Getting back to Stephen Adams specifically – did he talk much about himself? His life?'

Amy Hobbs swivelled back again.

'Oh, yes. Steve talked all right. Most of them do. Proud of his kids. Worried about his business. How he loved his wife really. All the usual shit.'

'You didn't think he was off the wall in any way?' Jacobson asked. 'Unstable mentally?'

'A married white Englishman? Service sector local business. Entry-level middle class. Heterosexual. A walking

236

instantiation of history's most redundant categories. Poor old Steve was *alienated* to fuck – but I wouldn't have called him mental in the ordinary sense of the word.'

Jacobson positively gaped at her.

'You're the first whore I've met with a sociological critique,' he said after a moment.

She drained the last of her tea before she replied.

'You should get out more, then. I've nearly finished my Master's. Then it'll be a research scholarship. UEA maybe. Or York. Bye-bye Crowby, anyway.'

'But you'll carry on working?' Kerr asked.

'If I have to. Beats waitressing or doing the ironing for some bourgeois cow who's too lazy to do it for herself.'

'Shagging for money with your daughter in the next room?'

'My mother takes her when I'm busy. I do four afternoons a week max. I earn more than I'd get slaving in an office.'

Unsmiling, folding her arms across her chest.

'Cool it, Ian,' Jacobson said, 'we came here about Adams. Nothing else.'

The toddler dumped the panda, picked up another toy.

'Lion,' she announced.

'OK. None of my business really,' Kerr said, coming as close as he ever did to an apology. 'What about the sex, then. Nothing odd in that way?'

'I could probably fit you in at the end of next week if you're desperate.'

Jacobson didn't entirely succeed in keeping a straight face.

'It's a legitimate question,' he said.

Amy Hobbs tapped her keyboard again. Spike and Drusilla.

'I dare say. But no, nothing odd. Blow job, doggie and missionary. Not the kinky type really, our Steve.'

Jacobson thanked her for her time. Kerr wanted to take the stairs back down but Jacobson insisted on the lift. Four small lads were stood near Kerr's Peugeot when they got back to it.

'We've kept an eye on your motor, mister,' the oldest-looking one said.

He could have been eight, possibly nine. Kerr made a quick tour of the paintwork, couldn't find any new scratches. He chucked a two-pound coin at the kid before he climbed in. On balance, he thought, it was a scam worth encouraging. Better than the usual number anyway: demand the cash up front, then mark the car and scamper the minute you were out of sight. He opened the passenger door for Jacobson.

'Where to next, Frank?'

Jacobson got in, leant behind the seat and lifted up his Kwik Save carrier bag.

'We ought to check with Mick Hume and company. Brian Bilston's hardly a criminal genius, he can't be *that* difficult to find. But first this,' – He thrust the bag at Kerr – 'Go on, take a look.'

Kerr looked inside: the *Daily Express*, two pairs of rubber kitchen gloves, a carton of lightweight cat litter, two boxes of dried cat food.

'Eileen Carter's cats, old son,' Jacobson said, finding his B and H packet. 'It's been on my conscience since last night. I phoned the RSPCA first thing. They can't do anything until Monday – so it's up to us meantime.'

Kerr turned the ignition, slipped the car into gear.

'Have it your way. I'd've thought more the *Sport* or the *Sun* for your average Woodlands moggie.'

Sheryl declined the offer of police transport this time, took the bus instead. Two buses really. One into Flowers Street, a second out to the hospital. She brought Lucy along too. Since Candice was being so decent about everything, she thought that it was time she had her place to herself – and Liam – for a couple of hours. Lucy was fine with it in any case, just took a lolly from the big jar at reception, made straight for the play corner as soon as they were shown into the room. The woman was still dressed entirely in black, looked more like a half-hearted dominatrix than a frigging shrink or a doctor.

'Anne-Marie' – she had a soft, gentle voice, Sheryl would give her that much – 'thank you for coming to see me again.'

Anne-Marie sat exactly where she'd sat before. In exactly the same silence. The woman had given Sheryl a mobile number yesterday, had said she could call her any time, arrange a meeting whenever she liked. Sheryl hadn't had much intention – until she'd found Anne-Marie with the plastic clothes line wrapped around her neck. There was an open packet of crayons on the table. Dr Claire Burke spread out a big sheet of white drawing paper next to them.

'I thought maybe you'd like to draw something today, Anne-Marie,' she said.

Anne-Marie kept her head down, still didn't speak.

'I thought you liked to paint and draw, love. That's what Mrs Harrison told me anyway,' Sheryl said.

Dr Burke took a few of the crayons out of the box, set them down within Anne-Marie's reach.

'Sometimes it's easier to draw than to tell,' she said.

Sheryl shifted her gaze from the woman to her daughter and then back again. You didn't need a frigging degree in psychology to see what her idea was this time. Anne-Marie had to find some way of dealing with what she'd seen, some way of letting go. Great. Only it didn't seem to be working. The world was full of experts, telling you what to do, what to think. But all it came down to was that they talked posh and you didn't; they'd passed some poxy exam and you hadn't. Half the time they were as much in the dark as you were, busking it. They might as well go home, she thought. Stop wasting the dreary cow's time. Stop wasting their own time.

Abruptly, Anne-Marie picked up a red crayon and a black one. She grabbed the sheet of paper and rushed away from the table – rushed away from them, it felt like – over towards the wide, tall window. Sheryl wondered if she should follow her but the woman looked across at her, gestured with her hand: leave her be. Anne-Marie knelt on the carpet. She used up the first sheet quickly. Then another. Then a third. More slowly, carefully, by then. She drew the same images over and over. A stick man hanging from a rope. A tall upright figure striking a smaller prone one with a shape like a stick. Thick red stripes zigzagging across the head of the figure lying down. A word balloon from the hanging stick man. *Help me.*

The search for a lead to Brian Bilston had diversified. Hume and Renbourn sticking with the Woodlands, Barber and the drug squad representative, DC Watts, covering Mill Street and the town centre dives. Jacobson and Kerr spent twenty minutes with the cats. The plan was to catch up with Hume and Renbourn in the Poets car park afterwards. Point one: assess the latest intelligence on Bilston. Point two: remind the Poets' bar manager, Terry Shields, that Crowby CID were still on his case. But Jacobson took a call from Sergeant Ince just as Kerr was starting up the car again, quickly changed his mind.

Kerr made the journey inside thirty minutes. Back into the centre of Crowby, back out to the Bartons. Not too bad, he thought, through the Saturday morning shopping traffic. The exterior of 3 Willow Court, aka Arcady, varied from the Adams' house at number eight by virtue, if that was the word, of its leaded bay windows and the faux Georgian Doric pillars on either side of the front door. An unpleasant, overweight Pomeranian, scenting black cat, snarled at Jacobson and Kerr as they followed Martin Warner into his front room. Kerr was neutral on dogs but Jacobson was mainly anti. A smart collie on a hill farm was one thing. Pampered mounds of hair, piss and crap on a suburban street were quite another.

Warner sat down on the sofa next to the dog. Jacobson grabbed an armchair. Kerr made do with standing, his back to the window. The story from Sergeant Ince was that Warner had phoned through to the incident room, had claimed he'd seen a visitor leaving the Adams' house in the early hours of Thursday morning.

''Scuse the mess,' Warner said, leaning forward and moving a cluttered tray – beer cans, dirty plates, an overflowing ashtray – from the floor onto a low, similarly cluttered table. Kerr studied his face, his expression. A guy about his own age or a couple of years younger. Smart haircut, recently shaved, ordinary casual weekend clothes. If you had to make an instant, superficial judgement you'd be hard pushed to say anything other than everyday, sane, normal.

'On your own, I take it?' Jacobson asked.

Warner leant forward again, righted a framed photograph that had been lying on its side next to a stack of magazines. Newlyweds popping champagne.

'She walked out six months ago. A bloke she met at some sales conference,' – he half laughed, half snorted – 'I wouldn't care really except she left me with this place on my hands. And the bloody dog. Both of them her ideas mainly. We had a nice little flat in town before we got hitched. Handy for the pubs, clubbing – everything.'

'You'll get a decent price if you sell up, though, surely,' Kerr said.

Warner patted the top of the Pomeranian's head.

'I guess so. So long as the "house of horror" doesn't put the buyers off.'

Jacobson studied the photo. Then:

'You didn't come forward until this morning. Two days after. Why?'

'I explained all that when I phoned. Didn't they tell you?'

Better than that, Ince had played him the tape of the conversation. But Jacobson wanted to hear Martin Warner's current version as well.

241

'Crossed wires as usual, Mr Warner,' he said. 'Maybe you could explain again?'

'Yeah, sure,' Warner said. 'I was in London yesterday and the day before. At the head office? I work for Fujitsu. I'm trying out for a move down there, maybe promotion.'

Jacobson didn't need the details of his CV but he let it pass.

'So you didn't know about the Adams family until you got back?'

'No – I knew before then all right. I heard it on the breakfast news yesterday. Radio Five. I must've phoned half a dozen times through the day, couldn't get an answer. Tried again in the evening, same thing. And it wasn't much easier this morning.'

Warner found a Marlboro packet and a lighter hidden under the February *GQ*. Jacobson mirrored him; only his third B and H of the day.

'Fair enough, Mr Warner. We do get plagued with nuisance calls on high-profile investigations unfortunately. Serial confessors, that kind of thing. Sometimes it's difficult for the genuine callers to reach us.'

Both of them lit up. Kerr coughed, his hand over his mouth.

'So – the early hours of Thursday. You saw something?' Jacobson asked.

'I couldn't get to sleep properly. That was the reason. I was wound up about wanting to make a good impression in London, kept thinking about what the set-up would be like down there. Head racing, you know?'

Jacobson nodded.

'Eventually I thought I'd grab a bit of fresh air, see if that helped. Took this tubby thing out with me. My sister was going to look after him while I was away. That meant he'd be getting even less exercise than usual.'

'The time?'

'I got out of bed dead on four am. I can still see the bedside clock in my mind. I had to be at the station by seven in any case – so I reckoned I'd be as well up and about as lying in bed not sleeping.'

'And you took your dog out for a walk?'

'*Her* dog, it's supposed to be. Fern Avenue. Rowan Court. Then back into Willow Court. A five-minute walk if I'd gone on my own, more like ten with his nibs in tow.'

Jacobson spotted a smaller ashtray that was only half full. He moved it onto the arm of the armchair.

'The Adams house, then. You saw what exactly?'

'It was when I was nearly back here. There's a service road behind the rear gardens on the other side of the street, shared with Rowan Court. Well, it's more or less straight. You can see right along it if you're walking past out on the avenue.'

Warner paused, sucked on his cigarette.

'Just as I was passing, I saw somebody coming out of number eight's back gate.'

'Description?' Jacobson asked.

'Hard to tell from that distance. But definitely a bloke anyway. Not young. Not old. Fairly tall. And he was carrying something under his arm. Like a parcel maybe.'

Kerr glanced out the window. There was a water feature, switched off for winter, in the centre of the lawn. A stone frog perched on a stone water lily. He turned his head towards the interior of the room again.

'You didn't challenge him?' he asked. 'A stranger sneaking out of the property in the middle of the night?'

Warner looked over at Kerr, shrugged.

'Would you if you weren't paid to? He didn't strike me as sneaking particularly. Could've been a friend or a lodger for all I know, could've been anybody.'

Kerr shrugged back. Warner, not him, was the one who'd have to live with it – if it needed to be lived with.

'You're certain it was number eight he was leaving from?' Jacobson asked.

'Positively. It's the very last garden, right along at the end. I *did* take a look across at the front of their house before I came back in here. But I couldn't see anything out of the ordinary. No lights on. Both vehicles in the drive.'

Jacobson tipped his ash.

'How did you get on with Mr and Mrs Adams as neighbours?'

'I hardly knew them. I've only been here just over a year. They were certainly friendly enough. Him in particular. He'd say hello, want to chat, any time he saw you. Always keen on parties and barbecues at the weekend in the summer. Open house to all the neighbours. Everybody invited.'

'But you didn't take up the invites yourself?' Jacobson guessed.

'Six months' argy-bargy. Then six months sulking on my own. I haven't really been in a sociable mood recently.'

Jacobson stood up. The Pomeranian was settling down for a snooze but still seething with enough canine malice to bark at him.

'Well, thank you, Mr Warner,' he said. 'We appreciate that you came forward.'

'Yep. Thanks. Sorry about your wife,' Kerr added, suddenly – unwillingly – thinking about his own.

# Chapter Thirty-Seven

Jacobson and Kerr called in on the crime scene. The wall and the pavement on either side of the lines of police tape were drenched in floral tributes and cards. From neighbours and school friends. But also from well-wishers: sympathisers who'd never known the family, who'd only learned about the deaths via the newspapers or the telly. Hardly any sod believed in God or politics or mutuality any more, Jacobson thought. Instead they grabbed a fragile, ersatz togetherness where they could find it. Football matches. The January sales. At the site of sudden, public deaths.

A constable he didn't know was stationed in the MIU. Watch duty. Inside the house, three SOCOs in white protective suits were still at work. Repeating certain procedures, they said: just to make absolutely certain. Jacobson persuaded them into an experiment of his own. He borrowed the plod's truncheon, found an unused wooden packing case at the back of the second Portakabin. When everything was ready, he closed the front door, stationed himself in the front garden. He sent Kerr to the side of the house and the plod around to the back. Upstairs, in the room where Mark Adams had met his death – where he looked to have put up a struggle first – the burliest SOCO laid into the packing case with the truncheon; trashed it as loudly and as violently as he could. Jacobson had asked him to remove his face mask, to shout and curse at the same time. Result: zero. Kerr and the uniformed heard nothing. Jacobson thought that *maybe* he might have heard a faint thump or two. But Stephen Adams' triple-glazed windows had pretty much muffled any noise from inside the house, would have done the same when his family were being slaughtered.

Kerr tried a new route back to the Divisional building. Over to Longtown first – via Derby Road. It was further in miles but it meant you could miss out the worst of the traffic headed for the Waitrose complex. They talked over Martin Warner's evidence on the way.

'He didn't strike me as a Looney Tunes merchant,' Kerr said.

'Me neither, Ian,' Jacobson replied. 'On the face of it. Don't forget his wife's buggered off, he's socially isolated. It's always possible he's an attention seeker, trying to boost his self-image, make himself feel important.'

Jacobson called Ince on his mobile. Ince had already checked Warner out on the PNC and on the local database; he confirmed that he wasn't Known To The Police. Not previously anyway.

'The thing is – suppose he is genuine, what then?' Kerr asked, slowing behind a delivery van that had no chance of beating the next set of traffic lights.

'We weigh it against everything else, old son. Especially the forensics. He could be genuine but mistaken, for instance. He hadn't slept well. It was early in the morning. Maybe he did just get the house wrong after all.'

*Were you awake during the night? Did you see or hear anyone or anything unusual or suspicious?* The questions had been included in every single interview conducted on the Bartons. But so far as Jacobson knew, only Warner avowed that he had.

Kerr dropped Jacobson off near the NCP car park. He could make the next calls on his own, Jacobson told him. What Jacobson wanted to do next himself, he said, was just sit down somewhere in peace and quiet. Just sit down and think.

\*

DC Barber and DC Watts ran into Jason Whitmore in the urinals of the Market Tavern. He looked about as pleased to see them as he'd been to see Mick Hume and Renbourn the day before.

'Starting early today, Jayce?' Barber asked him.

'Just a quick one. Hair of the dog, isn't it?'

Whitmore's body language was easier to read than the *Beano*. Leg it through the indoor market. Disappear among the crowds in the shopping centre.

'We need a word,' Watts said, blocking his path.

Whitmore did up his flies, dug his hands into his pockets.

'This is blinking harassment. I already spoke to your mate yesterday.'

'Different day, different word,' Barber said. 'The more you stand here arguing about it, the more chance somebody sees you with us.'

Reluctantly Whitmore agreed to meet them ten minutes later in Cake Break, a coffee bar in the specialist arcade which was mainly patronised by OAPs.

Barber treated him to a Danish pastry and an unconvincing-looking latte.

'Brian Bilston, Jason. What's he up to these days?'

Whitmore had his hood up, had insisted they move to a table as far away from the door and the window as possible.

'That mad cunt? I ain't seen him in months. I swear it.'

'That's hard to believe, Jayce,' Watts said. 'A mover and shaker such as yourself. In with the in crowd.'

Whitmore bit into the pastry, tore the top off a thin tube of sugar. Barber played the same game Hume had played the day before. Whitmore's next court appearance could go either way: more probation, more community service – or his first stretch in an adult nick.

'I'd help out if I could, mate. I swear it. But I ain't seen him – not to speak to anyway.'

Barber and Watts said nothing. Just waited.

'Sunday night. He was in a car up on the Woodlands. Charlie Taylor was driving – you could try asking him.'

Kerr stopped off at the Top Hat café on Copthorne Road, ordered two sausage sandwiches and a mug of tea. He thought about phoning Rachel just to hear her voice. Then he remembered she'd gone to Shropshire for the weekend, one of her rare visits to stay with her mother. She'd probably prefer not be disturbed. His own mother had been dead seven years now. But his dad was still going strong. Or so he always said. He was in Spain until the end of the month. Another one of his old leftist dos. A tour of Civil War sites and then some kind of conference in Barcelona. A piss-up as much as anything, he'd said when Kerr had driven him to the airport. *You know me, Ian. Still pissing against the wind of history.*

Somebody had left a *Daily Mirror* on the table. Kerr glanced at it while he ate. The story was more or less the same as in the *Express. Town Mourns Slaying of Perfect Family.* More or less the same pictures too. Stephen and Marion Adams beaming at the mayor. Sarah Adams dwarfed by a bouquet of roses and carnations. The two lads waving out of the window of the stretch limo. He ate up, finished his tea. He'd fitted an MP3 player in his car over Christmas, had spent a couple of days downloading music files. The thing he liked best was to set it on random play, just wait and see what came on next. He drove onto the Copthorne Road industrial estate with the Stones following the Hives: 'All Down The Line'. Blasting them off the planet, he thought. Without even trying.

The garage and workshop doors were locked up. The front office was empty but there were lights on inside and a woman's coat hanging on a peg. Kerr pressed the bell, waited, pressed it again. Linda Blackpole, Stephen Adams' sole office employee, appeared a few minutes later, entering the room from the door that connected it to the rest of the premises. Kerr had to hold his ID up to the window before she would let him in. He followed her through the office and into the workshop. Colin Paterson was checking stock, making ticks on a clipboard with a biro as he moved along the racks of aerials, decoders, amplifiers, satellite dishes. Jacobson in person had spoken to both of them on Thursday, had put them on his list of those he thought it was worth talking to again. The people you work with, old son, he'd said to Kerr earlier, a lot of the time they know you better than your own family. Kerr hadn't commented. Jacobson was the only other officer on the force who knew about Rachel. Or so he hoped.

'Just the two of you here, then?' he asked.

'Not much point for anyone else,' Paterson said. 'Not much point for us either, come to that. Someone's got to get the paperwork straight, complete the inventory. But after that it's down the dole office on Monday basically.'

The legal position of Adams Installations was unresolved. Stephen Adams hadn't kept his will up to date. In the event of his wife and children not surviving him by sixty days, his estate passed to his father. The fact that had probably got Kerr thinking about his own dad. Unfortunately Adams senior, himself a widower, was suffering from advanced Alzheimer's, was banged up in a nursing home in Wynarth. Paterson was correct: with bankruptcy already on the cards and the coroner likely to confirm Stephen Adams' death as suicide, the workforce were one hundred and ten per cent stuffed.

'Must be shit,' Kerr said. 'Especially when you've worked here for so long.'

'Ten years, mate. The firm's only being going for twelve.'

'I've been here for three years,' Linda Blackpole said. 'Nothing like as bad for me as for Colin. But even so.'

Paterson put his clipboard down, stuck the pen behind his ear.

'His whole family. I don't think I'll ever get my head round it.'

'You told DCI Jacobson he was a good boss,' Kerr said.

'Only because it's true. He never asked anybody to work any harder than he did himself, he paid the going rate, he treated you straight.'

'And that was the general view?' Kerr asked.

'You only have to look at the staff turnover,' Paterson replied. 'Folk joined and stayed on more often than they left.'

'He got a bit moody sometimes recently,' Linda Blackpole commented. 'Because of the downturn in business.'

'Moody, you say. What? Shouting, losing his temper?'

'No, nothing like that. He put a brave face on it. Laughing, joking – same as always. But you could tell he was worried deep down.'

She was more or less Amy Hobbs' age, Kerr thought. Scarcely less attractive.

'Don't take offence,' he said. 'It's something I have to ask. But some male bosses—'

'Nothing like that either,' she said, shaking her head for emphasis, not waiting for the whole question. 'He was a perfect gentleman as far as that goes. Some prat stuck a girlie calendar up one time. Steve told him it was inappropriate, asked him to take it back home.'

Paterson leant against the workbench where he'd placed the clipboard, rested his weight on his elbows.

'Like I say, he was a good boss.'

'A mate even?' Kerr asked.

'We certainly sank a few pints in the early years,' Paterson said. 'Maybe not so much recently.'

'Why the change?'

'The firm got bigger mainly. I think he felt he had to keep more of a distance. Be seen as the top layer.'

'So he wouldn't have confided in you, Mr Paterson?'

'Not about anything personal.'

# Chapter Thirty-Eight

Ray Coombs was the third name on Jacobson's list. But not because he thought he was worth speaking to again. The thing with Coombs was that he hadn't been spoken to at all. A couple of uniformeds had called at his house on Thursday night and again on Friday afternoon. No answer either time. Coombs lived on the Beech Park estate. The other side of it from Tom Kerr. Kerr drove to his father's house first anyway. He picked up the post and the freebie newspapers from the mat behind the front door, carried them through to the kitchen table, checked out the premises generally. By the time he reached Coombs' address, it was near enough one o'clock.

Two legs, covered in oil-stained trousers and ending in a pair of old, muddy trainers, protruded from the rear end underside of the Volkswagen Polo that was parked immediately outside. Six years old according to the registration plate. Kerr crouched down, said who he was, showed his ID.

'Two seconds, mate,' Ray Coombs said, tightening a bracket on an exhaust pipe that had seen better days.

When he was back on his feet, Kerr followed him indoors, Coombs stopping at the porch to kick off his footwear. The houses on this part of the estate all had their kitchens at the front. Coombs walked through, ran his hands under the tap and then shook them dry. Kerr told him about the two failed visits.

'Oh, I see, right,' Coombs said. 'The wife and I are always

251

out Thursdays. Over at the old Star and Garter. Line dancing. Tea any good to you?'

Kerr said that it was.

'And yesterday?'

'Depends when they called. The wife works at Homebase. On the checkout? So she's out all day for a kick-off. I went into town, had a look in the jobcentre. Nowt doing, of course.'

Coombs clicked on the kettle, found two mugs, two tea bags. Kerr put him somewhere between forty and fifty. An honest face is better than a handsome one, his mother might have said.

'Been with Adams for long?'

'Six months or thereabouts. The firm I was with before, they went bust an' all.'

'Too bad. Everybody says he was a good boss, though.'

Coombs lifted a carton of milk out of his fridge.

'Everybody in the crony brigade, mate,' he said. 'Don't get me wrong. It's a terrible thing's happened. I wouldn't wish it on anybody. But I wouldn't have stopped on there even this long if something else had turned up.'

Kerr asked him why not.

'I've worked for small firms like that before. Less than a dozen workers all told. Rubbish, mate. Complete rubbish.'

The kettle boiled and he made the tea, passed Kerr a mug and the carton of milk. They sat down at the kitchen table.

'Too cliquey, see? Adams, Paterson, a few others. Never totally honest with you, always bullshitting that everything was fine. Sugar?'

'No thanks,' Kerr said. 'And you don't think it was?'

Coombs spooned three heaped teaspoons into his own mug.

'Like buggery. Practically all we'd do is these daft, bloody reinspects. You know – revisit old customers, tweak their system free of charge. Plus try and flog them some new kit.

Half the time they didn't even want to let you in, never mind fork out more cash.'

His mouth broadened into an unwinning smile at the thought.

'The worst of it was if Paterson or Adams himself came out with you. Chucking brochures everywhere. I'm a technician, I told them, not a bloody salesman.'

Kerr decided the tea would need another minute to cool.

'So Colin Paterson was definitely what you'd call a crony?'

'Crony-in-flaming-chief, mate. The wife and I were out on the town a couple of Fridays back. A gang of us. Her youngest sister's birthday, see? Anyway, we're in Wetherspoons at one point. Late on too.'

Coombs paused, took his first sip.

'Guess who's propping up the bar? Knocking back the spirits? Adams and Paterson, that's who. Both of them well away by the looks of it.'

Jacobson checked into the incident room. Steve Horton, as thorough or as anal as ever, had run his computer program half a dozen times. Five young men had achieved correlation factors which Horton claimed were high enough to be significant. According to the local intelligence database, one of them had recently enlisted in the army and three of them were guests of the prison service. The fifth was Charles Edward Taylor, aged twenty, currently of no fixed abode. Bilston and Taylor were the same age. They'd been caught nicking together when they were eleven and again when they were fourteen. They'd been expelled from the same secondary school. Most consequentially of all, they'd both spent six months in HM Young Offenders' Institute Brinsford at precisely the same time. Jacobson studied the data, drew some meagre technophobic comfort from the fact that Barber and Watts had got to Taylor nearly as quickly – and by entirely traditional means. He assigned the coordinating role to Sergeant Ince. Give Barber and Watts time to dig Taylor out of his known hang-outs. If they hadn't got anywhere inside an hour, say, then Ince could release his details to other forces. But nothing to go to the media. Not at this stage anyway. They had witness testimony on Bilston, maybe eventually a forensic result from the tyre lever ditched under his bed. With regard to Taylor, they only had speculation so far. Mick Hume could handle that angle. Chase Ryan Walsh again, see if he could identify Taylor from his mug shots. Emma Smith and DC Williams were nearly finished with their cross-referencing. When they'd got to the end, they could join forces with Renbourn, carry on the general search for Bilston.

He nipped up to the canteen: cottage pie and baked beans, a glass of milk. Dr Claire Burke called him on his mobile. Anne-Marie Holmes might be on the verge of a positive breakthrough. But unfortunately there were no guarantees. It was only too conceivable that she could regress instead. She'd enjoyed Mr Behar's, by the way. He should come over to Birmingham some time, try out one of the original Balti houses. Jacobson said he'd like that. Then spent the rest of his mealtime telling himself that she probably didn't mean it, that she was probably only being polite.

The canteen was on the seventh floor. He'd taken the lift to get there but he walked down to his office via the back stairs. Under his arm he had everything on the Willow Court case that he felt was crucial. Robinson's preliminary and intermediary reports. The first faxed summary from the Birmingham FSS lab. Webster's diagrams and measurements of the crime scene. The crime scene video itself – on a disk which Steve Horton claimed he only had to shove into his computer and which would load itself up automatically.

He smoked a B and H. He didn't bother with the video for now, only skimmed the material he'd already studied. Anything new he looked at more carefully, making his own notes as he went. The NAFIS computer hadn't matched any of the fingerprints lifted from the scene: there was no evidence of a known criminal setting foot on the premises. Which was entirely as expected. Stephen Adams and both of his sons had all left prints on the resinous surface of the baseball bat. But the prints lifted from the smoothly polished mahogany banister, at the point where the tow rope had been slung across and knotted, came only from the father. Adams had been a heavy secretor, it turned out, his palms and his fingertips sweating onto everything he touched.

Greg Salter had requested that the Birmingham lab make the case a priority. But even so the summary stated that the DNA tests would take several more days to complete. An embarrassment of riches, Jacobson thought. Corruption or paucity of materials were the banes of the new science. But not this time. Sweat on the pillow case that encompassed the pillow that had suffocated Marion and Sarah. Skin cells on the baseball bat. Blood on Stephen Adams' dressing gown. Samples all over the bloody shop. Literally so. According to the summary, what the lab had done so far strongly suggested a total absence of non-familial DNA at any prime physical location within the crime scene. And some of the blood on Stephen Adams' clothes 'almost definitively' came from his sons.

He stubbed out the cigarette. He'd attended a seminar on the Elizabethan poet John Donne once. At a summer school when he'd been doing his OU degree. According to the lecturer, Donne had been obsessed with the idea of an actual bodily resurrection after death, had feared that if some part of you got lost in the dying – eaten by wolves, say – then you'd wake up at the final trumpet to find yourself minus an arm or a leg, maybe even short of your cock and bollocks. Poor old sod. He needn't have worried really. A string of fully unique DNA was so thin it could coil itself into a cell scarcely a millionth of an inch thick. So long as there was a sliver of fingernail or a bit of his dandruff around somewhere then a comeback could still be on the cards. Donne might have to sort out the daft-looking bloomers for himself, though.

He lit up a second B and H while the first one was still smouldering at the bottom of the waste bin. His desk phone rang. He was sorely tempted not to answer it. But his sense of duty got the better of him.

'Jacobson,' he said gruffly, picking up the receiver.

The caller was Peter Robinson.

'Frank. Glad I caught you. You've seen the forensic summary?'

'I'm wading through it right now, old son.'

'About the dog, I mean?'

'The dog?'

The dog was the least of his worries, surely, Jacobson thought. Killed in its basket. Throat cut. Belly slit open for good measure. A blooded Lion Sabatier kitchen knife lying on the floor less than a foot away. Stephen Adams' prints hadn't been on the handle. In fact *no* prints had been on the handle. It was an odd little fact, an anomaly. But the guy had probably just killed his entire human family. The whole point was that he'd acted oddly, insanely. Who would ever know the twisted logic that had zapped through his synapses? Wiping the handle of the knife that had killed the dog, not bothering with the bat he'd used to batter the life out of his sons.

'The dog?' he asked again, balancing the new cigarette precariously on the edge of his desk, the lit end pointing outwards.

Robinson had been diligent. Observing strict professional etiquette, he'd declined to carry out the post-mortem himself. Instead Boris the cocker spaniel had been ferried to a university department outside the region, had been sliced up by a professor of veterinary pathology. The professor had done his job properly too, had dispatched blood and tissue samples directly to the FSS lab.

'The knife went straight in through the trachea, Frank,

256

practically severed the head from the body. The poor beast must have been geysering blood all over the killer. And you'd expect other transference too. Hair or saliva for instance.'

'So what you're—'

'The tests aren't finished. But what the lab is saying is that so far they've found no evidence that links Stephen Adams with the death of his dog. Absolutely no evidence at all.'

# Chapter Thirty-Nine

Charlie and Lisa drove towards Coventry via the A452 and the A429. If you stayed on the route it brought you right in past the railway station. But Charlie turned off before they were too near the CCTV networks for comfort, finally dumped the Fiesta in Benedictine Road. It was only common sense, he thought, to keep a little bit of separation between your last move and your next one. He parked the car neatly, even locked the doors. They set off on foot, neither of them saying much. At the station he bought two day returns to Birmingham New Street. Again, no point advertising your plans any more than you had to. They made it onto a train which was just about to leave when they reached the platform. Lisa sat in the window seat, holding his hand tightly. The carriage was busy but the seats opposite them stayed empty until the train pulled into Birmingham International. A tall, young American squeezed in, straight from the airport it looked like, an airline luggage tag still tied onto his bulky backpack. He smiled hopefully across at them, asked how far it was into the city centre. Charlie told him ten minutes, didn't offer any elaboration, didn't smile back. The Yank took the hint, fished in the backpack, stuck his head behind a creased copy of *USA Today*.

Charlie exited the ticket barrier at New Street, joined the shortest queue at the ticket window. He paid in cash, bought two standard returns to Bristol Temple Meads. Lisa stayed behind the barrier, waited for him in the little WH Smith's, bought two cans of Pepsi Max while she was there. If the 9.42 hadn't been delayed, they'd have missed it, would have had to hang around until 10.13 for the next train out. But they caught it OK, managed to get two seats together. The journey was supposed to take an hour and a half. In the event it took more than two, the train finally winding into Bristol at twenty past twelve. It was a good hour after that before they found the address they needed, using buses and walking since Charlie had been wary of taking a cab. They'd slept most of the way – or tried to. Charlie had left their tickets out in front of him on the table. When the guard came along the carriage, she picked them up and clipped them without disturbing him. A sweet enough couple, she'd thought. A young lad and a young lass dozing side by side. Her head resting softly on his chest. His arm wrapped gently around her shoulders.

# Chapter Forty

*Fine. Everything bang on schedule. Hunker down in here until we get the order to move. They're not going to find us, the other side. No way. We'll track right along the edge of the wood until we're in the vicinity of the target. Then approach from the stream that runs behind the house. Classic. I'll go in with the first wave, obviously. Lead from the front. And follow the standard technique. There's three storeys if the surveillance is accurate. Secure them one at a time, inch by inch, room by room. The enemy will be right at the top. We'll need to be careful as we progress up, of course: booby traps, – or loose floorboards – anything that gives us away. If we can't surprise them, they'll go for broke. Death or Glory. Take most of our side with them. Hey, look, there's a magpie over there. Up in the high branches. No, two actually. The other one just behind. Can you see them? That's another thing they don't understand. The ones that laugh. The mockers. How you're out in the countryside, close up to nature. And all the time perfecting survival skills. Something you don't get if you're in an office all week, spending all your free time down the pub, pouring beer down your fat neck. The day it all breaks down, it'll be guys like me they'll all come running to. Fitness is the other thing. Keeping yourself battle ready. It's not that I'm against enjoying a drink, a good night out. Of course I'm not. But you need to have a balance, don't you think so? Even he understood that. Helping the lads with their soccer.*

*Coaching, training. Out and about in the fresh air. Getting off his backside. Putting something back.*

*I knew this would be good for me. That's the first time I've thought about him in an hour. Focus on the task at hand. That's the key. Stay busy. In any case, what's done is done. I could spend the rest of my life feeling guilty. I could walk straight into the nearest cop shop, give myself up. It wouldn't make any difference. Not a jot. It wouldn't bring any of them back. Not even the dog.*

# Chapter Forty-One

Eva Walsh buzzed DC Mick Hume into William Blake House, had left the door to the flat open for him when he emerged from the lift. The front room had been tidied since Jacobson and Kerr's visit on Tuesday night and since Smith and Williams had searched it the following morning. Dodgy goods dumped on dodgy purchasers or maybe just given away. Mainly what remained was Eva's cut-price leather suite and her big thirty-six-inch-screen telly. She was watching *Holby City* on UK Gold, didn't bother to switch it off.

'He's in his room,' she said, 'lying low.'

She was a sparrow of a woman in her mid-thirties. Bleach-blonde, thin, twitchy. Hard to credit that she'd produced a fat slug like her son.

'Ryan,' she shrieked, without rising from her armchair, 'CID. Get your arse in gear.'

Walsh wandered through from his bedroom a minute or two later, slunk himself onto the sofa.

'Now what is it?' he complained, trying not to look up.

'That's a nice one, Ryan,' Hume said.

Walsh had a black eye. A shiner. A real humdinger.

'Isn't it just,' said Eva. 'And no more than he frigging deserves.'

Walsh didn't want to talk about it but his mother did. Sheryl Holmes and Candice Thompson had been watching out for him, had nabbed him by the lifts last night when he'd been making his way home from the cop shop.

'I weren't expecting it,' Walsh said. 'They took me by surprise.'

'Big girl's blouse,' his mother commented.

And knickers too, Hume thought – but kept it to himself. He told Walsh why he was there, showed him Charlie Taylor's mug shots. They were less than eighteen months old, were probably still a fair likeness.

Walsh concentrated hard on the photographs – or pretended too.

'Ryan's good with photos,' Eva said. 'Good with nicking them from other folks' flats. Good with selling them to the newspapers.'

Ryan chucked the photographs onto the floor, shot clumsily to his feet.

'Fuck's sake, Mam. You don't need to tell everybody.'

According to Eva Walsh, Ryan Walsh had confessed the whole story to Sheryl Holmes and Candice Thompson when they'd ambushed him on the stairs, twisted his arm behind his back, threatened to break it. He'd been the one who'd sold on the snap of her and her girls. The one that had surfaced on the telly and in the papers.

'I only got frigging fifty quid,' he said, red faced.

Dejectedly he sat down again, picked the mug shots back up. It was a new experience for Hume. But he got into the swing of it easily enough: the mother as the nasty cop, himself as the good guy.

'Think about it this way, Ryan,' he said. 'You've learned a lesson. Now you can draw a line, start to move on.'

Walsh stared doubtfully at the three images of Charlie Taylor. Face front. Left side. Right side. He'd grassed anyway, he thought, he could hardly get himself into any more shit than he'd done already. If it came to court, he could always refuse to testify. Or just frigging lie.

The room had gone quiet. At some point when neither Ryan nor Hume had noticed it, Eva had turned the volume on the TV down to zero. He looked at his mother, looked at the copper, looked at his mother again.

'Yeah. All right,' he said. 'This is him. Monday morning. The bloke who was with Florida Boy.'

Jacobson answered a call from DC Barber. Together with Watts, Barber had just visited Charlie Taylor's sister in Byron House. She'd denied seeing her brother recently. She'd denied seeing him in the company of Florida Boy Bilston recently. She'd especially denied seeing either of them on Sunday night. The truth on all three counts, Barber reckoned, was precisely the opposite.

'Very likely, old son. Very likely,' Jacobson said.

He made two calls himself. Mick Hume – Ryan Walsh had ID'd Charlie Taylor. Emma Smith – still no sign locally of Brian Bilston's whereabouts.

He got up, located his surreptitious bottle of Glenlivet. He poured his usual measure into the bottom of his mug, replaced the bottle. At home he drank Glenfiddich for preference. But the Glenlivet had been a present from his daughter, Sally. It had been at the bottom of his filing cabinet for at least four years. A proof to himself, if to no one else, that he rarely drank on the premises. But sometimes – like right now – you needed something to blunt the senses rather than sharpen them. Something to dull the edges, leave your mind focused on whatever was troubling it – niggling at it – the most.

His phone rang again: DS Kerr. Kerr had driven from the Beech Park estate over to the Woodlands, had dropped in on Terry Shields at the Poets. Shields and one of the barmaids had confirmed that they'd seen Brian Bilston and Charlie Taylor in the pub on Sunday night. They'd drunk a couple of beers, played a game of pool, had left around nine. According to Kerr, Shields had described Bilston as 'an evil little twat' but denied that he'd had any special or particular grudge against either himself or Dave Carter. Shields also confirmed Amy

Hobbs' story. Stephen Adams had been meeting her in the Poets once a month or so, always on a Friday afternoon. He hadn't really spoken to Adams himself, he'd said, other than to serve him at the bar: double brandy for him, vodka and Red Bull for her.

Jacobson finished his whisky, his feet resting comfortably on the top of his desk. All the while he was thinking. All the while he was working. He smoked a third B and H down to the tip, seemed to have forgotten his recent health vow. Finally he sat up, found his pen and his notebook, opened it at a new page.

Dave Carter:

A low-level dealer who got too greedy.

Bilston and Taylor:

Apprentice hoodlums who bungled a punishment beating.

Conclusions:

carry on local search for B and T on back burner only. Sods almost certainly legged it. Best hope: will be spotted by other forces.

Stephen Adams:

Familicide followed by suicide. Possible evidence of mental instability: –
1) Depression 2) Abuse of drink/drugs 3) Compartmentalised poss. even Schizoid attitudes – "good family man" pose/reputation vs regular Friday sessions with Amy Hobbs. Also prepared to commit serious fraud to keep business going. Maintained

lifestyle spending despite drastic loss of real income:— SA unable to confront/accept reality of his situation.

## Anomalies in case:

1) Who killed the bloody dog?
2) Possible sighting of visitor

## Conclusions:

Repeat Bartons door-to-door enquiries one final time, seek confirmation of Martin Warner's claims. If unsuccessful, shelve case until full forensics in.

## Expectations:

Recommend no further police action, dog + visitor mystery notwithstanding.

When he'd finished writing, he phoned Greg Salter's home number. There were no press conferences scheduled. No television crews in the vicinity of the Divisional building. So Crowby's chief of detectives had buggered off to his upmarket flat in the Millennium apartment complex. His wife, Chrissie, answered. Greg was in his den, she told him, sounding like the keeper of the flame. Reluctantly, Salter authorised a further door-to-door sweep on the Bartons for tomorrow, Sunday. Jacobson could have the same complement of CID and uniformeds he'd had the day before. But that would have to be that. The budget was over-stretched already.

Jacobson grabbed his coat, mooched down to the incident room. Ince and Steve Horton were still hunched over a computer terminal. Kerr was back from the Woodlands. He'd made himself a cup of tea and was reading through a copy of the forensic summary. Otherwise the room was empty.

Jacobson spent another five minutes on the telephone, revised the rest of the team's current tasks. His assessment was that Bilston and Taylor were no longer in Crowby. All the local side could do now was to firm up the evidence for the Bilston–Taylor connection. And maybe pick up a hint of the duo's possible destinations in the process. More conversations with toerags. More visits to the town's underbelly. Mick Hume, Renbourn and Watts could crack on with that. Barber, Smith and Williams would relocate to the Bartons, restart the door-to-door sweep in advance of tomorrow's final operation. Now that the initial shock of the killings had faded a little, at least in his conscious mind, the Willow Court case had started to irritate Jacobson on a professional level. With the only suspect dead, it was hardly a murder investigation at all in the normal sense of the term. Yet the murder squad had to *act* as if it was, had to complete every standard check and procedure.

Ince looked up from the computer screen.

'Take a look at this, guv. Stephen Adams' mobile.'

Jacobson walked over to the workstation. Telephone records were a major data source in any serious inquiry. Who knew who. Who'd spoken to who. When. How long for. The log of calls to and from the land line at 8 Willow Court had been looked at already, had revealed nothing out of the ordinary. The last call of all had been made at 10.13 on the eve of the killings. Mark Adams phoning one of his schoolmates, asking if he could borrow a Ministry of Sound CD. Stephen Adams' mobile phone had been found in his home office. Now Ince and Horton were working on the log for his number: every call for the last seven days.

'What have we got, then?' Jacobson asked.

'Calls to his office, calls to his home,' Ince replied. 'He's phoned his bank, his suppliers. He's phoned his accountant a couple of times. Nothing untraceable or unusual.'

'Except for this, Mr Jacobson,' Horton said, not really

smiling – but still showing more white teeth than one person had a right to.

Jacobson squinted at the screen. Horton had highlighted an eleven-digit number. Also a date and a time. Thursday, 20th February. Two fifty-four am. Plus eight seconds. According to Robinson's post-mortem estimates, Stephen Adams would still have been alive then. And his wife and children newly dead.

# Chapter Forty-Two

'Remind me *why* you can't trace it, Steve,' Jacobson said. 'I thought that was the point of all this technology. Big Brother listening in every time anybody farts.'

Horton spelled it out. Adams' phone had been used to dial another mobile. Unfortunately the second mobile turned out to be pre-paid, unregistered. You could pick one up anywhere. High street outlets, garages, supermarkets. You bought it with cash, kept it going with top-up cards. The phone network didn't need a billing name and address because it didn't need to collect on a bill. The Home Office had huffed and puffed from time to time about the obvious criminal uses. But that was all they'd done so far.

'We could get some location data, though, surely?' Kerr asked.

Horton *did* smile this time.

'In theory yes, Mr Kerr. Usually the networks store signal-to-base records for at least six months. But the outcome's a bit of a lottery. It depends on how far the phone was from the nearest base station when it was used. You can get a fix down to five hundred metres if you're lucky – even closer in a city centre – or it could be as wide as a thirty-five-kilometre radius.'

Jacobson dredged his memory for something sensible to contribute.

'What about triangulation, old son? I thought I'd read that—'

Ince chipped in, tried not to sound patronising.

'Only works when the phone's actually switched on, guv. They measure the relative strength of the signal from the handset to the two nearest base stations and calculate the position that way.'

'We'd need a further authorisation before the network would release the information in any case,' Kerr commented. 'And, like Steve says, it might only tell us that the phone was somewhere vaguely in Crowby at the time.'

Jacobson frowned.

'I don't suppose we could check what *other* calls were made or received on the mystery phone?'

'That's less of a problem,' Horton said. 'Again, strictly I'll need a fresh authorisation. But if I explain the situation, the network *might* let me look at the data in advance.'

'Do it, then, Steve. And let me know as soon as.'

Jacobson had slung his coat across a desk near the door. He picked it up, began putting it on.

'Where to now?' Kerr asked

'The Brewer's Rest, old son. Coming?'

Sergeant Ince grinned.

'All right for some.'

'Strictly in the nature of business,' Jacobson replied, buttoning up. 'Liaison with the local press, to be precise.'

Henry Pelling was already ensconced at a table. With perfect timing his pint glass of Guinness was four-fifths empty. Jacobson got the round in while Kerr scanned through the latest edition of the *Argus*. Pelling had run a further feature on the Adams family, had spent nearly as much time on the leafy streets of the Bartons in the last two days as Crowby CID. Jacobson had reckoned it was worth a quick conversation – and the professional hardship of an afternoon glass of beer – to compare notes where appropriate.

The BR showed Channel 4 racing on the big screen on Saturday afternoons these days, trying to compete with the new sports bar on Silver Street. Pelling supped his Guinness, proved unwilling to say very much until the 2.40 race from Wincanton had finished: Pelling's horse trailing in at the back of the field.

'*Steve only wanted to get on in life,*' Jacobson said, quoting the newspaper article.

Pelling nodded.

'According to one of his ex-teachers, anyway. Though to be honest I don't think the old boy really remembered him, probably just wanted a mention in print.'

'North Crowby comp?' Jacobson asked.

'That's the one. But you're talking about twenty years ago. It was a reasonable enough school in those days. A rough catchment area certainly: the Son of the Bronx, even part of the Bronx itself. But neither of them were as bad then as they are now. Nothing like.'

Jacobson drank a mouthful of lager, couldn't disagree. The rot was only beginning to set in back then. There was only one generation on the dole, not three or four. Hard drugs were a novelty item, more or less a minority interest, had yet to develop into a general scourge.

'Still, you've got to hand it to him, Frank,' Pelling said. 'He grew up in the Woodlands, left school at sixteen. But he screwed the nut. Never out of work, married since he was twenty-one, own business at twenty-five.'

Jacobson took out his cigarette packet, offered one to Pelling.

'Not for me, thanks, mate.'

Pelling was using patches, apparently: his New Year resolution. Impressed, even chastened, Jacobson put the pack away without lighting up himself.

Kerr turned to the second page of the feature.

'*Steve Adams was Karaoke King,*' he quoted.

'According to the local publican, anyway,' Pelling said. 'The Catchpenny? Typical middle-class estate pub. Sunday

271

roasts. Quiz nights. Everybody talking house prices, pensions, terrorists. Everybody wanting hanging brought back for failure to mow the lawn to the regulation height. Adams was a stalwart, by all accounts, getting in more nights than not, setting the world to rights at the bar.'

Jacobson swallowed down another mouthful before he spoke.

'And I dare say you couldn't find any sod with a bad word against him?'

'No more than I expect you could, Frank.'

# Chapter Forty-Three

The gaff was a terraced house in the middle of a cramped street on the outskirts of St Paul's. Vincent, known as Vince, Charlie's mate from Winson Green, had seemed less pleased to see him than Charlie had hoped for. He'd been polite enough to Lisa, though. Respectful. There was an attic room at the top of the building. They could stop there for a couple of nights anyway, Vince had said. Until something else could be sorted. It was Vince's younger brother's room really. The dweeb was on remand again, Vince had said, *he don't need it right now.*

Attic shoebox was more the size of it, Charlie thought. A window the size of a cornflake packet. A tiny washbasin. A single bed that Lisa just chucked herself straight onto. Asleep again. Still exhausted. Charlie pulled the one chair to the side of the bed, so he could rest his feet on the edge while he sat down. He'd bought a *Birmingham Post* at Temple Meads, the closest paper he could find for the Crowby area. Florida Boy had made it to the bottom of page three. Brian Bilston, twenty, blah, blah. In connection with suspected arson and murder, blah, blah. The mug shot was the same one they'd used on the telly. Charlie read the report once, twice, three times. Trying to delve in between the lines. But there was no hint of a partner. Not much detail at all really. That bird from *EastEnders*, the one that everybody wanted to shag, had been in town to open a nightclub, took up most of the page to herself.

Vince knocked on the door.

'A spliff and two beers,' he announced. 'Welcome to the South West, mate.'

He proffered the drinks and the joint on an old Carlsberg tray, stuck it down on the top of his brother's rickety chest of drawers. Dirty white melamine. Vince had a big, broad smile when he felt like using it. And for some reason he seemed to have changed his tune.

'Come down when you're rested, yeah? And we'll talk. Make plans, arrangements.'

Charlie said OK, sure. When Vince went downstairs again, he lit the spliff, pulled open the tab on a can of Red Stripe. He nudged Lisa.

'Smoke?'

But she barely grunted, then turned over onto her other side. Charlie fetched his fleece, wrapped it around her for a blanket, sat back down with the spliff. He moved the *Post* onto the bed, folded it so that FB stopped staring at him.

He'd been barely sixteen when he'd got sent to the Brinsford YO over in Wolverhampton. FB had been banged up there just a couple of weeks beforehand. A lad had hung himself on Charlie's first night. He'd been on suicide watch but that hadn't stopped him. Nothing could stop you probably if you'd decided you'd had enough. There were kids from all over there. Some of them were the scariest fuckers he'd ever met. The kind that made you shit yourself. Out of control. Out of everything. You could get to a point in a set-up like that where you'd sooner give up the rest of your life than endure the next hour of it. The next day or week.

Charlie took an exploratory draw but the smoke hitting his lungs told him it was skunk. Like what he really needed right now was to get wasted. He put the joint out with his fingertips, swigged down some lager. FB had taken care of it pretty much back then. When he needn't have bothered.

Just because they were from the same town, the same streets. *Crowby boys against the world, old bean*, he'd said one time; kicking the arse of two Irish twats who'd fancied Charlie's phone cards – who'd fancied Charlie.

# Chapter Forty-Four

Jacobson and Kerr walked back to the Divisional building. In the absence of a more compellingly useful alternative, Kerr planned to drive out to the Bartons, help out with the renewed door-to-door effort. Jacobson told him he was going to review the paperwork in the case so far. His euphemism, as Kerr knew, for kicking his heels and waiting for something to happen.

Jacobson picked up the material he wanted in the incident room, took it to his own office. The Bartons witness statements mainly, efficiently collated and cross-referenced by Emma Smith and DC Williams. If you could really call them witness statements, he thought: when nobody had seen anything criminal, when the killer was being universally applauded as the ultimate Decent Bloke. He didn't light up a B and H, still astonished by Henry Pelling's unexpected resolve.

Pelling hadn't turned up anything new; apart from the retired schoolteacher, he hadn't spoken to anyone that CID hadn't spoken to. But talking to Pelling hadn't been a total waste of time. For one thing, he had a hack's instinct for an angle, a *story*: the kid from the Woodlands who'd got out, who'd got on, who hadn't looked back. One of the lucky ones. Maybe Adams *had* looked back, though. Maybe that was what Amy Hobbs had been all about. Not the sex part. But meeting her in the Poets, flashing his cash, needing to make a declaration of his success, his journey. I came from here. And now look at me.

Jacobson skim-read. Smith and Williams had done the first interviews in the Catchpenny themselves, had spoken to the publican – John 'Joe' Lodge – and to the regulars. Lodge had told them exactly what he'd told Pelling: Adams had been a popular customer, an unpaid *animateur* for special nights and occasions. According to his statement, Lodge had been the licensee for eighteen months. *Steve Adams and his wife and his friends made me welcome* – his words – *they really helped me to make a good go of the pub.* DC Williams, to judge by the handwriting, had appended a note on the last page. *Interview previous landlord also? Confirm impression?* Later – presumably – he'd countermanded his own advice. *No. No need.*

He paced to his window, watched the Saturday crowds in the square. Thoroughness was crucial to a murder inquiry. Assume nothing, check everything. But so was knowing where to draw the line, where not to waste time and effort. Especially in a case where the killer was safely tucked up in the morgue to start with. He phoned down to the incident room, spoke to Sergeant Ince. Horton was still waiting for the mobile phone data, Ince said. Nothing new otherwise.

Jacobson thought about lighting up again, rejected the idea. He thought about heading over to the Bartons or catching up with Mick Hume and company, ditto. Finally – just for something to do, just for something to occupy his time – he scribbled down the relevant details, decided to dot the *i* and cross the *t* himself.

Dove Road. The Beech Park estate. Hume and DS Renbourn walked up the path to the front door. DC Watts stayed with the car. Hume had suggested that three coppers would be counter-productive – over the top – for this particular visit.

Renbourn rang the bell. Lisa Pritchard's mother studied both of their ID cards carefully before she was prepared to let them in. Even then she showed them into the kitchen, told them she could live without the police force invading the privacy of her lounge.

'My husband's reading the paper, putting his feet up,' she went on. 'He works hard all week. He's entitled to some peace and quiet on a Saturday afternoon, surely to God.'

Hume didn't argue. Instead he repeated exactly what he'd told her on the doorstep. Her daughter wasn't in any trouble personally. But they understood she knew someone they were looking for. A lad by the name of Charlie Taylor: they needed to talk to him urgently about a serious matter.

She sat down at her table, left them standing. Uninvited.

'That waste of space. My husband put his foot down about him months ago. I'm not having that kind around my house, he told her.'

'So you don't think Lisa's been in contact with Mr Taylor recently?' Renbourn asked.

'Mr Taylor, is it? That's rich. No, she hasn't. Not as far as I know, anyway.'

She was a small woman. Forty maybe. Still attractive if her eyes had been less harried.

Hume heard a door open through in the hall. Then the husband appeared. A snatch of dialogue from some old movie followed him out, gunfire, the beginnings of a car chase. He walked into the kitchen, carrying his spectacle case. Hume ran through the entire looking-for-Taylor scenario a third time.

'She stopped seeing him,' Pritchard said, 'I put my foot down on that score.'

Renbourn was standing near the sink, taking care not to give offence by leaning on it.

'But Lisa's not here at the moment, you say?'

Mrs Pritchard answered.

'No. She's on a holiday. A short break. She's staying with a friend in London. A nurse who used to work in the hospital. An SRN,' she said, putting a spin on the family situation.

Hume asked when her daughter had left.

278

'Wednesday. Like I say, she's taking a short break.'

'Do you have an address? A contact number?'

Pritchard took off his reading glasses, stuck them inside the blue case. The unfashionable, outdated kind that the optician gave you for nothing.

'Why would you need that?' he asked. 'You said Lisa's not in trouble.'

Hume explained for a fourth time. He needed to ask Lisa herself about Charlie Taylor. Taylor needed to be found. And found quickly.

A single tear trickled slowly down Mrs Pritchard's cheek. Her fingers never moved to stem it. Her voice didn't waver.

'The truth is we don't know where Lisa's gone. She left a pack of lies on a daft note. There's a number all right. But the girl who answers says Lisa owes her money, says she hasn't heard from her since before Christmas.'

Jacobson took the lift down to the central records office on the second floor. The clerk on duty said that it would take her ten minutes to find the information. The decisions of the licensing justices hadn't yet been computerised, she told him. Not by the force, anyway. Although she'd heard they *were* now on the computer system at the magistrates' courts.

'But in-house only, Mr Jacobson. On the court intranet? Not much use to us on a Saturday afternoon, I'm afraid.'

Jacobson nodded like he was fluent in nu-speak. But gave the game away with a blank, uncomprehending smile. He decided to wait, idling his time by reading through the records office mission statement. And then just by staring at the arty calendar on the wall. February's playmates of the month were by Gauguin, the man who'd proven that you could work in a bank and still have the soul of a poet.

In the event it took the clerk quarter of an hour. When she returned to the service desk, she placed three black-and-white photocopies on the counter: three extracts from the minutes of three separate licensing meetings. Jacobson thanked her. He went out along the corridor and pressed for the lift. More waiting: he looked at the sheets, began to study the details. The big brewery chain that owned the Catchpenny had installed three landlords on the premises in the past five years. 'Joe' Lodge was the most recent, had been there for just over eighteen months. Exactly as per his witness statement. The first licensee had lasted twice that amount of time. Almost exactly three years. In between, there'd been a tenant who'd arrived and then left again inside a period of six months. His full given name was Terence Alfred Shields.

# Chapter Forty-Five

Ince and Horton cross-checked the data for him. There was no confusion, no clerical error. A year and a half ago, Terry Shields had been behind the bar in the Catchpenny, pulling pints for the petty bourgeoisie, Stephen Adams pre-eminently included. Jacobson was hugely, childishly, tempted to send a patrol car over, have Shields nicked and dumped in a cell until he was ready to talk to him. Shields' witness statement to DS Kerr, signed and dated scarcely two hours ago, had been a crock of shit. *I didn't know Mr Adams by name. But I recognise him now as an occasional customer in the Poets public house of which I am the licensee.* Arrest on suspicion of making a false and misleading statement. Grand. But in connection with what exactly?

The phone network had transmitted the call log for the mystery mobile number. Ince and Horton set to work on the new data. Jacobson boiled the kettle, made the drinks, tried not to get in their way.

'Done it, guv,' Ince said, ten minutes later.

The technique wasn't rocket science. Horton had an online link to BT's core reverse directory. The advantage this gave him over the geek in the street was that the core directory was constantly updated whereas the commercially available CD-ROM versions aged rapidly, never told the latest story.

Horton talked Jacobson through the results. The number had been used for the past four weeks, exclusively to or from three other numbers. Stephen Adams' mobile plus two land lines: both with the Crowby area code, both residential non-business numbers. Jacobson left his mug of instant coffee undrunk. He trawled the Bartons witness statements again, pulled out the names of half a dozen Catchpenny regulars. Each one had described Adams as a recurrent drinking companion over several years. He phoned DS Kerr: reinterview them ASAP, try and establish – *prove* – that Stephen Adams had been well known to Terry Shields when Shields had been the Catchpenny's tenant.

Horton clicked for a printout of the results, walked over to the printer tray.

'The phone log fits the typical non-legal profile, Mr Jacobson,' he said. 'Use over a short period of time, calls to or from a strictly limited number of contacts.'

Sergeant Ince nodded.

'And nothing at all since the call from Adams' number, Thursday morning.'

Jacobson moved to the whiteboard, picked up a marker.

'Suppose you're right, Steve,' he said, thinking out loud. 'Somebody using an unregistered mobile to cover up something criminal. Why didn't Adams and the other two do the same?'

Horton picked up his printout.

'Maybe their involvement isn't criminal? It's only the mystery party needs to cover up his or her tracks?'

Jacobson drew an imperfect circle at the bottom of the board

'That's one possibility. The other is that they're *all* involved. But things are going well, they're pleased with themselves – they feel secure. They're not really expecting to get caught.'

He scribbled the three names inside the circle, added an X for the unknown caller.

'Mr X – assuming it is a mister – might just be a different personality type,' he concluded. 'More cautious, more fastidious. Less of a risk-taker.'

# Chapter Forty-Six

Half an hour later Jacobson was driving towards the Woodlands. Solicitors and barristers had a saying: never ask a
question which you didn't already know the answer to.
Sound advice for the courtroom, Jacobson always thought.
But frequently worse than useless at the coalface. Right now
he barely knew *who* he wanted to talk to. Let alone what
might be said or unsaid.

Stephen Adams had called X in the middle of the night.
Between killing his family and stringing a clumsy, makeshift
noose around his own neck. As far as the unregistered mobile
was concerned, X had only ever spoken additionally to two
other people. One of them was Terry Shields. The other was
Colin Paterson, Adams' key employee. Paterson was also
Adams' mate, his *crony*, according to Ray Coombs, who'd
seen them pissed up together inside the last few weeks. It
was hardly a crime to get drunk with your boss. But for
some reason Paterson had lied about the fact when he'd
spoken to DS Kerr. As if he'd wanted to place a degree of
distance between the two of them. The RCS and drug squad
intelligence held that Terry Shields had been Dave Carter's
partner in the Poets' drug trade. And Shields, predictably,
had a record. All petty stuff and all of it *spent* in terms of
the Rehabilitation of Offenders Act. But at least he was an
obvious, uncontroversial candidate for toerag action. Unlike
either Adams or Paterson: neither of whom had ever graced
the PNC with their presence. X evidently linked all of them.

But Jacobson didn't know who X was or what the link entailed.

He reached the estate. He flicked his indicator, turned into Shakespeare Road, the main drag. Over to his right was the shabby row of two-storey houses where Shields had been living since he'd lost his brief tenancy at the Catchpenny – along with the nice, smart, live-in flat upstairs. It had cost Jacobson six telephone calls of his own before the chain of irritable, disturbed-at-home brewery apparatchiks had finally led him to the area personnel manager (hotels and licensed premises). Terry Shields hadn't worked out at the Catchpenny, it had been a bungled appointment, it hadn't been *his* decision. As far as the company knew, as far as *he* knew, Shields was doing better at the Poets. Why was Jacobson asking? Was there a problem? Jacobson had hung up without enlightening him.

He splashed his shoes and the bottoms of his trousers getting out of the car. Then he nearly dropped his keys in the puddle, trying to brush the water off. The place was dead when he went inside, caught in the lull between afternoon boozing and the night-time session still to come. The public bar was empty, the pool tables vacant. The two barmaids with nothing very much to do brought the total count of human beings in the main lounge to precisely six.

'Terry's in the—' the blonde one started to say.

But Jacobson was already lifting the counter lid, already making towards the grease-zone kitchen and the back room.

He found Shields sitting on the dusty sofa, filling in order sheets.

'Fuck's sake. This is getting out of—'

'Spare me the outraged citizen,' Jacobson said. 'I don't have the time.'

Shields shrugged, put the forms down. Jacobson kept it short. Shields had signed a statement to the effect that he hadn't known Stephen Adams prior to working in the

Poets. But CID now had several compelling statements to the contrary. They'd even seen a home video of a Halloween night at the Catchpenny: Shields hamming it up for the camera, presenting Stephen and Marion Adams with the third prize in the fancy dress competition.

Shields folded his arms across his chest, didn't speak. Jacobson knew that he was stretching a point. Kerr and the team over at the Bartons had only managed to re-interview two of the Catchpenny regulars so far. But it was true enough about the video. He showed him a slip of paper: X's mobile number.

'Whose number is it, Terry?'

Shields shrugged again.

'I don't recognise it.'

'Tuesday afternoon,' Jacobson persisted. 'A six-minute conversation. This number and your home number.'

'If you say so. I still don't recall it.'

Jacobson leant against the redundant snooker table which filled up the bulk of the room, took the weight off his legs.

'And you don't want to revise your statement about Stephen Adams?'

'I don't remember him from the Catchpenny. I can't be expected to remember every customer I've ever frigging served. Can I?'

Jacobson mentioned perjury, perverting the course of justice. But he had nothing yet really. He didn't even know what the crime was – whether there *was* a crime. It was only in the last minute that he'd even glimpsed the possibility of a relevant methodology. Something that might work.

'Have it your way, Terry. We'll talk again,' he said evenly.

Shields picked his order sheets back up, didn't bother to reply.

Jacobson started up his car in the potholed car park. Amy Hobbs was on the other side of the street, walking back from the local shops by the looks of it. A carrier bag in one hand. Her daughter, Cinnamon, hoisted on her shoulder. Jacobson pulled across, offered her a lift to Southey House. She gave him a quizzical look for a second. But he passed whatever test she applied for climbing into a car with a middle-aged man. He kept his speed down, mindful of the way she was bouncing the kiddie on her knee in the front passenger seat.

'I thought a bit more about what you asked,' she said, when Jacobson pulled up outside the block. 'About Steve Adams ever seeming strange. Well, there was one time actually. Just before Christmas?'

Jacobson switched off the engine. He'd finally learned to live with statements that ended up as questions. Not than anybody he met gave him much choice.

'Please, go ahead,' he said.

Adams liked to hang around for a while after they had sex, Amy Hobbs told him. Drink a cup of tea before he left her. She'd charged him extra, of course. Although probably he hadn't known that.

'Anyway, he's sitting there on my sofa, half dressed, prattling away about his wife and his frigging satellite dishes. Out of the blue he asks me if I've ever wondered whether other people really exist or not. What if we were all just in his imagination? Or what if he wasn't real himself? I laughed at first. But then I realised he wasn't joking.'

Jacobson watched her fussing with her daughter's jacket, making sure she was zipped against the cold.

'I explained about solipsism and Descartes – or tried to. How it was something that had been argued about for centuries? But I don't expect that helped very much.'

Jacobson decided he'd get out, walk around the car, open the door for her.

'No, lass. I don't expect it did,' he said.

# Chapter Forty-Seven

Vince wanted to show them around Bristol.

'Certain areas, Charlie,' he said. 'Certain areas of interest.'

Lisa had woken up. She didn't really look in the best of moods for sightseeing, Charlie thought. But the guy was putting them up and all that.

'Let's do it, Leez. See what there is to see,' he advised her.

Resigned, not saying anything, she went off to the bathroom. Charlie and Vince listened to her running the taps, splashing water. It took her half an hour, although, when she came out, she seemed only to have brushed her hair and done something minimal to her face. When she was ready, Vince drove them over to Clifton via the university area, detouring up and down side streets, pointing out specific bars, clubs, hang-outs.

He'd had a word with his associate, he'd told Charlie earlier. Given the whole matter thought. There could be some possibilities after all, he'd said. Real possibilities and serious opportunities. Just so the tour wasn't all work, he took them along Clifton Down as well, stopped for a while near Observatory Hill. So they could soak up a bit of greenery, he said. Finally he drove back to one of the streets they'd already seen, parked up outside some Latin American place where they seemed to know him.

Charlie liked the ornamental lizards on the walls. Students and hoity types crammed the tables, already planning their

Saturday night jollies. Vince ordered a Mojito for Lisa, a couple of Modelos for himself and Charlie.

'The Mojito will sort you out, girl,' Vince said. 'Rum and lime juice, a quick dash of the old soda.'

Charlie took a closer look around. Punters stuffing themselves at every table. He realised suddenly that he was famished, that he'd barely eaten a thing all day. When the drinks came, he took up Vince's recommendation: calamares followed by chicken fajitas and patatas bravas. Vince wanted a rib-eye steak but neither Vince, Charlie or the waitress could persuade Lisa into ordering anything.

Vince outlined his idea. Charlie could be the front end over in this area, get fixed up with a student union card, wander around with a book or two under his arm. It was the safest kind of trade there was. Especially if you needed to keep a low profile for a period of time.

'One thing about Bristol, it's where a lot of the rich kids go – if they're too thick for Oxford and such. Money to waste on getting wasted.'

He stopped to laugh at his own joke, lifted up his beer, clinked Charlie's bottle. 'There's a fair old bit of poppy waiting to be made, Charlie. A fair old bit.'

# Chapter Forty-Eight

Six pm. Like Terry Shields, unlike Stephen Adams, Colin Paterson was a bachelor. Or currently living as one. His gaff was a flat in Midland Road above a burger bar. Jacobson parked further down the street on double yellow, just outside the Happy Shopper. The stairs up to Paterson's door carried the smell of fried food with them. Paterson answered his door bell on the third ring. He'd been sitting in his front room by the looks of it: an open can of Stella on the little table next to the sofa, Sky Sports blaring on his digital TV.

'I spoke to one of your blokes earlier,' Paterson said, sitting back down, turning down the volume with his remote. It was dark outside now. Paterson had drawn a too-thin curtain across his window, failing to cut out the yellow glare of the nearest street lamp.

'Why did you lie, Mr Paterson?' Jacobson asked, inviting himself into an armchair that was more comfortable than it looked.

'Lie?'

Jacobson told him what Ray Coombs had seen in Wetherspoons, didn't tell him about Coombs. Paterson took a swig of beer.

'I-I must've got confused. Sorry,' he said unconvincingly. 'It's been a bit of a shock all this. It's not important, is it?'

'So Stephen Adams was still a mate? A drinking buddy?'

'Well, yeah, I guess. Now and again.'

Jacobson stood up, showed him the slip of paper on which he'd written the mobile phone number.

'This is a number that you've phoned twice in the last week, Colin. Whose is it?'

Paterson studied it, took another swig.

'No. I don't think so. I don't recognise it, anyway.'

Jacobson told him that there couldn't be a mistake. They'd checked the phone company records.

'Then they've got it wrong. It's all computers, isn't it? They're not infallible. I've got a mate who used to be a systems analyst. You should hear some of the stories he has to tell.'

Jacobson stayed on his feet.

'We'll be checking again, Colin,' he said, improvising – making it up. 'Some new software the telephone engineers are testing in the area. Automatically records the content of any calls over two minutes.'

He bought a cheeseburger on his way back to the car. He regretted it by the third bite but he stuck with it. On balance, it was probably just about better than nothing. He'd get his diet sorted out one of these days. Some time between cases. And along with the rest of his life. Shields was the seasoned toerag, he thought. But Paterson hadn't done too badly for an amateur. He binned the burger wrapper on the back seat when he'd finished eating. Before he drove off he got out and checked around the area on foot. Paterson's car, a red Astra, was actually stashed around the corner in Midland Crescent where parking wasn't restricted. The Happy Shopper was just about the ideal vantage point, as it turned out. That or outside Thresher's maybe. Either would give you a clear view of the flat, the vehicle and everything in between. He used his phone, started to put in place the arrangements he'd only very recently conceived of. Then he drove back along Midland Road towards the junction with

Mill Street. It could all be a giant waste of time. But there was only ever one way to find out. He turned left at the traffic lights, headed back towards the town centre and the Divisional building.

# Chapter Forty-Nine

Sheryl had the flat to herself apart from the kids. Candice had gone into Crowby. A girls' night out. She'd tried to talk Sheryl into going along, had even said she'd pay all of the babysitting herself. But Sheryl hadn't had the least notion of it, had preferred to stay here; close to Anne-Marie and Lucy. She could murder a cuppa, though. Maybe she'd slip through to the kitchen in a while. Put the kettle on. Have a ciggy while it boiled. Lucy was cuddled into her, watching the last minutes of *Toy Story 2* on video. Liam, Candice's lad, had complained, had called it a load of old rubbish. But now he was watching it too. Albeit that he was sitting at the other end of the sofa, trying his best to impersonate a grown-up.

Anne-Marie was lying on the floor, her arms propped on a cushion, surrounded by drawing paper and crayons. Still scribbling away. Claire Burke, the Woman in frigging Black, had given her a supply to take away with her, had told Sheryl it was the best sign yet. Sheryl had her doubts. But she didn't have any better ideas herself. She'd admit that much all right.

The film ended. Sheryl found the remote, pressed rewind, wondered what she'd do next to amuse them. Liam wasn't a bad kid, not really. But he was an only child. He liked his own way, wasn't great at sharing. Especially not – at his age – with two girls. The news came on while she was still considering. Wars. And threats of wars. The Prime Minister thinks this. The Prime Minister thinks that. The frigging big

292

shots causing trouble as usual. But they were never the ones sticking their necks out, getting themselves gassed and blown up. That was what you signed up mugs from shitheaps like the Woodlands for.

'Don't like this, Mum,' said Lucy.

Sheryl gave her a gentle squeeze.

'Why don't you see if you can pick another film, then, love,' she said.

'It should be my turn,' Liam whinged. 'It's my frigging house.'

Sheryl told him to shut it. Cheeky little sod. He had a telly in his own room anyway.

Some kind of exercise, she realised. That's what it was they were reporting. Chemical warfare drill. Soldiers trying on protective suits and masks.

Anne-Marie had stopped drawing, was staring at the TV screen. Liam stomped out of the room, slamming the door behind him. Lucy giggled.

'Shush, Lucy. Don't make it worse,' Sheryl said, noticing Anne-Marie.

'Those men, Mum,' Anne-Marie said softly, as if her voice had never been away. 'They look just like the man who helped Sarah's dad.'

# Chapter Fifty

Five past seven. A CrowbyCab pulled up outside the burger bar and deposited its customer. Emma Smith, DC Williams and Mick Hume watched him getting out. They'd parked a little way back from the Happy Shopper, more or less at the point where Jacobson had suggested. The cab drove off. Terry Shields looked up and down the street before he rang Colin Paterson's door bell. DS Kerr had shadowed the taxi from the Poets towards the town centre. Barber and Watts had followed it the rest of the way over. Hume whispered into his mobile, passed on the news to the incident room where Jacobson, Ince and Renbourn were sitting by the phone lines.

Shields and Paterson emerged onto the pavement ten minutes later. They were on the other side of the street, but they were still headed their way. Hume ducked down on the back seat just in case. Williams pulled Emma Smith into a phoney clinch. Or maybe not *that* phoney, according to the gossip that Hume had heard Barry Sheldon spreading at a rugby club booze-up. Hume had warned him off. Whether it was true or not, he'd said, it was nobody else's business. Williams, sitting in the driver's seat, still had a clear view. He watched them walk around the corner into Midland Crescent, saw Paterson unlocking his Astra and both of them getting in.

The Astra was facing towards Midland Road. Paterson pulled out towards the corner, turned left when the way was clear. He drove along past the burger bar and his flat, back towards Mill Street and the inner ring road. They tailed him by relay. Williams to Barber to Kerr to Williams. It was easy enough in town. But the traffic thinned on the approaches to Copthorne Road. Williams dropped back, even lost sight on occasion. The three pursuing cars met up with each other at the BP filling station, the one just before the roundabout that gave access to the industrial estate. A quick decision was needed. Kerr had seniority on the ground: Kerr was *it*. He took Hume and Watts with him, told the others to stay put for now. DC Barber was to contact the security company, make sure their patrols kept well out of it.

He set off in the direction of Adams Installations, driving slowly. He stopped outside a unit called Carpet Kleen, tucked the Peugeot in beside a Ford Transit. They walked the rest of the way. Until he saw the red Astra parked outside, Kerr had no way of knowing whether he was the hero of the hour or the guy who'd fucked everything up. The unit opposite Adams' place was some kind of building supplies outlet. Kerr, Hume and Watts crouched down in an office doorway, hoped that no one would see them who wasn't seriously looking.

They watched and waited. Every five minutes or so, the workshop doors opened. Paterson would unlock the boot of his car and Shields would pack something inside. From this distance they couldn't see exactly what. Twenty minutes passed. Kerr had his phone on a low ring volume, answered it at the first tone. Emma Smith: a Citroën Xsara had just driven onto the estate. They crouched lower to the ground, shrank further into the doorway. The Xsara turned up thirty seconds later, pulled in alongside Paterson's Astra. The driver got out and stood outside the workshop doors. Either Paterson or Shields, or both of them, must have heard the car arriving since the doors opened from the inside without any sign of knocking or ringing the bell. When the doors closed again, Kerr whispered into his phone: *let's do it.*

# Chapter Fifty-One

There were legal niceties involved. Even though Jacobson's guesswork seemed to be proving true second by second, no magistrate or judge in the country would have issued a warrant on the strength of it. Colin Paterson had been entrusted with keys to the premises by his employer. Even though that employer was dead, he had at least an arguable *pro tem* right to be there, to permit others to be there. And parked up in the loading bays, the Astra and the Citroën were as much on private property as if they'd been inside the building. But if a police officer *saw* a potentially criminal activity taking place, everything changed. An Englishman's home was his castle. Except that if a copper looked through the window and noticed him strangling his wife, he was fully entitled to barge in and stop him.

Kerr ran across to the front of Kwik-Fit, squeezed himself in flat against the wall. They'd see him if they came out and looked to the left. But he'd see them too, see exactly what they were up to, what they were carrying. A minute passed. Two minutes. Nearly three. He thought he heard footsteps behind the workshop doors. And then there they were. Stepping out one after the other. Paterson unlocked the boot. Shields and Mr X stood waiting with their arms full.

'Police! You're nicked,' Kerr shouted, walking towards them.

Paterson stayed where he was. Maybe just for the hell of it, maybe not seriously expecting to get away, Shields dropped what he was holding and ran. He sprinted around the side of the Astra, directly into the path of Hume and Watts. He aimed some kind of Kung Fu kick at Hume's head, losing his balance in the process. Hume ducked, nutted him, pinned him over the bonnet. Mr X shoved Paterson out of his way, tried to follow Shields. Kerr grabbed him, somehow got him to the floor. The guy was strong, knew what he was about. But by now there were headlights, cars, uniformed back-up. Nowhere really for him to go.

# Chapter Fifty-Two

Ten pm. Jacobson and Kerr sat in the police canteen, waiting for their turn in the interview rooms. The drug squad and DS Renbourn from the RCS were going first. They were interviewing the arrested suspects sequentially, using what they learned in one session to help them with the next. Kerr tried to phone Cathy. He knew she was there – where else would she be? – but she didn't pick up. He left a message anyway, kept it neutral, just said he'd be home as soon as he could. Jacobson drank his coffee, didn't comment. Amazingly for this time on a Saturday night, it tasted very nearly fresh. He played with his B and H packet and his lighter. But persuaded himself that he didn't need a cigarette with every single cup.

Clean Harry Fields walked in. He'd been called in to supervise the search at Adams Installations, had stayed on to monitor the interviews.

'He's all yours, Frank, if you're ready,' he said.

'So what's the latest?' Jacobson asked.

'Shields is still playing it cool – and your lad. Paterson looks like he might be about to crack. He's more or less admitted already that you panicked them into trying to get rid, offload their supplies elsewhere. Not that it matters too much if none of them utters another word. The street value in the haul has to be in excess of a hundred K. Plus all three of them were caught *in flagrante*.'

Kerr got to his feet. Jacobson waved his coffee cup.

'Just a minute, old son. I'll be right with you.'

He took a final sip. Shields and Paterson could go to hell for all he cared. They'd certainly go to prison. But they weren't really his problem any longer. Jacobson's business was solely with the third arrestee: Stephen Adams' accountant, his friend from schooldays. Mr X was Alan Jones.

# Chapter Fifty-Three

Both Harry Fields and Jacobson played by the book when it mattered. Jones had been checked out in the medical suite after his scuffle with Kerr. He'd been allowed rest time between interview sessions. He had a paper cup of tea on the table in front of him. And the duty solicitor sitting alongside, dispensing advice.

Jacobson switched on the tape recorder, spoke the names of those present. Jones didn't wait for the first question.

'I'd no idea there were drugs on the premises,' he said. 'The only reason I was there was that Colin Paterson asked if I'd help with the stock-taking from an accountancy point of view—'

'Stow it, Mr Jones,' Jacobson interrupted. 'You're talking to a *Guardian* reader. If I had my way, I'd legalise the lot tomorrow, eliminate the criminal incentives. Let the social services and the doctors sort out the problem cases.'

He sat down, pulled in his chair.

'No. I don't give a monkey's about any of that. I need to caution you that this interview is about the deaths of Stephen Adams and his family.'

He coughed, cleared his throat.

'I think you can help us clear up exactly what happened. I think you can help us a great deal in that line.'

Jones drank some tea from the paper cup. His hand was steady. If Jacobson had surprised him, he kept it well hidden.

Jacobson ran through some of the basics. Stephen Adams had made a mobile-to-mobile telephone call after he'd killed his family. The call had been answered and it had lasted for four minutes. The drug squad raid on Alan Jones' home earlier this evening had unearthed the mobile that Adams had phoned. As a result of that discovery, a separate warrant had been issued pertaining to the Willow Court inquiry. Certain other items of interest had been discovered and these had now been removed for forensic examination.

'I've no idea what you're talking about,' Jones said.

'But you admit that Adams phoned you, at any rate?'

Jones took another sip. Then:

'I admit that you've told me you found this phone in my house. But can you prove it's mine? Can you prove where this phone was at the time you say Steve phoned me?'

Jacobson smiled.

'Sergeant Kerr. Any questions for Mr Jones?'

Kerr asked him to confirm that he was a member of the Territorial Army.

'I'm a lieutenant. I've already been through all this in the other interview.'

'And you were training today?'

'You already know I was. And tomorrow. Everything's going up a gear at the moment.'

Jacobson yawned.

'Your wife witnessed the search of your home this evening. She works for NatWest, says she was at the Swindon branch on Wednesday and Thursday.'

'She's on an appointments board. She goes all over.'

'Which means you were at home on your own when Stephen Adams phoned you in the middle of the night,' Kerr said.

'I was alone on Wednesday night. I'll agree to that much. I've never claimed otherwise.'

Jacobson made a show of consulting his notes.

'That's right, Mr Jones,' he said. 'But only because you didn't think you'd need to.'

# Chapter Fifty-Four

Vince took Charlie to somewhere called the E-Shed. Down by the harbourside. Needed him to get a feel for the scene, he said. It was a cool enough place. But Charlie just didn't want to be there. Lisa had refused point blank this time. After a day like today she wasn't going anywhere, she'd said. Charlie stuck it as long he could. Eating, keeping yourself together, was one thing. Clubbing or partying was another. Vince pulled some bird anyway, was the kind who pulled easily, pretty much lost interest in his role as tour guide.

Charlie risked a cab back to the address, probably couldn't have found it on his own at night. A guy called Tipper, who was dossing in the basement, let him in. Lisa had gone to bed but she wasn't sleeping. Vince's brother had left an ancient TV set in his cupboard. Charlie had dragged it out earlier, mended the fuse on the plug, reattached the aerial. Lisa was propped against the headboard, watching some kind of science fiction bollocks. Her face seemed paler than pale.

'You was on the news,' she said flatly. 'You and Brian. Right at the end, just before the sport. They showed your picture, said the police needed to speak to you about arson and murder. You was dangerous, they said. Not to be approached.'

Charlie squeezed down next to her on the narrow bed. He'd rescued the unsmoked spliff from the waste bin, thought maybe he'd use it now.

'Don't mean nothing, Leez,' he said.

He was trying to convince himself, trying to get a grip.

'It'll only be news for a couple of days, then they'll lose interest. And the dibble got hundreds of people they're after. Maybe even thousands.'

He dug in his trousers, found a lighter.

''Sides, they'll be looking for two geezers. Not a couple.'

He offered her the joint when he'd lit it. But she didn't want it, went back to watching the telly. He put his free arm around her shoulders but she brushed him away. He got up again and took the chair over to the tiny window. It was clear and frosty down this way and there were stars visible above the rooftops.

The skunk didn't help the memories. All that shit with him trying to strangle her, with thumping his head. And then dealing with the mess, the blood.

# Chapter Fifty-Five

They should just have left him, after all. Left him and taken their chances. But when they were ready to go, they'd gone upstairs, given it one more try. Charlie had tried to wake him; shake him and wake him out of his drug-shit sleep. Nothing. Lisa had gone to the nearest bathroom, had taken a copper kettle from the landing with her. A heavy antique jobbie. A typical Tim and Nichola decorative item. She'd filled it from the cold tap, emptied it straight over his head. He'd woke up then all right – from Christ knows where. He'd lunged at her, grabbed her by the frigging throat, wouldn't let frigging go, roaring his stupid, fuckwit head off. *Cunt and bitch. Cunt and bitch.* Holding her throat. Slapping at her face. Charlie clocked him with the kettle – what else could he do? – had to do it half a dozen times before the twat let her go. Then Lisa took over. Grabbing the kettle from Charlie. Banging it down on FB's head. Banging it down and banging it down again. *Nobody treats me like that, Charlie. Nobody.*

They'd hardly spoken afterwards. Just worked together. Quietly, efficiently. They'd wrapped the body in the bed-clothes, dragged it downstairs that way. Charlie had thought about burning again. But couldn't see a way to do it without the risk of blazing the whole gaff, bringing instant, unwanted attention. In the end they'd done the best thing he could think of. They'd dragged FB through to the swimming pool, stripped him, pushed him in. Then they'd burnt his clothes and the bedclothes in the Aga, tidied up as best they could. They'd showered, washed their own clothes, dried them in Nichola's massive tumble dryer. None of it was perfect. Charlie was no expert but he knew they'd still have left traces, couldn't not have done. Plus he'd been mouth-swabbed when he was seventeen, had his DNA taken. Two killings. Plus arson, damage to property. It was the kind of thing you'd get fifteen years for, be dead inside when you got out.

The only good things left were all temporary. A few more days until Tim and Nichola came home. A few days more days until somebody recognised him or shopped him. A few more days with his head rested on Lisa's sweet tits. If she'd let him.

# Chapter Fifty-Six

Kerr and Jacobson both gave last orders a miss, both drove home after the interview. Jacobson nursed a Glenfiddich, watched the news, glanced at a few pages of *Summer Lightning* before deciding that he wasn't really in the mood to give Wodehouse a fair trial. He went to bed before twelve, slept better than the night before.

He got up at eight, showered, shaved, ate a proper breakfast. To go with a clean shirt, he chose a silk tie that Sally had bought him a couple of birthdays ago. He'd phone her later in the week, say hello. She was still living in London, although she'd finally given up fashion photography. The last time she'd called, she'd told him she wanted to do something less trivial with her life. Teaching maybe, she'd said, or social work. Jacobson hoped he hadn't passed on his own defective gene. The one that made you give a fuck about the human race: when no sod else did.

He didn't think about the case until he was in the car, driving towards the town centre. The drugs angle was pretty much wrapped up at any rate. Adams and Jones had been the instigators. Adams had been desperate to save his hard-won pile. Jones had the know-how to launder drugs cash through the Adams Installations accounts, was probably just an everyday greedy bastard. Shields, Dave Carter (deceased) and Colin Paterson completed the business synergy. Shields and Carter provided the necessary criminal contacts. They controlled a prime outlet between them, probably had expansion plans for others. Paterson had been the storeman. He'd looked after the product, kept it secure and hidden from accidental discovery by the rest of Adams' employees. It was the kind of scheme that could only ever have worked long-term: keeping the Birmingham firm's profits up, filtering your own stuff in slowly here and there. But Stephen Adams had been a man in a ruinous, short-term hurry.

He took the lift straight up to his office. There was a message from the hospital on his voicemail. Eileen Carter was dead, had suffered a relapse in the middle of the night. Sergeant Ince phoned him from the incident room: no reports from other forces regarding Brian Bilston and Charlie Taylor. Not so far. Jacobson looked at his watch. It was still only 9.30. He'd make a start on his report, he thought. He could always fill in the blanks later.

He'd already decided to wait until the afternoon. Or possibly the evening. There would be no solid forensic results from the FSS lab today. But at least they'd promised an initial assessment. A statement of what was possible and what wasn't. Likewise Claire Burke needed time to make her assessment, to decree whether Anne-Marie Holmes was ready to make a formal witness statement or not. Jacobson had no intention of rushing her. The little girl's recovery, if it could be accomplished, was the one piece of light to set against the darkness. He loosened his collar, slackened his tie a little, took out his pen. Alan Jones wasn't going anywhere anyway. He'd let him play silly buggers last night. He wouldn't let it happen twice.

# Chapter Fifty-Seven

*I expect I'll tell them, make a full confession. If that's the right terminology. Not today maybe. Maybe not even for a while. Wait and see if they work it out for themselves. Wait and see if they can prove it. Tell them before the trial anyway. No reason not to, is there? It might even help my case. There might be some kind of legal spin or angle in it. Mr Jones has cooperated fully with the police in another matter, m'lud. That kind of thing.*

*I'm stuffed otherwise because of the drugs. A middle-class professional of previous good character. His motive was greed, m'lud. Unabashed, wicked greed. Well maybe. But not entirely, surely? It could have worked, after all. Dug old Steve out of his hole, kept his family afloat. It's not as if there's any shortage. People wanting it. People selling it. Banging me up isn't going to stop any of that, is it?*

*Jesus. This is a shithole right enough. No wonder the old name, rank and serial number routine doesn't always work. They stick you in a place like this long enough, eventually you're glad to spill the beans: just to talk to somebody, just for the sake of a bit of variety. They've taken my computer, apparently. And what they're describing as 'certain items'. The chemical warfare suit, no doubt. I should have got rid of it straight away. It'll be critical, I expect, if they're going to prove anything. Fibres, bloodstains, all the usual shit. I washed it, of course, cleaned it up. But you can't get everything off, can you? Still, it worked in the other direction. No traces of yours truly on the banister, on the rope, on poor old Steve.*

*It's hardly as if it's murder anyway. Not in the real meaning of the word. And don't forget, I nearly didn't go round at all. I wouldn't have known a thing about it if I hadn't left the mobile switched on when I went to bed. Down to Terry Shields, that one. He'd said he'd phone early in the morning. He thought he'd found a buyer for the stuff who wasn't offering a totally insulting price to take it off our hands – after our little difficulty with the gentlemen from Birmingham. They're to blame as much as anybody when you think about it, doing what they did to Carter. Steve felt cornered after that. Finished.*

*What would you do if your best mate phoned you up in the middle of the night and said, 'Help me. I'm mad. I've killed everybody'? I thought it was a sick, stupid joke at first. Then, when I started to believe him, I very nearly dialled 999. Of course, that's also when I thought about the files on his computer; the bits and pieces of paperwork that could do with tidying up – or with vanishing altogether.*

*So I dithered, basically. It's not how we're trained to react. Action, decisiveness, leadership. That's what extreme situations call for. But I admit it: I dithered. I spent maybe half an hour dithering before I did go round. He'd already strung himself up, was already more than half gone. All I did really was to help him on his way. Tighten the noose a bit, block his airways. Assisted suicide would be a better term than murder. A fairer description, don't you think?*

*I can't honestly say I feel bad about it. Not for my part anyway. I had a strange feeling when I was there, too. Like someone was watching me? Imagination really, I guess. And only for a minute or two anyway. When I was actually doing it, when I had my hands around his neck. The feeling left me after that, I think. Certainly before I went back downstairs.*

*Oh, and the dog? Well, that's easy. I never liked it. And it was old, incontinent, always moulting. It just crapped on my carpet once or twice too often.*